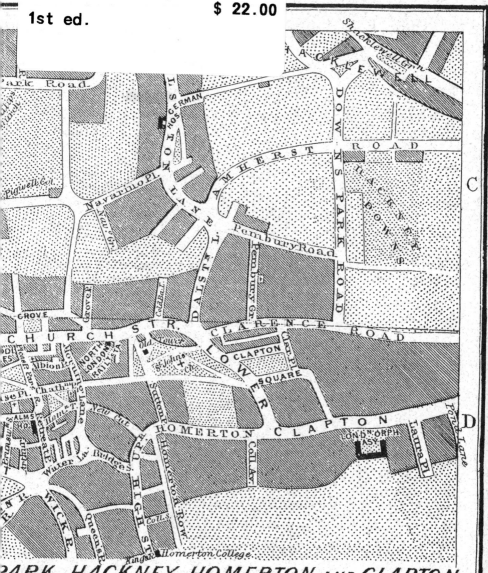

PARK, HACKNEY HOMERTON AND CLAPTON.

DRAWN & ENGRAVED BY R. JARMAN.

Selene of the Spirits

Selene of the Spirits

Melissa Pritchard

The Ontario Review Press
9 Honey Brook Drive
Princeton, NJ 08540

Distributed by George Braziller, Inc.
171 Madison Avenue
New York, NY 10016

Library of Congress Cataloging-in-Publication Data

Pritchard, Melissa.
Selene of the spirits / Melissa Pritchard.
p. cm.
ISBN 0-86538-094-5
ISBN 0-86538-095-3 (pbk.)
I. Title.
PS3566.R578S45   1998
813'.54—dc21   98-28729
CIP

First Edition

Excerpts from *Selene of the Spirits*
have previously appeared, in a slightly different form,
in *StoryQuarterly* and *Ontario Review*.

ACKNOWLEDGMENTS

For generous support during the writing of this novel, I thank The Writer's Voice of the Scottsdale/Paradise Valley YMCA, especially Julie Hampton. Thanks to Margo Tamez, Sena Jeter Naslund, Pamela Painter, Sharon Sheehe Stark, Antonya Nelson, Mary Clyde and Deneen Jenks, careful readers of various early manuscript drafts. Also, I am indebted to my agent, Kim Witherspoon, and her assistant, Gideon Weil.

Special thanks to Allyson Stack, research assistant and lifelong friend, Colette Korry-Hatrick, healer and intuitive reader, Mary Osmond, psychic reader extraordinaire, and Matthew Baker—all beloved companions who have played their parts in guiding and supporting me.

To all of you, including Raymond Smith and Joyce Carol Oates, who believed wholeheartedly in this book, I extend love and gratitude.

For

My Mother and My Father

—D.D.D.L. and M.B.—

and

My Sister, Penelope

CONTENTS

Selene of the Spirits

Dobbs' Pantry
20 Battersea Rise
Battersea, South of the Thames
April, 1886

Young Jenny Dobbs, the grocer's wife, her black merino shawl slipped down over one shoulder, stood before the upstairs window overlooking Battersea Park. Everything appeared motionless, drenched in spring sunlight and freshest green. Here, on the other side of the begrimed window, the atmosphere was fetid, seasonless, oppressive with burning tallow and the stench of sickness. For three days now, the woman in the bed behind her had maintained an inexplicable grace, inexplicable considering her history, as Jenny had heard it, had raptly listened—a steep decline from fame and beauty's fortune to this.

The emaciated figure in its linen chemise with a rich embroidery of scarlet honeysuckle about the neck and wrists, attempted sitting up. Hearing her efforts, Jenny turned from the window. A vein in the woman's neck swelled like softest lilac cording, her chestnut hair lay pasted in thin vines around her shoulders. Her hooded eyes seemed fixed on a place or a thought far beyond the room she was in, their once fine colour given over entirely to an expanding blackness of the pupil. Her skin's humid whiteness suggested a root or bulb brutally brought up from its underground chambers. The bedclothes, the sheets and counterpane, held an ominous fated stillness. Pat and Jenny Dobbs' only tenant, scarcely thirty years old, was dying of pneumonia in a cheap flat above their grocery, where a bad drain smell crept from beneath the warped flooring, and a small stove gave off a thin raveling of warmth. The woman lifted her hand in a gesture weak but nonetheless urgent.

"What is it, Selene? What is it, dear?"

The hand lapsed back upon the quilt. Jenny moved in the direction it had seemed to suggest toward a black leather trunk across the room. Raising the lid, she saw, set atop a neat stack of books, an envelope sealed with a blood bright orb of melted wax.

Envelope in hand, Jenny recrossed the small room. "This?" she began to ask, but when she came to the bed, it was too late to receive any living answer. Selene Cook's face bore an expression of what could only be described as calm, cold peace.

With wetted fingers, the grocer's wife extinguished the several candles surrounding the bedside. The goldfinch in its domed cage she would carry downstairs as Miss Cook had insisted—a gift. And the old-fashioned, dark blue dress she had asked to be buried in— the same dress she told Jenny she had worn in all her seances— that needed to be prepared as well. As for relatives, there was only a sister in Kensington to be notified. What more? The letter. As she studied the address, it occurred to Jenny to say nothing to her husband. He was a cautious, short-tempered man, and she found herself wanting, purely for her own adventure, to take the omnibus to Mornington Road and deliver poor Miss Cook's letter herself. That would be the best thing, the thing Miss Cook no doubt would have wished her to do.

Unluckily married, yet still awake to the possibilities of ro- mance, Jenny Dobbs stood on the room's threshold, the finch's cage in one hand, the letter to Sir William Herapath in the other, regarding the silent, diminutive figure upon the bed. Fancy what a world! Here was someone familiar with the dead, at one time famous for being so, now, within the past hour, become finally, everlastingly, one of them.

THE HACKNEY SEANCES
1873

it grows worse.
instructions. mischief. powers.
a trembling throughout.

6 Bruce Villas, Eleanor Road
Hackney, London
January, 1873

Mathilde, or Tot, as she preferred to be called, took her time lighting the coal fire. The girl was face down upon the bed, still in her corset of scarlet flannel, her petticoats tangled about her, while her pet finch, freed from its domed cage sat perched in the girl's loosened hair, regarding Tot with a fierce, indolent eye. A checked muslin gown, a black woolen cloak, a green shawl, all lay heaped upon a chair. Muddy black boots stood beneath them. Tot ignored the sleeping girl, grateful to be relieved of her usual morning's routine which would have involved returning at least twice before the brat bothered to wake up and demand that Tot unlace then retighten her corset, help fasten up her teacher's dress, comb and pin up her thick, unruly hair. Meanwhile the younger sister, Octavia, would have eaten her breakfast, memorized her bit of French and be waiting coolly beside the front door for her ride to Miss Cliff's where she was an obedient and tractable pupil, while this other, this one, was said to be a most eccentric and bad-tempered teacher.

Yesterday's news of Selene's dismissal from Miss Cliff's School for Young Ladies, of the consequent loss to the Cook household of thirty pounds a year, of the forfeiture of Octavia's education due entirely to her sister's selfish behavior, had plummeted the family into unexpected crisis. All this, with its dread implications, had fairly unhinged Tot, as had the evening's outbursts of hysteria from all save Mr. Cook, who remained calm because he had known enough to stay away.

Tot left a fire blazing hotly in the girl's room. Three more days passed in this same suspension from routine. The front steps accumulated unswept snow and a treacherous sheeting of ice formed underneath. Indoors, lamp chimneys darkened with soot, vegetables sprouted waxy tendrils, furniture became lightly cloaked in dust and the culprit, Selene, continued to lay as if dead, in a fit, with Tot obliged to carry upstairs and back downstairs, platefuls of uneaten toast, while a morose Octavia plucked listlessly at what lay on her plate before locking herself back in her bedroom. Mrs. Cook launched herself about the house on opposing tides of rage and melancholy, working her hands as if they might produce something in their constant wringing to save the situation. And Mr. Cook, a man much weaker and more precarious in his health than his wife, fell ill but took himself out of the house anyway, beyond range of catastrophe.

On the fourth day, as Tot sprinkled wetted tea leaves over a muddy footprint on the hall carpet, preparing to whisk the whole mess back up with a handbrush, she was rapped on the head by her employer.

"Tot," Mrs. Cook loomed above her, reeking of bacon. "Go upstairs and bring Selene and Octavia down from their rooms. We are going to demand of those spirits responsible for this crisis what it is they would have us do. We are on the very brink of ruin. What, I will ask them, is to keep you from losing your employment and the rest of us from falling straight into the workhouse?"

So Tot, terrified of spirits, of devils, of ghosts, of all things that refused visibility, stood outside the girl's bedroom, crossing herself repeatedly, until she summoned enough courage to open the door and rouse a creature whose body had become a shadowy crossroads, a meeting place for the unholy or at the very least, the unseen.

Shall I say it?
I am going mad.
Moments of such terror, my own name eludes me.
And my family—strangers gazing at me,
their eyes like barbs in my flesh.
All night I was awakened by a voice calling itself Phoenicia.
At her instruction, I rose from my bed and wandered over the
dark house.
Then she said I must go outside and wash with snow.
This I did.

Bathe in fire, the voice said.

I feel a great iron heaviness in all my limbs.

Denis Cook's worsening grippe convinced him to quit work early and travel straight home to bed. He dreaded the mare's nest that would no doubt greet him, but hoped the sight of his nightcap on his head and the bedcovers sealed over him at four o'clock in the afternoon would persuade his family to leave him in peace.

As he stood in the foyer, knocking snow off the tops of his boots after having nearly been assassinated by a bit of ice hidden on the stoop, as he unwound the red woolen muffler from his inflamed throat and lifted off his bowler hat, Denis Cook became aware of an eerie silence.

"Mrs. Cook? Tot? Octavia?" He stepped gingerly, tiptoed in stockinged feet about his own house. Were they in some plural faint, poisoned or run off? When he cracked open the double doors to the parlour, his discovery scarcely comforted him. The patterned drapes were closed tight, the room itself dark except for a coal fire in the grate by fitful light of which he saw the women of his family seated, hands clasped in a ring around the parlour table. A fourth figure, he could identify its pear-shaped bulk as Tot's, was present as well. Whatever the women were doing in that circle, heads thrown back and eyes closed, Denis Cook felt chiefly disappointed. He had wanted Tot to prepare him his favorite horehound syrup, the usual mustard poultice for his chest.

As he stood there, Selene, Octavia, even his wife of eighteen years (whom, out of some misplaced awe, he still called Mrs. Cook), even his houseservant, paid him not the slightest heed so rapt were they in their trance. He experienced a distinct sympathy for himself as he closed the doors upon their bizarre little tableau and made his way, throat burning as if a small hot cinder were stuck at its back, up to his bed.

Halfway up the draughty stairway, he was stopped by a thump from below. As if, he thought, a heavy object (a table perhaps?) had been hurled across the parlour and struck heavily against the wall. He heard Mrs. Cook shriek. Tot's short huffings and declarations, he could hear those too. Did they have need of him? In a paralysis of illness and indecision, he heard again the stifled whump of furniture.

Neither sealing himself into his bed nor striding manfully into the parlour, Denis Cook crouched outside its doors, his eye fitted to the keyhole like a scarab in its setting. His eldest daughter was talking in a voice at once coquettish and demanding. He heard no respondent. Through the keyhole, he glimpsed a puzzle piece of his wife, the crook of her elbow. She appeared to be writing something down. Denis Cook heard mention of a Navarino Road, a little street he knew well, not far from their own. There was a decent pub on Navarino, The Sword and Garter, where the owner would gladly fry up a chop if he brought one along to accompany his beer. Due to recent poverty, he hadn't been there in a fortnight.

Oh, pish. He stood up irritably. They've gone mad. First the one daughter, now the rest of them hysterical as queens. For a second time, Cook trod the stairs which now seemed steeper and colder, climbing upward toward the comfort of his nightcap, the little oblivion of sleep.

Queer this becomes,
Madness.
Now a second voice, not hers, but a man's,
speaking through me to mother. I am, it says, to be taken to a place
on Navarino Road. I am, it says, to become a great medium.
Octavia is so angry she won't speak except to insinuate I've
deliberately ruined her life, that I've no regard for anyone but
myself, that I indulge myself in theatrics, that everyone pays for my
behaviour.
Does she think I can command myself any differently?
I feel as if I am inhabited by a host of selves, only one of them the
sister she knows. The others are strangers to us both, and they are
cruel, mischievous, indifferent, what is happening to me, what is
happening to me?

Mother is frightened. Wit's end, she says. These new instructions
relieve her. Something to do.

This afternoon I woke, having slept again all day. The new servant
girl was standing beside the bed, staring down at me with a most
peculiar expression. She was, I think, praying.

Harriet Cook stood with her two daughters before a red brick Georgian terrace house, regarding the plaque affixed to the door.

THE DALSTON ASSOCIATION OF
INQUIRIES INTO SPIRITUALISM
74 NAVARINO ROAD
THOMAS BOYNTON, SECRETARY IN RESIDENCE

Selene interrupted her mother's awed contemplation of this address given them by Spirit.

"Good Lord, it's just a house, isn't it?" With that, Selene raised her black-mittened hand and briskly reached for the brass knocker in the shape of a fox's head, rapped three times, dislodging a tiny heap of snow between its sharp brass ears. On the several blocks' walk to Navarino Road, they had had to traverse Richmond Road, pass directly beneath the row of tall, claret-draped windows of Miss Cliff's School for Young Ladies. This had greatly vexed Octavia, who had not ceased brooding over the circumstance of her expulsion from that avenue of learning. Now however, Selene turned on her booted heel and descended the steps to the brick sidewalk, the first of their party to admit the pointless effort of their walk. Thus she only overheard, rather than observed, as did Octavia and Harriet Cook, the door draw open, the voice with its gravelly thread of cough, "Yes, I am Mrs. Boynton, Thomas's mother. Leave your card. No, I cannot. Give your card, I'll tell my son. I'm no spiritualist. The dead haven't told any of us a thing we need to know." The green door shut with sterner emphasis than it had opened.

The three women walked back. In the late afternoon, rooks scudded heavily from wintry branch to wintry branch, and the sun burned with a silvery whiteness. Crossing the various streets, returning the way they had just come, they stepped cautiously, avoiding the unswept horse dung from carriages. Back home, they would await the response of the Secretary of the Dalston Association to their modest visiting card.

*

Thomas Boynton arrived at 6 Bruce Villas the next day by hansom cab. With neither hesitation nor inhibition, he mounted the icy steps, knocked at the door and waited until a giantess in a pink servant's dress answered. Thomas Boynton found himself ushered into a scorching-hot dining room where Mrs. Cook sat none too patiently mending one of Mr. Cook's perpetually damaged shirts. Octavia sat at her desk conjugating French verbs, while the object of his visit, Selene Cook, lay draped upon a gold brocade sofa in a languid, heavy pose.

Mr. Boynton was a youngish gentleman, short, too short, Mrs. Cook adjudged, with a well-proportioned but rather pimply face topped off by an unruly mop of black hair well in need of pomade. She couldn't abide untrained hair on a man. He had a sparse beard, mournful black eyes and a strangely pendulous lower lip. There he stood in his black frock coat, top hat in his hands, sober and silent. Much like an undertaker's assistant, Mrs. Cook thought.

She spoke to the point, describing the recent, peculiar history of her eldest daughter, of Selene's fits and trances, tantrums, the seeing of orbs of flame, the hearing of voices. Mr. Boynton listened, perched on the edge of Mr. Cook's favourite, much stained chair. He listened with a solemnity which Mrs. Cook would later come to recognize as his way of showing a very intense excitement. He declined tea or any sort of refreshment, for which Tot, batting about like a moth in the doorway, was grateful. Their supply of food in the pantry was much reduced these past weeks. Boynton asked if he might, however, return the following evening for a seance. He wished to observe for himself the girl's powers. Mrs. Cook, having just stabbed her finger with the needle, nodded consent as she sucked at the dot of blood.

Mr. Boynton assures me I am not mad. He says I am gifted with psychical talent but have not yet been taught to govern my powers and so they frighten me. Mother told him my most recent history of lying cold and rigid, nearly pulseless, hours on end, unable to be roused, of my constant sleepiness, sensation of heaviness, of the voices I hear, have heard since I was fourteen, of my walking at night while asleep, of the orbs of flame I once saw passing in front of my vision, day after day, great hoops of fire. He asked about my childhood. Always in bed, Mother said to him, always lung complaint, fever, cough. Given to daydreams, staring into space, as if she were never here with us but elsewhere. I told him of my grandmother, my father's mother, who lived with us before she died. How I saw her in a trance a number of times when I was seven and eight years old.

He wrote nothing down but again assured me I was in possession of a gift, not a pack of devils as I feared (or as Tot is convinced I am). He comes back tomorrow night and will help us prepare a seance as he is well trained in this.

Octavia was an ungrateful sulk. When he politely addressed her, she snubbed him. She is jealous, I suppose, but why? I have suffered this "gift" as Mr. Boynton calls it, endured it, been terrified of it, been fearful of my sanity, that this is my first gleam of hope, why should she begrudge me that?

To:
Balfour Lodge, Editor
The Spiritualist Magazine
61 Lambs Conduit Street, London

Sir,

I wish to describe some recent manifestations witnessed at the residence of a gentleman by the name of Cook, in Hackney, whose daughter has mediumistic gifts, as yet untutored, and therefore unpredictable in occurrence. These have appeared within the past fortnight or three weeks. The young lady (aged sixteen) and her mother were sitting at a table on the afternoon of 26 January, when among other communications, they were urgently requested "to go at once to 74 Navarino Road, where they hold seances." They accordingly called at my residence. I afterward paid them a visit, and a seance was arranged, the sitters consisting of Mr. and Mrs. Cook, their daughter Selene, another daughter, Octavia, and myself. The light was removed, whereupon Miss Cook was immediately "placed" upon the table, and upon my holding her hand, was "removed" from the table onto the floor, and onto the table again several times in a manner which convinced me she was being floated in the air. The table, a heavy oak one, was then thrown with great force over into the fireplace, and Miss Cook carried very rapidly round the room. Articles were carried about the room as well, and Miss Cook stated she saw several spirits and lights during the evening; also one spirit, known to the family, shook her by the hand, and kissed her.

I was privileged to sit with them a second time, the circle consisting of Mr. and Mrs. Cook, the one Miss Cook and myself. Previous to the light being removed, the table gave violent tilts; when the light was extinguished, Miss Cook and her chair were repeatedly removed from the floor onto the table. A chair was twice placed over my head, without its legs first touching me; then a portion of Miss Cook's dress was removed, and after being whisked in our faces, was thrown over my head, whilst a hassock was thrown into my lap, as well as a vulcanite necklace which Miss Cook had been wearing. Table movements of a very powerful nature ensued, whilst the raps were remarkably loud and distinct. On the gas being lit, Miss Cook was entranced, and with her head turned from some paper and resting on the table, wrote, for the first time under spirit influence, many interesting communications. On my asking the reason for the condition of darkness for some of the communications, she wrote, "Light destroys our conditions"; and on request for a few words in French, "*Je suis un esprit*"; with the translation, "I am a spirit." Another was "Get Selene (Miss Cook) to come to your seances, it will be well for both parties." In answer to other questions of mine, the spirits intimated she was to become a most powerful writing and speaking medium.

Mr. Lodge, I wish to invite you on Wednesday evening next, 7 o'clock, to attend a seance at my home on Navarino Road whereupon this same brave young lady will demonstrate her considerable though as yet untrained powers of spirit communication. I have also invited Mr. Charles Blackburn. As you and I well know, Mr. Blackburn can be wonderfully munificent when it comes to supporting those spiritual interests he believes in. He is always eager to hear of yet another manifestation of spirit evidence which reassures him of vitality beyond the grave.

> THOMAS BOYNTON
> Secretary of the Dalston Association
> of Inquiries into Spiritualism
>
> January 30, 1873

*

"She spies. And when she walks behind you, I've seen her cross herself backwards and forwards. A ridiculous girl. And so fat. Selie, you've got a mole right there, can you feel it? Isn't it odd how we cannot see our own backs?"

Selene burrowed under the covers while Octavia, propped on one elbow, scratched her sister's warm back, a ritual they had perfected from years of sharing a bed. Octavia had come into her sister's room to look for a misplaced copy of *Aesop's Fables*. Now she bunched Selene's linen nightdress higher up upon her slender shoulders and moved her fingers in light, lazy patterns.

"Crossing herself until she's dizzy. No doubt our Tot considers you *un diable*. They say Catholics see ten devils for one angel. I'm surprised she stays."

"What is it you are writing across my back?"

"My own name. Mademoiselle Octavia Cook. Now yours. Selene. Here's Pappa's name, now Mamma's."

Selene felt the feathery scripting of her sister's cool fingers.

"Do another name. Right over there. It itches. Octavia? I am sorry about Miss Cliff's."

"Quite all right." As if to further convince herself, Octavia repeated what she had just said. "Quite all right. I'm used to my new independence, reading what I like, as I like." She hardly dared consider why she lied and so extravagantly. She would think about it later, in the privacy of her room.

"I'm so glad you no longer blame me. Anyway, it was a hateful school. But surely you miss poor Monsieur Archembeaults's calisthenics?"

At the memory of the exercises they had been forced to perform, their legs "developing muscular energies," feigning movement beneath starched petticoats, crinolines and horsehair bustles, they rolled about, laughing.

"Now me," Octavia flopped on her stomach, hoping Selene might, for once, give her an equal turn.

"Will you go to Mr. Boynton's seance with me tomorrow evening?"

Octavia snorted into a pillow, her voice muffled, "We may well encounter husbands."

"Yes, well. Mamma looks out for us on that account."

"What of Mr. Boynton?"

Recalling the man's houndlike expression and protruding lip, Selene and Octavia stuck their heads under pillows and shrieked, drumming their feet into the mattress.

"Oh, Octave. Now my side pains me. *J'ai soif.* Tot? Oh, Tot? Are you, as Octave assures me you are, peering in through the keyhole? We'd like our tea, dear Tot."

"Yes. Tea, Tot." That sent Octavia into another fit. She hammered her feet and howled. "Tea, Tot."

Frustrated at having seen nothing to report to the priest at St. Jerome's, Tot wished her own back could be scratched. It ached from the day's work and ached more, anticipating the next day's work. If she didn't manage to sneak away, her back would have to continue its labour, preparing tea for these two, late as it was. Devil's hours.

"She was there, Octave, just as you said, but she's gone now."

"How would you know? I shall creep across the room, fling open the door, pounce on her. Then she can get us our tea."

"No. I see Tot has gone upstairs to her room which is cruelly cold." Selene had begun to speak in that superior, dreamy tone which so irritated Octavia. "She is unfastening her dress, it has a small tear at the waist. She is very downcast. No one to touch her or to talk to. Oh, we should be much, much kinder to her."

"Pish posh! She's our new servant, and not a very good one, and I quite hate how plain she is. It is impossible to look upon such a ham and remain cheerful. One cannot cultivate pleasant thoughts when one is forced to contemplate ugly objects. I wish Mamma had not hired her. She came cheap, that's why."

"You must try for a less cold heart, Octavia. She cannot help how plain she is. Besides she's only plain by your judgment, which is society's."

"Well, your ghosts or spirits or whatever they are mislead you. My heart is perfectly fine. And that was the worst cheat of a backscratch ever. I'm going to bed."

Octavia had turned cross. Though her sister's disturbing new power seemed to offer a fresh sort of adventure in the world, beginning with tomorrow's invitation to participate in a seance at Mr. Boynton's, still, it was a world Octavia was not privy to. She could neither study it nor learn spirit voices nor would she wish to. These so-called spirits elected their human instruments, one did not summon them to oneself. One was chosen, as was Selene, or excluded, as herself. It was chary business and once again, her sister dominated and triumphed over her own hard-won, real achievements. No one cared how well Octavia could write in French, or how perfectly she danced the tarantella. Always it was Selene who effortlessly drew notice. And now, in addition to her sister's visible charms, her obvious beauty, Selene was now possessed of invisible powers as well. A cold heart. No, an irritated disposition from not having her backscratch returned properly. As usual. On her way, Octavia tapped on the domed birdcage.

"Your bird's in a fit as well. A malevolent spirit has lodged in it, no doubt."

Then at the door, half desirous of their earlier merriment, Octavia turned. "Perhaps tomorrow we can kindly ask our *beautiful* Tot to heat us a bath and *kindly* help us to wash our hair.

Mine feels absolutely thick. We must be prepared to enchant our dear *petit homme.*"

"Oh Octave. I feel it's you he's smitten with. I imagine his lip droops even further, past his chin, at the merest mention of you."

"Dreadful image! A drooped Boynton. By the way, Selie, it was his name I've been writing up and down your back all night. Thomas Boynton."

A black slipper went hurtling through the air but missed Octavia's departing figure and landed harmlessly on the floor.

*

At the moment, Octavia hated her sister enough to lie. Enough to pretend it was all right to have been betrayed. All right to have been taken out of the one atmosphere where, though she had no friends (her intelligence denied her that frivolity), she felt appreciated and fulfilled. Selene may have loathed Miss Cliff's, felt tormented having to teach girls not much younger than herself, but to Octavia, school, the hours spent learning, was bliss. And before this, before her fits and trances, Selene had been able to charm her way out of any trouble. When they quarreled, Octavia had always forgiven first, given in first. Her sister, no doubt, assumed this time would be like all the others. But Selene's betrayal of their unspoken pact—that she preside as the beautiful and charming older sister, while Octavia be given the part of the plain, but brilliant, younger one (and how eagerly she had looked forward to taking over Selene's teaching post)—this betrayal cut to the quick of Octavia's existence. She had wanted nothing more, and Selene knew it. To be a teacher, and one day mistress of her own school, not Miss Cliff's but Miss Cook's ... and if she entertained the possibility of a husband, always he appeared as an instructor like herself.... Now it was ended. Finished. She hated Selene for what she had heedlessly thrown over—her one dream—then blithely apologizing! Octavia could not even speak frankly about it. The damage was so great, so irreparable, it had to be buried.

Octavia got out her sketch book, sat on her bed and by candle-light began to outline in charcoal the large, double schoolroom, then sketched a trio of Miss Cliff's young ladies insulting their pianos, vying for the most tortured interpretation of some defenseless composer. She composed a group of other girls, dressed in their gowns of silk claret and long white gloves, standing in pairs, conjugating German and French verbs, then reciting whole passages from Woodhouselee's *Universal History*. Along the west wall, Octavia drew three of Miss Cliff's charges in wooden chairs facing the cream-coloured wall, some mischief having placed them so. She sketched them sitting stiff and still as handbells, each with a stubborn back and huge puffed skirt, their profiles falsely repentant, long sausage curls dangling from hair pomaded smooth as glass to each of their heads. She remembered, but did not sketch, her last noon dinner at Miss Cliff's, the platter heaped with overboiled tongues frilled with a sticky collar of broccoli tufts, the white, runny pudding—at least she would not miss the food. But her sketches only made her feel worse, as did her attempts, over the next several days, to set up a schoolroom for herself in her bedroom. She sat, assiduously copying out an essay, her face pinched with strain. Then she went into Selene's room when it was empty and located a copy of M. A. Johnston's *The Ladies College and School Examiner*, thumbing through its thin pages to find the questions marked for each day's lesson:

Whose are the expressions, *L`état c`est moi, Après moi le déluge,* and *Qui ne sait pas dissimuler ne sait pas régner?*

What do quadrumana and pachydermata signify, and how are these families represented in Europe?

Name the last three Laureates, and their chief works.

Some account of the Escurial.

Who was Deucalion?

When was the Bank of England established?

Who always ended his speeches in the senate with "Delenda est Carthago"?

Since the answers were at the back, Octavia looked them up and diligently copied them down. As she leafed idly through other pages, she came across Selene's handwriting, put down in one of the margins, a list titled "My Questions":

Why do I hear voices when no one else hears them?

How could this stupid dress be any uglier?

How could life at Miss Cliff's be any more of a torment to my
aching brain?

What is to become of me?

Perhaps, Octavia guessed, Selene had been busy writing this
when the schoolroom grew ominously silent and Miss Cliff
surprised her by lifting the book from her hands. When all twenty
pupils, including Octavia, stared at Miss Augusta Cliff, a stout
woman, encased in a tunic of dark green rather like an opera
costume, towering above Selene, who said something defiant to
which Miss Cliff responded by raising one thick arm and rapping
at the girl's shoulders with her long, ivory-tipped cane, and when
Selene stood, wrested the cane from Miss Cliff and flung it to the
floor, kicking at it with her boots, Octavia vaguely remembered
the ploffing sound of her own silk dress collapsing to the hard,
waxed floor, vaguely recalled Monsieur Archembeault's arms
raising her up...hearing the awful sucking sounds he made with
his yellow teeth, hearing him alternately reassure her, then bitterly
complain that his hour of calisthenics had been usurped, sacrificed
to the miscreant. By the time she had felt well enough to be helped
to a chair beside Monsieur's dumbbells and wooden poles, Selene
was already removed from the schoolroom by Miss Cliff, and the
din in the place had resumed, loud with scandal and speculation,
until the calisthenics instructor strode to the front of the room, stood
beside Selene's now empty teaching post, clapped his hands,
sucked at his teeth, and by shouting *Attendez, attendez-vous!*,
restored some fragile order. Selene had been expelled, and as a
consequence of her temper, her fit, her selfishness, whatever it was,
there was no money for Octavia to continue her schooling, to pursue
what had been, after all, a modest dream.

*

Since the seance with Mr. Boynton, Selene had heard no more
voices. She and Octavia were getting on better as well. She had
apologized and, it seemed to Selene, Octavia had forgiven her.
Tomorrow night was to be her first formal seance at Mr. Boynton's
home on Navarino Road, so she now stood before her oval looking
glass, laboring to improve her image, namely removing a compress

from the stinging gap between her eyebrows where she had just plucked out several offending hairs. She waited before applying the mixture of gall nuts, oil, ammoniac salt and vinegar that would darken them. The solution was to be left on all night and, in the morning, she would wash her brows with tepid water. On the cluttered surface of her dressing table stood a tiny pot of *rose en tasse* rouge, a bowl of powdered starch and another containing a freshly concocted mask of barley flour, honey and white of egg. The truth was, she did not think herself very attractive, having neither the oval face nor the rosy cupid's mouth, nor the thinly arched eyebrows that were the current day's ideal. And poor Octavia was no nearer conventional beauty, or for that matter any sort of beauty, than herself. Selene wished desperately for funds so she could go back to Piesse and Lubin on New Bond Street where she had been last Christmastime. Piesse and Lubin carried toilet powders, scented oils, perfumed soaps, cold creams, scented waters, glycerin jellies, fruit syrups, vegetable lip salves. She especially longed for some of their famous powdered French chalk, *craie de Briacon*, so she could stop using the kitchen starch that clumped and spotted on her skin. She had tried some at Anne Fletcher's home. Selene's mother had a prejudice against cosmetics, saying only creatures of the *demi-monde* or low-moraled actresses used makeup, rouging and enameling their faces into shiny, cheap plates for sale. Mrs. Cook's code of beauty was this: avoid cold air, eschew excess water on the face and over-rich food, do not sit close to any fire or out in harsh sunlight, refuse any excess of emotion or disturbance of the mind—these, she claimed, were natural methods which denoted good breeding. Unfortunately, Octavia adhered to these methods and the gain was negligible. Her sister was unredeemably plain, and Selene only half allowed to herself that she benefited from the contrast.

Struggling to keep the eyebrow solution from dripping off the sides of her face, her skin prickling beneath the sticky mask she had applied with a bit of chamois cloth to her forehead, cheeks and chin, Selene lay upon her bed wishing for a chaise lounge. All the ladies in the novels she read possessed chaise lounges. They seemed *de rigueur* for a sufficiently dramatic life, and Selene wanted a dramatic life, though not necessarily a distressing one. She longed for a life like Maggie's in Mrs. Alexander's *The Wooing O't*, the daughter of a chemist in love with a brilliant man of the world who rescues her from the unsought attentions of a half-mad second cousin. Or better, Nell L'Estrange in Miss Broughton's novel, *Cometh Up as a Flower*. Even now Selene held that novel high above her head, turning its pages with aching arms as her brows blackened and her pasted complexion strove for a translucent whiteness. She read aloud: "Great tears are standing in his honest, tender, agonized eyes—tears that do not disgrace his manhood much, I think... and as he so kisses and clasps me, a great blackness comes over my eyes, and I swoon away in his arms."

Her own arms dropped down, the pages of Miss Broughton's novel temporarily abandoned for the delicious sensation they had just induced, a delicious sensation which Selene, eyes closed, heart racing and skin prickling, endeavoured to sustain.

*

By half past six, Mrs. Cook had convinced her husband to hire a carriage. It would hardly do, she said, to have them traipsing on foot to Mr. Boynton's like chimney sweeps. This was no luxury but the necessity of maintaining a proper appearance. Thus she appealed successfully to Mr. Cook's fear of social ineptitude.

Nevertheless, they arrived late. Tot had misplaced Mr. Cook's whitest collar, Selene had an attack of nerves and threatened to stay home, and the hired coachman, a mound-shaped old mole, had driven recklessly and with so confused a direction that it took them, Denis Cook complained, twice as long to be driven as to walk. He paid two shillings less, and the driver cursed him extravagantly before lashing his poor beast into a lopsided clatter down the cobbled street.

As they walked up the clean swept, well-lit steps, Cook eyed his family—wife in a ribbon trimmed mantle and modest bonnet, one daughter demurely clad, the other stamping from foot to foot with unbridled anxiety. As the butler opened the front door, Denis Cook heard hymn singing, distinctly baritone. By the foyer gaslight, he squinted worriedly at his pocket watch; nearly half past. A second servant removed their cloaks and jackets, hats and scarves. That accomplished, the butler waited until the final verse was finished before circumspectly drawing open the library doors. The

Cooks recognized only Thomas Boynton who rose delightedly and with a rare animation, crossed the room to greet them. Mr. Cook, Mrs. Cook, Octavia and Selene shook hands round the small circle. Present were Mr. Henry Wilkes, founding member of the Dalston Association, Mr. Balfour Lodge, editor of *The Spiritualist*, Mr. Frank Herne and Mr. Charles Risdale, renowned mediums and friends of the Dalston Association. Another guest, Mr. Charles Blackburn, was regrettably absent but sent regards to all.

High-backed chairs of green Spanish leather were brought forward and the assembly enlarged by four. All were seated around a circular table covered with green cloth, Selene between Mr. Boynton and Mr. Lodge, a gentleman whose muttonchop whiskers took up nearly half of his parsnip-coloured face. Octavia was seated on Mr. Boynton's other side. With each sister forced to grasp one of his hands, they later decided such seating had been, with insidious foresight, prearranged by Mr. Boynton.

With a long wooden pole, the maid deftly turned down three or four gas lamps in the library. The company was now seated in pitch darkness. Having glimpsed how complete and distinguished a library this was, Octavia wished she could browse amid the rows of leather-bound books rather than be ensnared, as she was, in the circumference of this spirit circle. Indeed, before the seance was fully underway, while it was still in its early stage of dreary hymn singing and psalm recitation, Octavia could not help but cast a longing, if blind, glance around a room dedicated to knowledge. The owner of these volumes, Mr. Boynton, seated on her right, suddenly began to pump at her hand as it lay in his as though it were an accordion. Startled, Octavia leaned forward to better view her sister, but what she saw on that account alarmed her still more. Selene's eyes were turned dramatically back, her lips moved soundlessly. And now, Octavia's hand, entrapped as it was in Mr. Boynton's, was made to inscribe the air in little circles, as if their two hands conjoined had taken on a separate life. Octavia, forced to endure the evening, questioned if her sister's behavior wasn't a clever fraud to draw male attention to herself. The evening progressed into such strange events as Mr. Herne and Mr. Risdale alternately speaking in both feminine and masculine spirit voices, delivering messages from those deceased, invisible guests of Mr. Boynton, who wafted freely in his library. The sonorous voice of

John King, a famous pirate and governor of Jamaica, Frank Herne's spirit control, spoke at length and ramblingly. Near the close of the seance came a showering down upon the table of small gifts or *apports*, cigars, embroidered handkerchiefs, tokens from grateful spirits. Selene was restrained until the moment she placed her head upon the table as if asleep and spoke in a deepened much altered voice that announced itself as John King's daughter, Florence, who said she wished to speak through the young medium Selene Cook. A grand accomplishment on her sister's part, Octavia noted bitterly. All the gentlemen, with the exception of her father who was asleep, gazed past Octavia to Selene, transfixed with admiration.

Afterward, when the gas lamps were turned up, restoring the library to its usual brightness, Mr. Herne and Mr. Risdale spoke to Mr. Cook in the foyer. They arranged with his permission, a series of appointments with his oldest daughter. Under chaperone, she was to come to Mr. Boynton's house and sit in private spirit circles with them. Her gifts, they assured Mr. Cook, would advance rapidly under their trained guidance. And the rewards of a medium in communication with the dead, were many. Meanwhile, Mr. Boynton had called a cab for the Cook family and paid their fare in advance.

It was a quiet ride home, with Mr. Cook thinking how prosperous Herne and Risdale had seemed, how he had never been in a home as fine as Boynton's. Mrs. Cook's thoughts were not far off course from her husband's. Meanwhile, Octavia and Selene mimicked the dry squeezings of Thomas Boynton's hands, described the loathsome drop of perspiration that had shone at the tip of his nose and hung there till, defeated by gravity, it had dropped to the table.

Thus Selene Cook was placed under the professional tutelage of Mr. Boynton and Mr. Lodge, Mr. Herne and Mr. Risdale. And thus were the material appetites of Harriet and Denis Cook whetted as they saw their way clear to a prosperity newly awarded them by the voices of the dead, through the medium, quite literally, of their daughter.

Today was my first meeting with Mr. Herne and Mr. Risdale. They were both enormously kind, and Mr. Risdale reinforced what Mr. Boynton had first told me, that psychical powers such as mine must be managed properly or they threaten the very derangement of the self.

Mr. Herne, who is the more charming of the two, asked had I ever ridden a runaway horse? No, I replied, I had never even been seated on a horse that stood still, much less upon one that ran away. In fact, I told him, I had only seen horses from a distance in Regent's Park. A pity, he said kindly, for you would understand more what Mr. Risdale is trying to say to you. Think, he said, of the psychical gift as a horse that needs bridling, reining in, needs training to get control of its wild impulses until it becomes an instrument useful to man, and the medium (yourself) becomes of service to others. Otherwise, this power becomes a very dangerous animal indeed.

We had tea then, and I repeated the little awkward history of myself. Mr. Herne showed great interest and Mr. Risdale none. He repeatedly glanced at his watch, holding it up to his ear most peculiarly. Finally, just as I had started to tell about the voice named Phoenicia, he stood up ungraciously and interrupted me. Well, let's get on with it, Herne, shall we? I'm sorry, Miss Cook, but we have another appointment directly following yours.

So I was given my first "lesson" in Mr. Boynton's library on Navarino Road as to the management of my powers. I came home elated, only to find Octavia once again jealous, pouting over the attentions paid to me. Perhaps if you would cultivate a spiritual talent of your own, you too might receive attention, I teased. No thank you, she snapped, plunging her head back into another of her books. I'll educate myself honestly.

Three times now I have met with Mr. Herne and Mr. Risdale and really, what they are capable of is nothing short of astonishing! While my chaperone, old Mrs. Boynton sits by the door of the library, knitting and falling asleep, I have been instructed in the producing of spirit raps of numerous kinds—it is so easy!—ticks, thumps, even loud slaps. Also the art (as Mr. Herne calls it) of being tied up so as to easily slip loose, the use of a telescopic "reaching rod" made of aluminum which hooks into the handle of a trumpet to make it float, or fits into the trumpet as a tube through which the medium can whisper, or a thin rubber tube can be slipped into the trumpet, lying upon the floor, so that spirit voices issue from that. Invisible hands playing the chimes, or a tambourine, a mandolin, even an accordion—the directing of thin veils of vapour around a darkened room, the floating of a luminous spirit arm (and even near the ceiling, with the use of a chair!)—all by means of a bit of pulverized luminous paint powdered on the arm! The concealing of bent pins and Chinese silk thread under one's skirts, used in such a way as to cause a table to glide on its casters across the room. There is more—phosphorescent lights, ringing bells, objects flying, it is all too exhausting to write down.

But when I looked incredulous, which was, I confess, often, aren't these tricks, I wanted to say, aren't you tricking people, deceiving them? When I first ventured this question, breathed the word trick, Mr. Risdale, if it were possible, drew his gaunt frame up even straighter than it was and delivered a great, thunderous lecture, his left arm powdered in luminous paint, a spirit trumpet in his right hand, and a black beard coming unglued from his chin... a lecture on the <u>duty</u> of the medium to deceive, on the medium's <u>responsibility</u> to his sitters, on how disastrous it would be to depend upon the fitful, often fickle response of spirit power... parlour seances demand consistent performance and these, he waved his glowing arm and trumpet about, were the innocent aids to such. Certainly I must be aware as he and Mr. Herne, as all spiritualists operating in London were aware, of how quixotic one's own unseen powers could prove... how mischievous and lazy... and so with these "assists" as he called them, a medium became infallible. Thus, his greatest obligation—no, <u>duty</u>—he was again thundering—that of insuring the sitter's faith in a divine afterlife remained unshaken...a duty, he glowered at me, greater than that of your average curate, Miss Cook.

Mr. Herne, who had stood to the side seeming amused, now spoke. Do not underestimate, my charming Miss Cook, the power of showmanship. A rambunctious spirit is always more attractive to its audience of sitters than a sedate one. Think of it, dear child, as God's theatre. Even our Lord realized how slow-witted his creatures were. Even he performed miracles. We perform them too, simply on a more modest scale.

Didsbury, Manchester
May, 1873

Charles Blackburn had arrived at his current despondency by a long and torturous route. Since his resolve to journey to London and deliver his daughter a second time to the Brooke Asylum in Upper Clapham, his depression had so thoroughly cast itself over the humid, sultry day that he scarcely noticed what he usually loved, hedges greening and stippled with fledgling blackbirds, his orchards in fragrant, alabaster bloom. A fire burned in the grate opposite the bed where his daughter lay, her eyes closed, her lips reciting a language of foreign syllables, reversed consonants, unintelligible phrasings. Around her wrist, narrow as a peeled twig, was knotted a slender ribbon of robin's-egg blue, fastened at its other end to her father's wrist. Eliza's symptoms had returned— the refusal to eat or to sleep, outbursts of eerie laughter, con- sumptive coughings, an occasional paralysis of limbs so severe she had to be carried, and worst, paroxysms of violence followed by a vacuous docility.

Blackburn toyed with the ribbon he'd gotten from his deceased wife's sewing room, turning it this way and that. When Eliza stirred, he could, he reasoned, feel the direction of her movement and thus sometimes rest without ceasing to protect her.

Through the diamond-shaped window, he could see the sun lowering behind his orchards like a slow unfolding fan of fire. Its light, as if in final claim for the day's radiance, set a temporary jewel upon Eliza's face. His own face was in shadow, grimly set at the thought of tomorrow's journey. Neither he nor his wife, Jane, had ever ceased marveling at their child's beauty (and Eliza was no longer a child but a young woman of nineteen), beauty with scarcely any awareness of itself. Her ivory skin was marked with a starring of freckles like those dun spots on the pale eggs of thrushes and nightingales. Her hair, grown past her waist, was a marvelous, deeply crimped torrent of auburn. Her eyes were the remarkable colour of wild violets, the eyelids tinged lilac. And what of the perfection of her former temperament, a nature selfless and sweet, obedient and gay, always gay. Her madness was a mystery per- secuting him.

During the three years since his wife's death, Eliza, too, had been lost to him. Physicians could neither explain the cause of her insanity nor offer hope for its cure. Of what use was his wealth, of what use or pleasure, any of it. His wife and now his daughter, on whom he had lavished such pride, were equally gone.

He looked at the sun's play of fire along the edges of his property, unable to stop himself from envisioning tomorrow's cruel destination. Upon reaching London and settling Eliza in her room at the Brooke Asylum, he would call on his old friend Thomas Boynton with whom he had recently been in correspondence. Boynton had sent a most sympathetic reply to his news, promising a seance for him at the Cook home. Since her first public appearance, their daughter Selene, he said, had advanced in her spiritualist powers. Her displays were as fine and numerous, as thrilling as any shown by better established mediums in London. As fine as Mrs. Guppy's or D. D. Homes's, even surpassing Frank Herne's. In his last letter, Boynton had included directions to the Cook home on Eleanor Road which was, he said, near his own place on Navarino.

Charles Blackburn had visited a great many mediums since his wife's death, witnessed luminous spirit hands and faces, heard accordions and harps played in lively manner by ghostly hands, seen floating lights, felt furniture tilting and spinning, read messages written on slate by the hands of invisible spirits. He was a member of both the Dalston Association and the Ghost Club, an organization whose members believed all nations were run entirely by ghosts and were instructed to address one another as Brother Ghost. His donations to these organizations, to the editors of the several spiritualist newspapers in London, his constant patronage of psychical activities, had made him a popular figure (some would say target) among spiritualists. Here was a gentleman with little use for his own money, whose generosity could be depended upon; in return, he was surrounded by a circle of high-minded companions who indulged his yearning for contact with the spirit world.

That night, at his estate in Didsbury, Charles Blackburn studied his daughter's face, delicately featured as any faerie queen's, now defaulted from all womanly purpose or ambition. He dropped to sleep in her small brocade chair, the ribbon shifting slightly, as a filament of web might shimmer in the wake of a breeze or a thought or perhaps a spirit, invisible, passing by.

*

With uncanny genius, Eliza immediately understood where and why he was taking her. She fought being dressed in her lavender silk travel dress, struggled against any arrangement of her hair and when he was for one instant distracted and the ribbon loosened, she ran off from him. He found her cowering beneath her own bed, but not before coming across what she had already done. His consequent anger lent him the strength he needed to turn her over to Dr. Munro at Brooke House. She had entered his library, broken open his glass collection case which held row upon row of the birds' eggs he and Jane had made a tranquil but fastidious hobby of collecting on their walks together. In shock, he regarded the damage. She'd smashed them all, every one, utterly destroyed the collection, insulted his wife's memory. How, in her madness, she seemed to hate him!

Not an hour after this, Eliza Blackburn was taken, dress askew, shoes wrongly fastened, taken off by her father under a warm misting of spring rain, traveling first down the green and muddy lanes, then the elm sheltered roads toward London where he envisioned himself stopping first at Brooke House in Upper Clapham, being met by Dr. Munro and the same Miss Pettingal who had cared for Eliza before, and then, if he was steady enough, he would manage to get himself to the Cook girl's seance.

This afternoon was to be my final lesson with Mr. Herne and Mr. Risdale. Mr. Herne was not yet there when I arrived and Mr. Risdale was in the library with an enormously fat woman he introduced as a Mrs. Guppy. He explained that he and Mr. Herne were protégés of Mrs. Guppy's and that she had come today to see the schoolgirl medium they had been prattling on about. Of course, I had heard of Mrs. Guppy. She was considered London's foremost medium and famous for her apports—showering sitters with gifts, mainly fruits and vegetables. Indeed, I have read of you, I spoke breathlessly for it seemed, despite her grotesque appearance, an honor to meet the great Mrs. Guppy, who had once been levitated all the way from her kitchen where she was tallying receipts and in fact had just finished writing the word "onion" when she found herself whizzing through the air and landing in a heap upon a large table where a seance was in progress. Now, however, she eyed me very coldly, leaning close as she spoke, her breath so thick with gin it took everything in me not to be sick. Fortunately, Mr. Herne showed up, apologizing for his tardiness. Another of your tiresome assignations, Robert? Mrs. Guppy sneered. I really found her quite atrocious.

Our last session did not go well, and I believe it was her fault. And though Mr. Herne answered my complaint after she had gone by saying she was much better behaved in seance, I was not convinced. He even promised to take me, if I liked, to one of her seances on Lamb's Conduit Road to see for myself her remarkable feats. Only last week, he went on, Lord Arthur Russell had asked for a flower and, in an instant, a six-foot sunflower, roots and all, had landed at his feet, clumps of dirt still sticking to it! I have, Mr. Herne said, seen Mrs. Guppy cause live eels and lobsters, seawater and starfish, to drop down upon the table, and once, upon a woman she clearly disliked, a little bucket of tar, so the woman had to be led out of the parlour and cleaned up. She has traveled all over Europe, Miss Cook. Particularly Italy, where she was a guest of the Duchess d'Arpino. You may not like her, she is not an agreeable woman,

*still, she has met a great many titled personages and been treated to
a great many luxuries.*

I don't care. I find her a sinister presence, I said and meant it.

I suppose I am glad it was my last meeting with these men, for I
am more than a little confused. Am I to strengthen sitters' faith
with my new skills or profit from them? And what of the original
powers I displayed, however roughly? Mother says a series of
seances has already been set up for me by Mr. Boynton and is being
advertised in Mr. Lodge's newspaper. And these men, Mr. Boynton
and Mr. Lodge, I have learned, paid Mr. Herne and Mr. Risdale a
stipend to "educate" me . . . though apparently not enough, for Mr.
Risdale was always eager to end our lessons and never stopped his
habit of peering at his watch.

What is my most compelling reason to continue on this path?
Relief from the madness I feared would consume me. For weeks
now, there have been no voices about my head, no heaviness.
Whatever the dangerous animal was in me, it is momentarily stilled,
due to the influence, I suppose, of these two men. And for that I am
grateful.

"Tot, you're behaving like a proper fool! Quit crossing yourself and help me."

Hopping from one black-stockinged foot to the other, Selene attempted buttoning up her best set of pantalets, the ones trimmed with anglaise embroidery and set with white ribbons at the knees. Her dress was still in a heap on the floor; it was a plain, dark blue, the one she wore for all her seances. Without giving Tot a chance to help her, she rushed over to the open window and gazed up and down Eleanor Road, praying that she see neither her mother's new spiritualist friends, the Corners (along with their horrid son Elgeron), nor Mr. Blackburn (said to be a wealthy widower), hoping they would all be, as she most certainly was, late. Her panic made everything in the room look stupid. Especially Tot, who moved with all the haste of an expiring cow. She turned back to the window. Their little brick street, spaced with leafy elms and empty of all traffic, now produced a reverse anxiety—Selene imagined the dreadful prospect of no one showing up at all.

"Tot! Do you think I need toast? What could it be that I need? I feel as if I'm fainting."

Furtively crossing herself on her way over to Selene who had dropped to her knees before the window ledge, Tot considered the bread and bacon she would miss if she quit. This thought persuaded her to go on assisting in these weekly, fiendish preparations. Always there was a screeching display of nerves and peevish temper. Twice she had been slapped for not moving fast enough, for dropping an earring or a comb. A curious contrast to the sweet, child-like creature who would appear downstairs in the darkened parlour, the neat head bowed modestly, the voice angelic, the movements ethereal, all otherworldliness. Yet, on the whole, aside from these preparations for seance, Selene was tolerably affectionate. Certainly kinder than Octavia, who treated her as a servant to be demeaned. Selene had once given Tot a petticoat, only slightly torn, and a mother-of-pearl hair comb, broken but pretty to look at. Selene had made her a trusted confederate in these preparations, and if she was sometimes irritable and overwrought, she could be equally generous in her displays and tokens of affection.

At the dressing table, Tot brushed the girl's dark hair and, with a practiced, calming gesture, arranged the fringe on her high, slightly oily forehead. Stepping back to regard the lustrous oiled ringlets neatly falling to the sides of Selene's anxious face, she then tried, without success, to picture what her own hair might look like, done up so.

*

What a preposterous hive of superstition this house has become! Fuming, Octavia stood at her window, looking down as yet another carriage pulled up beside their curb. Her sister's reputation was well established now in London's spirit circles. Each day monogrammed visiting cards were dropped off, gifts arrived—today's a box of preserved apricots from Fortnum and Mason's—the whole household was hypnotized by her sudden celebrity as a spirit medium. And Selene, at hive's center, queen bee. Utterly noxious. Every one of them, even stupid Tot, under a dodo's spell of superstition. No one eats, no one uses the earth toilet, no one steps from indoors to outdoors without consulting some spirit or other as to how. Ridiculous how prosperity alters people. In her own mother's actions these past months, since that first seance in Thomas Boynton's library, Mrs. Cook's shrewd nature, long frustrated by no material to exercise itself upon, had outdone itself. Her appetites, all of them, had grown apace. She ate rolls, cakes, meats, blood puddings. In front of her own daughters, she shamelessly pinched and diddled Mr. Cook. Like some retired general set newly in charge of a grand military campaign, her mother stormed about, spewing orders, particularly in the direction of Mr. Cook, who had begun to fancy himself an entrepreneur of sorts, wheedling favours and gifts, promising invitations to private sittings with his eldest daughter if perhaps a jewel or a fine watch might be delicately proffered in exchange. All his own distorted ideas of what a gentleman should be burst forth in a manner as unseemly as his wife's. Octavia was deeply mortified. Only she remained proudly uncordial, deliberately aloof. As for myself, she thought most injuredly, kneeling beside the window spying on the Corners as they emerged clumsily from their carriage, only I remain uncompromised. But whatever comfort she derived from her superior standard of modesty and good taste was, she realized, mainly small and distinctly bitter.

Mother manages me as though I were a business.
Father acts the fool.
Octavia despises what I do.
I have become an organ grinder's monkey.
Still.
The voices no longer torment me. And I no longer fear madness,
though I do dread exposure. Unmasking. Disgrace.

In the small suite of rooms at Brooke House, neither of them could eat the meal Miss Pettingal had carried in, the haunch of boiled beef, stewed rhubarb and suet dumplings. Eliza's two rooms had only a single latticed window with bars of iron covering its outside; the dismal view was of a walled-in grass yard with a dirty gravel border. The yard was mainly under water, and when he questioned Miss Pettingal about this swamp, this malodorous bilge of space he and his daughter were forced after their supper to walk around and around for their meager exercise, she answered that Dr. Munro, at his expense, had tried twice in the past fort-night to have the yard drained, but to no avail. Charles Blackburn simply could not recall prior conditions having been so dismal. Yet he had inspected other private, licensed houses, including Finch's and Blacklands House, and their conditions, if it could be fathomed, were worse.

The anguish Eliza demonstrated upon his taking leave of her affected Charles profoundly. He left only to return for a few minutes more. He promised to return in the morning. He promised if she were well, he would take her back to Manchester. And on his way by coach to the address on Eleanor Street, Hackney, he realized he had promised her falsely. The guilt he experienced crushed him so that he hardly knew how he found himself standing on a freshly whitewashed doorstep, staring dejectedly at a window box of red geraniums and white mignonette. When the door opened, he clumsily introduced himself.

"Oh, Mr. Blackburn, good evening. You've never, I'm certain of it, seen a sight to match Selene in one of her trances. Our house has been turned upside down these past months. We scarcely know, unless some spirit or other directs us, if we're here or there, and it's all I can do to keep up with the notice being paid our Selene." Harriet Cook, who would not tolerate melancholy in any man, lifted and set his large feet onto the same needlepointed footstool that had hurled itself through the parlour the previous week. "We're blessed, I'm sure, to have so many dead souls want-ing to speak through our dear daughter. Tot will bring refreshment presently."

No fool, Mrs. Cook already knew a great deal about the stout widower seated before her. The only surprise, since she'd never before seen him, was his bald pate which sported huge tufts at the sides. His short, yellow waistcoat was blotched with brown gravy and a white rose drooped from the lapel of his frock coat. He looked not so much wealthy as neglected. Deftly, she inquired of his family, his interest in spiritualism, his cotton manufacturing business (even going so far as to invent a cousin who had dabbled in the same). She attained superlative heights of hospitality. The cost of these weekly seances was nearly killing them, and they could no longer survive on preserved apricots and fancy bouquets. And lo! Into their home comes Mr. Blackburn. Harriet Cook found that her native solicitude was positively *inspired* by hope of gain.

*

A SEANCE WITH FACE MANIFESTATIONS WAS PRE-SIDED OVER BY MISS SELENE COOK ON TUESDAY, MAY 31, 1873 AT SEVEN O'CLOCK IN THE EVENING AT THE COOK RESIDENCE, ELEANOR ROAD, HACKNEY, LONDON. PRESENT WERE MR. CHARLES BLACKBURN, MR. BALFOUR LODGE, MR. THOMAS BOYNTON. DENIS COOK, HARRIET COOK, OCTAVIA COOK, AMELIA CORNER, COUNCIL MEMBER OF THE DALSTON ASSOCIATION, AND HER THREE GROWN CHILDREN, SARAH, ISABEL AND ELGERON.

The Spiritualist
June 4, 1873

*

Charles Blackburn found himself escorted downstairs to a queer sort of half basement-breakfast room where a monstrous wooden corner cupboard stood as spirit cabinet for the medium. His intent was simple: to compare hers to other seances he had attended, to test her reputation. He found ten guests already crowded into the room. Boynton, of course, and Lodge, both of whom greeted him with effusive sympathy and fondness, then a family by the name of Corner, a mother, two lacklustre daughters and a son, Elgeron, who devoted himself mainly to the grooming of his hair, Mrs. Cook, Mr. Cook, a second daughter, plain and rather petulant, and lastly, himself, Old Hummums, as his daughter once called him, in happier times.

Seated, or rather squeezed round a table, they were commanded by Mrs. Cook to grasp hands and cultivate high-minded thoughts so as to prepare the atmosphere for spirit visitors. Then Boynton intoned a dry prayer and launched into the opening verse of "Footsteps of Angels," until a sturdy domestic girl led the young medium into the room, looking as though she could scarcely walk but was determined to do so. Charles Blackburn observed that the medium was exceedingly pretty, nearly childlike in stature. Her hands fluttered about her person, tremulous as birds. She seated herself directly across from him, her mother on her left and the young man, so egregiously vain, on her right. After she had settled herself, a series of rappings commenced, percussive and brittle, in various corners and parts of the room. Then a brass bell, near him, its mouth open upon the Turkey carpet, rang seemingly of its own power. Rang once more while disporting itself airily, as if it were a feather, onto the table. Then, with Miss Cook's face upturned in rapt concentration, a cool breeze wafted over everyone as the table gave a long, low shudder and began to wallow from side to side beneath the company's tightly clasped hands. Then, abruptly, it stopped and became a table upon which the medium's head rested, turned to one side. As if this were a signal, Mrs. Cook brought forth paper and a pen from her skirts and laid them beside the inert, limp hand which by its own will grasped the pen and began, rapidly, to write. The hand scrawled, stopped, then took up its ghostly activity one more. The medium gave a small utterance and pushed the paper away. Mrs. Cook took it up, handed it to Mr. Lodge who read aloud:

> *Mes Amis! Je suis en esprit.* You will see I write in the hand of one who has most dearly loved one of you now present, indeed has been wife to him. The yellow waistcoat he knows to be my favourite, for I sewed it for him some years ago. But the poor rose, how wilted it appears, there in his dear pocket! And that you know this message is truly mine, I give you the private name our beloved daughter has always called you by... I write it down for you to see. *Au revoir*, dear husband!

Charles Blackburn experienced a profusion of tears in his eyes. Then all swiftly changed as a female voice sounded thrillingly from another part of the room, announcing itself as Florence King, spirit control of Selene Cook. Selene, the voice commanded, was now to enter the cabinet.

The conceited young man and Boynton unclasped hands and rose to escort Miss Cook into the large, cheap cupboard, empty save for a Windsor chair. When she was seated, Boynton placed a coil of rope in her lap and firmly closed the cabinet door. Urging the others to join in, Mrs. Cook took up the singing of "Footsteps of Angels" once more until stopped by a definite sound from inside the cabinet. Boynton opened the door to reveal Miss Cook tied to her chair by the neck, wrists and ankles, her face in a profound trance, her body in a swoon. He shut the door again. With dampened fingers, Mrs. Cook extinguished the candle. All sat in darkness. Through an aperture at the top, a tall vapourous face, eyes unblinking and features defeated of life, seemed to float awhile in the opening, then vanish. Mrs. Cook prompted the company to sing again, stopping only when a second face appeared, this one black, the eyes rolled backward.

After an interval, this black apparition vanished too. After some additional minutes, Boynton creaked open the door of the cabinet, Mrs. Cook re-lit the candle and all saw Miss Cook, still tied to her chair, insensible to the world around her.

Both her father and mother went to her. They pinched, lightly slapped and roused her by name. The medium managed barely to stand. She claimed to remember nothing of what had occurred. Supported on either side, the girl was led by her servant out of the room.

Charles Blackburn, damp eyed, thanked the cheerful Mrs. Cook. She invited him to return the following Sunday. In all likelihood, he assured her, he would do so. Her daughter, he said, was enchanting, and her youth a most convincing argument for the truth of the experiment. He then asked if he could have the trance note, for he wished to see what name the spirit had written down.

Having already glanced at the scrawled writing—not her daughter's hand—and seen the word *Hummums*...really, Selene's psychical powers threatened at times to unnerve her, Harriet Cook pressed the note into his hand, making him promise he would, indeed, come back to see them.

   This morning I took Octavia with me by omnibus to New Bond Street where, at last, we were able to go to Piesse and Lubin. With some of my first cheque from Mr. Blackburn, I bought her things she liked and myself as well. We both purchased tins of craie de Briacon for our faces. I suppose I wanted to show her how whatever attention I receive by my mediumship benefits her as well—if we make the effort to get along together. On the ride home, I confided in her as to how some of the false things in seance are done, a mistake as her reaction was decidedly cool. I knew it, she said. You are a fraud. In my defense, I trotted out Mr. Risdale's argument, certainly one my parents seem easily to accept, but Octavia was unmoved by my borrowed idea that the deception was done only to enhance a faith that should exist in people in the first place. I serve people, I said. No, she said, you deceive them. I dangled her package, fancily wrapped from Piesse and Lubin, in front of her. But you will be the prettier for it. She laughed but there has grown up between us a perceptible chill that I greatly regret.

June 6, 1873

To my Trusted Friend and Colleague, Dr. Franklin Worthy,

What a place London is! No doubt I'll miss it, but with this loathsome hot spell, the air smells of brick dust and horse dung. The city, mainly a hodgepodge of villages, is being built at such tremendous pace, construction on every corner, that for blocks the air is clogged with red brick dust and smells burnt from the quantity of working kilns. That and the abominable stink of piss and manure, the incessant noise of iron carriage wheels on brick and cobblestone, the hordes of beggars, hawkers, and foreign street musicians (some with monkeys and bears!)...have I made you content to remain in Boston?

I hope you are well, Frank, and the practice not too burden-some. On this side of the Atlantic, your friend has had a rare experience. Two evenings ago, I attended a full-fledged SEANCE. You've heard of those people calling themselves spiritualists, who sit in dark parlours causing sticks of furniture to fly about yet never managing to bash anyone, a happenstance for which our skills might come in useful, where strange termite rappings come from the walls and whatnot...we've had our case in Boston with the Fox sisters...all this to supposedly prove life beyond the grave.

At any rate, I had called upon William Herapath, a brilliant seeming, though most saturnine scientist and photographer (you know of my interest in the camera). Through an acquaintance I had been referred to Herapath and while visiting him in his laboratory (a splendid place tucked right into his home), he received a letter of invitation to a seance that same evening. Turns out he's something of an investigator in that field as well. I expressed some curiosity, and before I knew it, we were on our way to a drab section of the city known as Hackney. As we rolled smartly along in one of the newer hansom cabs, the driver more than once taking us round corners on two wheels, Herapath chatted on, unperturbed, though my heart was in my ear and myself nearly in his lap. I was relieved to be finally stopped in front of an ordinary terrace house which would, I reasoned, contain within it ordinary domestic English life. What a prema-ture supposition that proved to be! No ordinary occupants live within that commonplace exterior I can assure you.

The point is: I have now observed how the English chat with their dead, and the conversation, as I heard it, is very much subdued.

A servant girl unceremoniously yanked the door then left us as she padded upstairs. Herapath and I made our way toward the sound of voices, going downstairs until we came into a small, badly-lit kind of eating room which smelled hideously of flatulence and stewed cabbage. The woman of the house, a plump woman who blinked like a pigeon, by name of Mrs. Cook, greeted us, as did her husband, a shifty-eyed fellow whose glance kept returning to my gold watch chain. Herapath and I were seated around a table with the other guests—a small, pockmarked gentleman with something of the mortician's cast to him, a second gentleman sporting a yellow waistcoat much splotched with his dinners and an odd trio, two girls looking as if they had been kept on vinegar fasts and a young fellow who fancied himself a sort of human prize. I have never seen anyone, so many times, put his hand back to smooth his hair which was blond, heavily pomaded and as waxed as your parlour piano. Which would be the medium, I whispered to Herapath, who shook his head and cracked his finger joints by way of response. Mrs. Cook then instructed us to grasp hands in a circle. The dull little man started up with a prayer, then in a dyspeptic soprano, the pigeon warbled..., stopped to dislodge something from its teeth, then quavered again into song. I held hands with the man of the house and was glad of it... to have hold of such a paw that seemed as if it mainly wanted to crawl over my chest and make off with my watch. My other hand was attached to one of the vinegar sister's and a fishy, humourless hand it was.

All heads turned at the sound of rustling skirts coming down the hall. Propped up by the servant girl, in came THE MEDIUM. I could not take my eyes off this instrument of the spirits. Oh, to be a spirit, able to take up lodging in such a creature! And it is this that has brought your dear old fusty bachelor to his current state: as she swept her eerie gaze around the table as if to take soul's measure of each one of us, her eyes stopped longest upon mine and then, I swear it, Frank, she winked.

As for the seance, considering what I had heard of such things in America, this was pretty dull stuff. A few termite rappings, a jolt or two of the table, a bell rolling on its own across a carpet and then whizzing up to the table, a husky voice from behind the washstand commanding Miss Cook to enter the corner cabinet. The medium seated herself on a little chair, a large ball of twine on her lap. The cabinet door was shut by the little undertaker, opened after a hymn or two and there she was, cleverly knotted to the chair. The door was shut, the door was opened, open sesame, still tied! After that, we watched several faces appear in a hole at the top of the cabinet. I recognized those faces—all hers—as any student of physiognomy knows, a single face can be contorted into any number of masks. Children do this all the time, upturning their eyes to resemble gargoyles and griffins. Mainly I was impressed by the little medium's athletic prowess, how she managed to get up from her chair, poke her veiled face into the aperture, then knot herself back into the chair. I'm sure our dreadful singing had something to do with her facility. The yellow-waistcoated gentleman who had been spoken to by the voice of his dead wife (this the single authentic-seeming episode), blotted up tears and trumpeted his nose. Then it was over. The girl was roused rather viciously by her parents, then led as if she were a consumptive from the room.

The point being this: your old Arthur finds himself infatuated by the most unlikely of candidates, a young English spiritualist...unlucky shot from Cupid's quiver!

I have secured a small villa in Sandowne on the Isle of Wight for the remainder of the month and whom do you imagine I intend to invite for a brief visit, along with her Mamma, of course? Though I am somewhat worried that my Aunt Edwina, a formidable old battleship who died January of last year, might decide to reprimand me through the instrument of Miss Cook.

I plan on being home in time for whatever epidemic is to strike us next in Boston. By far the silliest plague I've seen here is this outbreak of spiritualism, and yet your Arthur finds himself with unjaded eye fixed upon a certain delightful young English medium. Laugh if you will, my friend, I am happy.

Affection to All,

A.

Mrs. Cook was working to conceal, by an artful bunching of her own cream silk scarf, a pinkish wart on the side of Selene's neck. A blemish easily overlooked, and one Selene had had ever since she was a child but, today, every impediment to the successful capture of Dr. Purdon must be removed. Clearly though, the scarf drew rather than diverted attention. Harriet fussed with it because something larger worried her. Selene's behaviour had become increasingly peculiar and morose over the six-hour train journey out of London's Paddington Station toward the Isle of Wight. Of Dr. Purdon himself, his nature or qualification as a possible match for her eldest daughter, Harriet Cook knew only enough to speculate inaccurately. He had appeared, an uninvited sitter, in the company of the well-known William Herapath, at one of their seances. After some unsubtle digging about, Harriet had determined that Dr. A. E. Purdon was an American bachelor and physician. Still, she must not have been overly impressed upon meeting him, for when his letter arrived, she struggled to match a face to the invitation. It was colourless to her memory, a cipher. But he was unmarried, of some means, and apparently much taken with her daughter, who at this moment, could be mistaken for a lummox.

Indeed, when the letter arrived, Mr. and Mrs. Cook agreed that here was a second bit of fortune resulting from their daughter's career as a sensitive. Before their eyes stretched an imaginary but profitable vista—courtship, marriage, life in America. With skillful encouragement from Harriet and the natural enticement of Selene, a proposal was surely in hand. This would not, they further agreed, interfere with their first and primary bit of fortune, the patronage of Charles Blackburn. Over dinner, Denis had tapped a knife on his glass for attention and cleared his throat while Harriet read the letter aloud. Selene's response was cool. What man is he? Oh, well. A trip to the sea? A villa? Listlessly, she drove the baked cod around her plate with her fork. Mrs. Cook wanted to slap her. Was it that fop, Elgeron Corner? That walking advertisement for bear grease pomade? Marry that young sap, you'll be in the public halls giving seances and turning over your petty wages for him to go spend on himself. Mrs. Cook thought all this and more but said nothing. She really wasn't certain if Selene's moodiness had anything at all to do with him.

Meanwhile, Octavia offered to go. "I'll simply impersonate my sister. How will he know the difference, it's so dark at those sittings. Besides, I recall him distinctly. Sandy haired, long whiskered, modern spectacles, watery blue eyes."

The apparent seriousness of her sister's offer roused Selene.

"We'll have to go to the stores tomorrow. If I go, I shall be needing new things."

Octavia scraped back her chair, sobbing, calling Selene a spoilt, wicked prig, destined for an eternity in Hell. Hearing that, Tot fumbled with and dropped a dish of *pommes de terre*. Heedless of the potatoes rolling about his feet, Mr. Cook dribbled more port into his glass and wondered where the devil he had put the Cuban cigar Purdon had given him last week.

A letter of acceptance was swiftly drafted and dispatched by Mrs. Cook. Funds were outlaid in excess of what they had, by means of credit, in order to provide Selene with the most alluring of accessories. As for Octavia, her parents agreed that once Selene was married off, they would look to her frankly dismal prospects. They were convinced she read too much and was in danger of ruining her eyes.

But now, nearly arrived and thereafter scheduled to take the ferry boat, Mrs. Cook realized they would be in the company of the eligible Dr. Purdon in less than two hours. With Selene beside her, stupid as a shoe.

"Liveliness, child! A man enjoys a woman with bloom in her cheeks!" The girl was selfish. Didn't care whether her mother drifted straight into the workhouse and from there fell into an unmarked pauper's grave. Didn't care a whiff for anyone but herself. Well, the bill was being footed by Dr. Purdon, wasn't it, and if Selene could so easily attract one man, surely there would be others. I won't, Harriet resolved, spoil my part of the excursion. Selene was not the only one who had never seen the sea, much less stayed in a villa. Harriet pinched Selene's arm.

"Never mind. Let's enjoy ourselves, shall we?"

She stuffed the cream silk scarf back into her portmanteau. A man who's a physician might just find a wart entirely attractive.

*

As she waited with her mother on the Isle of Wight's landing, Selene brushed and patted down the rumpled skirt of her fawn-coloured dress. Their luggage stood heaped about them, an uneven, penetrable barricade.

"That's probably him, Selie! In the white carriage, trimmed with scarlet. Lovely."

Outfitted in a fashionable dogstooth checked suit, dove-grey bowler and matching grey gloves, Arthur Purdon got down from his carriage, which was indeed white and trimmed in scarlet, and greeted his visitors in a slightly nasal, flat-sounding American accent. Bowing to Mrs. Cook, then to her daughter, he produced from behind his back two nosegays of violets, white for Harriet, royal purple for Selene, who barely sniffed at their wilted, moist fragrance as she gazed past the man to the sea.

"Selene's stunned, Doctor. She has worshipped violets ever since she was a child."

The driver, instructed by Purdon to return in an hour's time, hefted the luggage into the open carriage and whipped the horses past the boardwalk where a great many seaside visitors were walking. There seemed to Selene to be a hot dazzle of activities and random noises, boot heels scuffling against wooden walkways, the sea, the exhilaration of its green and white sound, its crescendo and yawning sigh, then the desultory rise and fall of human conversation. Purdon purchased them each a pale Italian ice which they ate while standing near an organ grinder with his four monkeys, each of whom wore an embroidered vest and a flat maroon, green-tasseled cap. The monkeys somersaulted, leapt up, rubbed at their faces, while the organ grinder's lugubrious music rendered their quick antics all the more amusing. Finishing their ices, the three made their way further down the boardwalk, Harriet's fringed parasol raised against the glaring sun. Occasionally, progress was slowed by a congress of parasols, their owners forced to lift or slightly dip their black or white silk parasols to permit smoother passage. It was just past three o'clock. The afternoon was hot, cloudless and only partially relieved by currents of salt air blowing off the sea; these buffeted Selene's hat, brown velvet with a cluster of artificial cherries and a netting of fawn tulle. One of the hat pins had come loose during the day's journey, so the hat itself wobbled slightly on her dark brown, precisely curled hair.

Purdon guided them good-naturedly, determined to give the two women pleasant passage through the weekend crowds. He brought them to an excellent vantage point from which they could observe a Punch-and-Judy show set up on the sand. Harriet Cook was delighted by everything she saw, and her enthusiasm was matched by Purdon's. Without intending it, these two found themselves sharing an unabashed capacity for pleasure.

Selene lagged, her pace tentative, almost clumsy, in contrast to the elegance of her slight figure. She felt mesmerized by the sound and flecked colours of the sea. Beyond the elevated boardwalk where a bright tapestry of human activity flowed, she heard only the rhythm of the sea, heard nothing of the gay, temporal conversations of people. She could neither distinguish nor translate any of their speech, it was as if they were all sealed over in a sudden, heavy silence. The sea had taken up its broad soliloquy with her, courting, invading, shocking her with its rhythms.

She stood beside her mother, her cheeks flushed, a rivulet of sweat trickling down her back. Harriet Cook and Purdon watched with exclamations of delight as Judy clouted Punch with a red and blue pointed staff. The puppet husband bobbed back and forth, whispering to the crowd his intended revenge. Selene, hemmed in by strangers, felt weighted, unable to breath, hearing nothing, yet seeing everything. Without willing it, she began, quite literally, to see the fates of those nearest her. The Punch-and-Judy ended with a thump of unfurled curtain, followed by shouts and applause. Then a conjurer in a red satin stovepipe hat pushed the legs of a blue table into the sand and began to perform a series of mystifying tricks, putting cards into both his trouser pockets, moving three black hats about, then causing these same cards to float up from each of the black hats.

Selene knew precisely what he was doing, how extraordinarily simple it was to deceive people, aided by their own desire to be lifted up from their lives and given hope. As a fan of images arranged themselves, like photographs, around the head of each person she happened to look at, Selene saw each man, woman and child's life unfold, hesitate, then close into its unique appointment with death. The young woman standing beside her would bear a child who would die in infancy, a second child who would flourish and a husband who would leave her widowed and bitterly poor. She saw destinies as vividly as her mother and Dr. Purdon saw the red-hatted conjurer, his back to the sea, busy with his dream of tricks and bafflement. With shy dread, she glanced at her mother but saw nothing, simply the sea air, brilliant and gauzy. Dr. Purdon, however, would never marry, would prefer it so until one evening, and how clearly she saw it—twilight on a congested street—he would be run down by a pair of horses half a block from his home. This would happen soon, for in her vision he appeared much the same age as he did now. Selene moved from her place in the crowd and walked quickly down a slope of greyish sand until she reached the edge of the sea. She stood on a dark collar of sand wetted with ribbons of kelp, spotted with bits of shell. Across the Channel lay France. Better to gaze out upon the sea than to have to look at people ignorant of what was to befall them.

Then Dr. Purdon was beside her, his face inclined close to hers, inquiring if she were tired. He escorted her back up the sandy incline at the top of which Mrs. Cook waited, her face beneath the fringed parasol bearing a shadowy expression of delight replaced by agitation at the sight of the front hem of her daughter's new dress, scalloped with sea water and a thick beadwork of sand, her new kid boots wet and ruined as well.

In the same white carriage, Purdon and his guests departed from Sandowne, riding out through a cool, deeply wooded area, eventually coming upon a bright, wide field of sunflowers. Selene begged the driver to stop so she might step down. Purdon stood patiently beside the carriage, not hearing Mrs. Cook prattle on, watching the broad yellow heads of the sunflowers sway as Selene floated among them.

It took an exasperated Harriet the rest of the short ride to Dr. Purdon's rented villa to brush the sticky gold pollen off Selene's new jacket.

*

The largest of two lace-curtained windows faced east and overlooked the sea. Selene stood there, picturing herself a heroine in one of the novels she and Octavia had read, preferably one of Miss Broughton's. A hand mirror of carved pearwood lay on the dressing table. She walked about the room, the mirror held out before her. At moments, in certain lights, her features greatly pleased her—she almost did, she thought, resemble a heroine whose life was passionate and dramatic. She imagined being wife to Dr. Purdon, with his too-eager, watery eyes—no—that gave her a greensickness face, an image she wanted nothing to do with. Still, the room itself was peaceful. It implied a life of order and elegance. Selene unbuttoned and drew off her damp shoes, lay back on the bed, holding the mirror above her face, imagining what a lover's face (and not Dr. Purdon's), looking down upon hers, would see. She particularly admired her eyes and her creamy skin and wondered again why it was she could never glimpse her own destiny, see anything clearly of her own fate.

*

Harriet Cook discovered her daughter on top of a handsome four-poster bed, asleep, her brown velvet cap still on, her white kid boots, stained with sea water, thrown onto the apricot-hued carpet. On a small wicker table beside the bed, a bag of saltwater taffies purchased by Dr. Purdon, seized her attention. Mrs. Cook saw no reason to curb her love of sweets, especially now, when she could feel the agitated palpitations of her heart. She rustled several of the candies out of the bag and chewed, wiping the clouded drool that caught at the downturned corners of her mouth. Her daughter's talents had won them this luxury. Popping several more of the sticky white candies into her mouth, Harriet agonized over the evening ahead. Selene did not perform seances outside their home, and now, with her behavior so like that terrible time they had to seek out Thomas Boynton's help, perplexed by Selene's spells of stupor, her outbursts of hysterics, now—on this trip— came the possibility, the ominous threat of—recurrence. They had less than an hour to prepare. These were wealthy strangers whom Selene must both charm and persuade. She must deepen Dr. Purdon's infatuation, move him toward that nuptial instinct which Harriet perceived had made, as yet, only a fragile inroad into his bachelor's mind.

Behind heavy green tapestried drapes substituting for her medium's "cabinet," Selene, bound with tape and rope to a ridiculously highbacked, gold velvet chair, could manifest nothing. Nothing. From that doomed moment during dinner when Lord Brompton had risen to his feet over a plate of turkey *à la perigeux*, portentiously announcing he would tie a string from his ankle to that of the young medium's in order to note any suspicious movement within the cabinet (surely the charming medium from London had no objection), from that moment on, Dr. Purdon's guests grew increasingly fractious. Herded into the parlor after dinner, the seven or eight titled guests reacted to Mrs. Cook's instructions like spoilt, unruly schoolchildren. They refused to sing "Footsteps of Angels." Lady Brompton, as a Roman Catholic, pleaded ignorance, along with her husband, of such a hymn. Why, if the point was to muffle the medium's movements with song, could they not simply bellow "God Save the Queen"? Wouldn't that do as well? All Harriet's attempts to manage the seance were undermined. As a foreigner, Dr. Purdon was unaware of the subtler insults and jibes being aimed at both mother and daughter. When the tapestries were drawn back a third time, Selene was found to be in a dead swoon, stemming from humiliation or spiritual seizure, no one knew but everyone, depending on his or her degree of skepticism, had a boisterous opinion. In any event, the pretty imposter, as Lord Brompton, string still around his ankle, declared her, was escorted upstairs by her mother. The rest of the evening proceeded blithely enough for Dr. Purdon's guests, though upstairs, Harriet would be tormented by all that she had overheard as she had paused with Selene, who really was ill, on the dark staircase.

"Perfectly forgiveable, Purdon. These sorts issue mainly from the lower classes. Shamelessly clever types who perform these sorts of ghost shows in order to worm themselves into the upper classes. Nearly every month Lady Brompton and I hear of yet another young medium marrying well above her class, and whatever highminded discourse with ghosts she had previously conducted is curiously replaced with inquiries as to prices of silver cutlery and names of fashionable dressmakers. Perhaps in America, such fraud could not succeed. She is an attractive creature, your Miss Cook. I'd venture to say the mother has her matrimonial eye firmly fixed on you, Purdon."

*

Breakfast the next morning was served on the broad, greystone terrace. Joining the doctor, Harriet ate three slices of jellied toast before taking the opportunity to repair Selene's endangered reputation. Arthur Purdon sat across from her in a claret paisley dressing gown, an unattractive tinge of mustache above his lip, listening to Mrs. Cook blither on about evil spirits, notorious for overtaking seances and causing dreadful mischief. If conditions were not right in the circle of sitters, the medium could be rendered helpless to perform. As a rule, sitters were screened with care; even if skeptical, they must prove sympathetic to the purpose of the evening. Last evening's seance was...

"Last night's difficulty, if I understand you correctly, can be traced to the impropriety of my guests? Tonight, then, Mrs. Cook, I propose the three of us conduct our own private seance. I will insure that your spirits feel more comfortable. The good ones, that is. The others, the malefic ones, will be—what?—repelled by my impeccable behaviour?"

Harriet had the disquieting sensation that, much like Lord and Lady Brompton, he was making fun of her, though she had no proof. Not knowing what else to do, she agreed, then helped herself to a fourth slice of toast and an only slightly deflated enjoyment of the sunlight and the sea view.

When Selene finally appeared, Purdon was cheerfully practicing his croquet game on the velvety turf below the terrace. Harriet was sitting in a spot of sunlight, finding bliss in unaccustomed idleness. Her daughter wore a pearl-coloured dressing gown and looked as suited to the opulent surroundings as Harriet could have hoped. Even Purdon, stopping in mid-swing, appeared much taken with her appearance, though Harriet did not fail to note a degree of reserve buried like a troubling seed within the pleasant inquiry as to the quality of his guest's sleep, as he tapped his mallet into the flank of a wooden ball.

The second half of the day passed swiftly enough. Too swiftly for Harriet, who had begun to savour an existence entirely devoted, it would seem, to the circulation and re-circulation of pleasurable sensations. In the late afternoon, they drove back into Sandowne, where Dr. Purdon rented Selene and her mother a bathing machine along with two black bathing costumes. Her mother's shameless affectations of delight mortified Selene, as did that foolish drowning look in the doctor's weak eyes whenever he looked at her. Angry with her mother's obvious zeal to marry her off, Selene thought it a good idea to walk straight into the sea and punish them both.

Abruptly, she left them seated on beach chairs beneath a huge black umbrella, where Dr. Purdon was explaining the uses of photography in the diagnosis of disease to her ridiculous mother...oh, nevermind! She grabbed up her bathing costume and marched along the shore, taking in great lungfuls of salt air. She was working up nerve to go into the bathing machine, a horse-drawn contraption—a box on wheels—within which she would no doubt have to stand bare-legged in this stupid costume while it sagged with the cold weight of seawater. As if she were already inside it, she envisioned the marbled blue slab of sky above her head, and the sun-shot darkness within the wooden enclosure, the sloshing salt water, the poor horse up to its rotting hocks and facing the shore, and herself, standing in a watery coffin, oppressed and suffocating. She would then be expected to step outside, take hold of one of the hemp ropes hanging at the back of the wagon, swing herself into the surge and push of the waves. There was her mother waving from where she sat with Dr. Purdon in an orb of shade upon the sand. Gripping the still-dry bathing costume, Selene started back toward them. Had Octavia been with her, she might have had the enthusiasm to try.

That evening, Purdon was taking a practice tap with his favourite croquet mallet and feeling increasingly uneasy with his exquisite little medium. Still fascinated, he stared at her covertly, much more he knew, than was respectable. Her moodiness alarmed him. Was she on the verge of hysteria, madness? He had treated two such cases in his own practice, had read articles about treatment for female hysterics—from leeching of the genital region to the latest, most extreme recommendation for surgical excision of the disturbed portion of the genitals. Surely, it would not benefit his career to be afflicted with a child-wife who had lost her wits. His medical practice and his peace of mind were equally predicated on dependability and habit. His patients knew and trusted him. Belching lightly before sending the wooden ball rocketing triumphantly through a series of three wickets, Purdon made up his mind to stare as much as he liked, stare himself blind until tomorrow morning when the train would carry the pretty medium and her tiresome mother back to their drab little borough of London. He had no cause to disrupt his life in pursuit of an unstable wife. He would not see her again.

*

Fleetingly, a face appeared in the crack between the tapestried curtains. A female spirit hand gleamed and flitted with a charming luminosity just outside the curtain. And near the end of this seance attended only by Dr. Purdon and Harriet, a masculine voice, rather choked and high timbered, instructed the doctor to be most cautious in his travels, to watch where he was going, particularly when crossing streets.

Arthur Purdon's opinion became quite fixed. Selene Cook's seances addressed a need people had to see some proof and promise of resurrection. He and his colleague in Boston, Franklin Worthy, would discuss this in the months before Purdon's death (in six months to be exact), always concurring that mediums thrived on exploiting those whose Christian faith had eroded.

*

The three-day trip had ended in defeat. Any hope of a marriage proposal had been dashed. Harriet, though she tried to appreciate the elegant room she had slept in, the terrace at breakfast, the generous hospitality—even now, a willow hamper filled with food sat at her feet—found herself tormented by the bitter experience of exclusion. Oh, a life like Lord and Lady Brompton's could only be glimpsed. Impenetrable walls stood between people like herself and people like the Bromptons. A fierce thought bore in on Harriet. Had she been her own daughter these past three days, she would have brought Arthur Purdon to his trousered knee, pledging her everything he owned. Instead, here they were, not an hour from Hackney, a basket of upperclass crumbs at their feet, being returned by train to the same straitened circumstances Harriet had lived in and put up with all her life.

*

Seated on the needlepoint bench before her dressing table, Selene drew her hand backwards out of the cage and perched the goldfinch on her shoulder where it strutted sideways, pricking her flesh with its cool claws. It was past midnight and she was not the least tired. On her dressing table lay an opened letter from Charles Blackburn. His usual cheque had already been turned over to her mother. The letter expressed plans to soon be in London to attend yet another of her remarkable seances. Had she enjoyed her stay at the Isle of Wight? He had never been, had heard it was a place of great natural charm—in contrast to the noisy, soot-drenched city he lived near, Manchester, all cotton mills, warehouses and banks. Had she ever visited Paris, he inquired in fresher, darker ink on the reverse side of the stationery. He planned a brief trip next month. Would she consider joining him?

In the oval mirror, a single candle flickering before it, Selene's reflection was well satisfied. It was good to be home, recovering from her mother's mortifying ambitions and savouring a possible journey to Paris.

A flurried rapping at the door was followed by Tot's pink-capped head thrusting itself into the room.

"What in heaven is the matter?" Selene coaxed the startled finch, which had flown to the floor, back onto her finger so she could pop it back in its cage. "Why have you disturbed me?"

Tot's facial expression, eerily lit by the candle she held before her, was unfathomably grave. Following a step behind her down the dark hallway, Selene saw how badly the pale taper, in its holder, trembled.

"*Qu'est-ce que c'est*? Whatever is the matter with you?"

The guiding candle, which reeked of beef tallow, stopped outside Octavia's closed door. Crouching down, Tot beckoned to Selene to take her turn spying through the keyhole.

"Piffle! I scarcely need to peer through a keyhole into my own sister's room. Give me that candle."

Selene opened the door. Octavia's bedroom was dark save for a second candle flame winking at the far end of the room. Selene went in its direction and found her sister sitting bolt upright on her bed, in a trance, scrawling away on a sheet of monogrammed stationery, the pen wandering unevenly up and down the paper. The messages, insofar as Selene could read them, seemed marked by a cunning mimicry and were mostly taken up with the subject of Charles Blackburn's daughter, Eliza. As Selene watched, the rambling, impassioned missive came to a close with a block-printed signature at the bottom of the page: WRITTEN BY L. GORDON—

SPIRIT CONTROL OF OCTAVIA COOK. Selene stealthily exited her sister's room, nearly falling over the figure of Tot, who waited to tell her that Octavia's trance-writing had started the very day she and Mrs. Cook had left for the Isle of Wight.

*

Soon after Octavia claimed to have received the spirit voice of L. Gordon, less than one month before Selene was to leave for Paris, she and her mother accepted an invitation from Thomas Boynton to enjoy a day trip to the Crystal Palace and dinner aboard a rented yacht, during the course of which they were to enjoy the summer fireworks from Sydenham. But that morning, Harriet complained of rheumatism and a neuralgic headache and declined leaving the house. These ailments seemed to Selene excuses for her mother to stay home and scheme up new ways to ingratiate Octavia more deeply into Charles Blackburn's favor. Octavia had already received her first cheque from him in support of her newfound talent. Well, Selene would let them see how little their conspiracies affected her. She would go to the Crystal Palace unchaperoned and somehow manage a marvelous outing with a dull, dyspeptic man.

But could she confide in Thomas Boynton? Since the night Selene had witnessed her sister in a trance, a poisonous atmosphere had begun to infect the household. Subtle war raged and to what purpose? To establish supremacy of psychical powers, more pointedly, to see which sister could best capture the remunerative attentions of Charles Blackburn. Tot had become Selene's ally; it was Tot who had shown her Octavia's secretly drafted letter to Mr. Blackburn, thick with lies about his daughter's mistreatment in the asylum. L. Gordon claimed to hover above Brooke Asylum, claimed to have witnessed Eliza's abused condition. According to L. Gordon, the only person with spirit authority to assist in this dire matter was Octavia. Bitterly, Selene observed her sister and mother sacrificing whatever she had gained for them in order to more ambitiously serve themselves. No doubt her mother was now plotting to marry Octavia to Mr. Blackburn. Fine. Let her hope. Selene would enjoy herself with Mr. Boynton and within three days' time, travel across the Channel to Paris where she determined she could easily recover Mr. Blackburn's affections and loyalties.

*

Selene said very little, strolling with Mr. Boynton a second time around the large, circular Sydenham pond. Across the glaring puddle of water (as he called it), and through the pale green summer foliage, she made out the long necks and strangely configured heads of enormous, prehistoric dinosaurs. In winter, Mr. Boynton said, following her gaze, these grey concrete creatures presided with a somber and ancient dominance over skaters skimming the ice like dark birds, iron skates scraping. Might he anticipate the pleasure of taking her skating this winter? He spoke so earnestly, holding onto her arm and gazing so sincerely, that she could not help laughing at his expression. Then, so as not to hurt his feelings, she said, yes, absolutely.

Wearing a mauve dress with a rich black stripe, her hair bundled in a full chignon capped by a small black feathered hat tilted fashionably forward, she barely kept pace with the brisk step of Mr. Boynton in his plain black frock coat, fawn-coloured trousers and curly brimmed top hat. Fleetingly, she fancied herself Mrs. Boynton of Navarino Road, before being distracted by a magnificent pair of white swans gliding across the lake. She admired their fiery red beaks, the snowy S's of their long, lanquid necks.

"They can be quite fierce. In a twinkling, grace becomes aggression." Mr. Boynton possessed an aggravating talent for commenting on whatever she was seeing. Still what he said about the swans reminded her of Octavia. The misleadingly docile appearance, the glacial eye. Affectionate one moment, peevish and rude the next. Why? She had tried to be kind to Octavia. Tried to make it up to her. She could hardly be expected to curb her own nature could she? One must lead one's life regardless of other people's resentments or criticisms.

"What is it, my dear girl? You seem quite caught up in rumination."

"Forgive me. It is so terribly hot."

Indeed, moisture from the huge pond seemed to have gathered around them like a shroud of humid cloth. Even the massive trees in the huge park seemed weighted, stilled, desirous of relief.

Soon after, Thomas Boynton and Selene were taken by hired barouche the short distance through a wooded park to the Crystal Palace. It was July, and those Londoners who could had taken refuge in the cooler countryside. Thus, Boynton dryly observed, was the suffocating heat compensated for by unobstructed progress. Seated beside her irksome companion, Selene playfully twirled her mother's black parasol, leaning forward to catch a glimpse of the Crystal Palace. When she was twelve and Octavia ten, their father had taken them to see three of the exhibits— Manufactures, Machinery and Raw Materials. Vividly, Selene recalled to Mr. Boynton the hodgepodge of machinery, great lumps of coal, steam engines, a Nubian court, some Indian miniatures, a hall of rubber plants, and what she and Octavia had liked best of all, the Empress Josephine's palm tree, a fifty-foot tree imported from Fontainebleau and dragged on a cart by thirty-five horses from a horticultural nursery in Hackney. She and Octavia had begged their father to allow them to see the fourth exhibit—Fine Arts. Selene particularly had pleaded and wept to see the water fountains and white marble statues, but their father remained stubbornly fixed upon the dominant themes of the Great Exhibition—Machinery and Trade. Trade, which brought all peoples together under imperial British rule, and Machinery, that new covenant for all the world's ills. Well, this time, Mr. Boynton assured her, she should see all the exotic courts she wished to within the Fine Arts exhibit.

"We may indeed be a nation of shopkeepers, my child, we do cultivate a rather tasteless fetish for the Machine, it is our new Messiah, but I see no reason you and I should bow down before a jamboree of shop shrines today."

The barouche stopped between two Sphinxes which framed a flight of heavily balustraded stone steps leading to one of a dozen entrances. Selene stepped down with the help of Mr. Boynton and gazed awhile at the splendid fairie edifice of glass. What was it he had said, nineteen acres of glass, so many million, thirty million cubic feet of glass?

"John Ruskin first named it in *Punch*, 'the giant cucumber frame.' The designer, Joseph Paxton, was trained as a horticulturist and went on to become a designer of hothouses. Yet the effect is spectacular. Each time I come here, the sensation of pure light as it is divided by the many thousands of iron ribs, the sensation of clearest light outstrips any other architectural feat... it gives one the perspective of infinity itself. One has only to see all this," here Boynton gestured expansively, "to be forever convinced of the superiority of the English people. What nation upon the face of the earth, my dear, has achieved anything so extraordinary, so massive, so perfectly conceived?"

Though she had been nowhere else in the world, Selene was compelled to agree. They climbed the first series of steps and found themselves on one of a dozen terraces, each with a rectangular granite pool bordered at its corners by a life-sized statue. Selene touched the sculpture nearest her, a voluptuous, heavily veiled female figure.

"Splendid, isn't she?" Again, he had followed her gaze. "If I raised you onto this ledge you would no doubt be mistaken for one of these alluring ladies."

"I rather think I am not suitably attired."

"Well then, we would find you a great many white draperies, wouldn't we? No matter, for I am about to extend a rare compliment, I, who am not much given to swelling the heads of others, Miss Cook: you would be any sculptor's crowning achievement."

"How extraordinarily flattering, Mr. Boynton, though I scarcely think it's true." Looking directly at him, she suddenly saw the woman he would marry. An older, sickly widow with a sizable inheritance and an anemic complexion. Poor Mr. Boynton would fade, a disappointed but stalwart husband. He would die years before his wife and his mother, of cholera. Selene dreaded the dismal images clouding people when she looked at them. And why—why?—could she never see a single image of her own future?

They proceeded up yet another flight of stairs until they reached an entryway of the Crystal Palace and walked along a broad avenue of fountains, huge ferns potted in enormous urns, exotic lilies and orchids, glyphed white columns and marble benches. They crossed through the transept and pursued a course to the left, entering the western division of the nave and coming upon a maze of exotic courts, the Indian Court, the African, Canadian, West Indian, the Medieval Court, the Cape of Good Hope Court, the English Sculpture Court. The whole impression was vertiginous, overwhelming, the sensation very nearly mystical. As they walked on, Mr. Boynton lecturing to her, Selene gazed down the long spacious corridors of light. Beneath this translucent-skinned beast were hundreds of exhibits, from methods of photography to the latest coal mine lights, here was both shop and shrine dedicated to the genius and industry of man, and English exhibits took up well over half the space.

Having finally traversed the Fine Arts Exhibit, they entered the Music Court where Mr. Boynton had purchased tickets for the afternoon's concert. Selene listened to the rather squat-figured tenor, Tiejans, sing "Let the British Seraphim" while Boynton, to her right, drummed his fingers like slender peeled sticks upon his black-clothed knees. He seemed particularly stirred by the trumpet obligato, which came after Tiejans, and jumped to his feet along with others in the audience, calling for an encore. Several other behaviors of his seemed odd to her. Once they had got inside the Crystal Palace, he had taken up the practice of conversing with himself. She caught words, phrases of his monologue, a dull running response to whatever he was seeing or hearing. He also sniffed repetitively, clearing his throat and plucking fitfully at the edges of his nostrils. Her fantasy of being Mrs. Boynton did not survive these peculiarities. Besides, she had seen, without wishing to, his romantic destiny: the anemic wife with gout in one toe.

That evening, on board the rented yacht, Selene watched the feathery upward plashing of fireworks and found herself, for Thomas Boynton seemed a person sympathetic if not half in love with her, confiding in him. She related the particulars of Octavia's jealousy, her mother's cultivation of that jealousy, how her spiritualist's gifts had been exploited for the profit of her family, how Octavia's supposed spirit guide, L. Gordon, whom Selene knew to be a fake, now claimed superior powers and an intimate knowledge of Eliza Blackburn.

It seemed he had no advice for her. The fireworks had ended and they stood together at the side of the yacht. Except for the rhythmic slap of water upon the hull, and the occasional sound of the man's dialogue with himself, all was quiet.

"I've got it!"

"Got what?"

"Outwit her. Exceed your sister's abilities."

"What more can I do? I've perfected all I can, and whatever I do, she copies."

"You have produced spirit faces, hands, an occasional arm. Yet I've read in Mr. Lodge's paper and several other spiritualist journals, about mediums in America who are now able to produce, in trance, full-form manifestations. Not just a ghostly head or a floating hand. An entire spirit body steps forth from the cabinet and addresses the sitters in the room. There lies your future. If you can accelerate your powers to that degree, Octavia will be defeated."

*

It occurred to Selene on the cab ride home that evening, the horses' hooves clopping out a slow, ringing rhythm, as she remembered the statues on the terrace outside of the Crystal Palace, veiled in their marble draperies, graceful figures of mystery, it came plainly to her how, with some small, not too costly effort along with a private meeting with Mr. Herne, she might accomplish such a triumph.

8 September 1873

My Dear Mr. Blackburn—

Your medium has triumphed beyond imagining! Last night,
in the presence of Mr. Boynton, Mr. Lodge, Mrs. Amelia Corner,
her children and of course, Mamma and Pappa, I achieved what
those two great mediums and my early guides, Mr. Herne and
Mr. Risdale, have not yet succeeded in doing: Congratulate your
medium who has brought forth the full-form manifestation of
Florence King!

Last evening, Florrie (as she tells us she likes to be called)
emerged from the cabinet and strolled about the room while I
sat in a cold, heavy trance behind the curtain. I will not deny the
tremendous exhaustion I experienced from this, but such victory
exceeds, does it not, fleshly complaint? I wish urgently that you
come down from Manchester to see for yourself, I feel certain
Florence King, now so firmly in command of her instrument—
my poor self!—will appear a second, third, oh, any number of
times. For now, may I content myself with a small recounting?

It was a smaller sitting than we are normally accustomed to,
held not in our kitchen but moved to the upper rooms. Tapestries
were hung by Pappa and Mr. Boynton across the doorway
between rooms. I was searched, along with all of my clothing,
by Mrs. Corner and her daughters before being seated behind
the curtains and tied to the chair. Mr. Boynton, Mr. Lodge (who
this moment composes an excellent article about me for *The
Spiritualist*) and the others (excluding Octavia who claimed to
feel seedy and kept to her room, a pity, she missed what all agree
was a most capital event) took their places in the circle.

Faintly I heard them singing "Beulahland," then "Footsteps
of Angels." I say faintly, for I felt peculiar, as though I were a
bird trapped, fluttering in its cage. I fought to breathe until a
heavy sensation and a voice from outside myself clamped down
on me. I remember nothing past that. Here is what I am told
happened:

Upon the closing line, "...such as these have lived and died,"
the curtains drew a little apart and the white-draped face of
Florence King appeared. The curtains then drew more widely
apart and a tall, graceful figure emerged. She was bare-armed,
bare-legged, covered in whitish shroud. She stood fixed a minute,

Mr. Lodge told me, before gliding to one side of the room and seeming to float or hover, illumined by the weak glow of gaslight. She took, Mr. Boynton noted, quite a lively interest in her surroundings. After several minutes, she returned to the curtains, boldly regarded each of the sitters before gliding backward, head lowered, between the curtain's opening and into the place where I sat.

Roused by my mother and informed of what had occurred, I agreed to repeat the experiment in three nights' time. Who knows what progress I will have made by the time you arrive?

With all tender regards,

Selene Cook
Your faithful medium

*

As she signed her name to the monogrammed stationery, freshly ordered by her mother, Selene called gaily to Tot. Outside, it was a black, wet afternoon; indeed, from the west window, the sky flashed lightning. Selene's room was cozily lit by kerosene lamps, a small coal fire in the grate, and her own excellent humor. Tot had just delivered yet another gift, this a bouquet of white lilies, the attached note congratulating her on the previous evening's triumph. Not an hour before, Mr. Boynton had sent over a large green silk fan ornamented with hand-painted swans. Now Selene sniffed the lilies and twitted the fan under Tot's nose... "the lamps in the parlour must be cleaned before tonight's seance. The chimneys are horribly smoked. And I wish a hot bath, though now I think I must rest, I'm much too excited to sleep. Paris in a week's time, dear Tot, to Paris and meanwhile, tributes! Oh, at last I am having a dramatic and marvelous life. This fan is ugly, don't you think? Mr. Boynton is kind but he lacks taste. Or do you like it, Tot? Would you like it as a gift from me?"

*

Charles Blackburn read the letter with its astounding news and as soon as he could departed from his home outside Manchester. He wished to observe for himself this newest reward for his patronage. He would find himself, the following evening, treated to the most convivial, nearly mischievous spirit play of Florrie King as she moved about the dim-lit room. He would watch as Florrie merrily tied up Thomas Boynton, fastened him to his chair, covered him over with a tablecloth, then an antimacassar, bidding him keep still while a small chair with an arrangement of fruits was precariously balanced upon his shrouded head. When she vanished behind her curtain and the gas lights were raised to their fullest by Mr. Cook, a great deal of hilarity would erupt at the sight of poor Tom Boynton.

The following evening found Florrie inviting this same poor Tom to feel how real she was. To the expressed delight of the spirit, Boynton exclaimed there seemed to be a great hole at the back of her head. "Oh, then, I have neglected to finish myself," she laughed. Even Blackburn found himself teased, poked at, tickled under the whiskers by the marvelous spectre and asked in a naughty whisper if he would ever squeeze her. Mrs. Corner's black merino shawl was plucked from around her shoulders and wrapped around the head of Mr. Lodge. Mr. Cook was mortified by the spirit's calling him "Cookie" and advising that he use slightly less Rowland's Macassar Oil on his hair, as it left greasy rings upon the furniture and bedsheets.

They tell me I do things in trance, as Florrie, that have never been heard of. They say I, or rather Florrie, possesses a mischievous nature and that she is very fond of men and enjoys teasing them. I would not know.

Something rather terrifying is happening, all <u>unpredictably</u>, the sensation of heaviness, of struggling to breathe, of being trapped—much as I described in my letter to Mr. Blackburn, like a bird beating its wings against its cage. I recall nothing afterwards.

What I fear is having no control. Who is Florence King, and what if she will not leave my body? I sometimes hear her laughing, I think, and I grow afraid she will deny me my own body, that she will inhabit me so permanently that I, Selene, will be forever lost. It is, I suppose, the loss of control which tests me, as well as my own madness. So far, after these figure manifestations, I have always returned. So far she has departed when asked. And my success, <u>or Florrie's</u>!, has been astonishing—it has happened so quickly and much is expected of me, of us.

"Quite a sensation you've become, child." Denis Cook rattled one of three Spiritualist newspapers he had brought home. There were front-page articles about his daughter's full-figure manifestation in every one. Selene lay recumbent on the parlour sofa, scarcely breathing. The Florence King manifestations had taxed her beyond endurance. Her mother, meanwhile, had taken advantage of Selene's indisposition to arrange a meeting between Octavia and Mr. Blackburn. Octavia, overshadowed by her sister's spectacular new talent, continued receiving messages from L. Gordon. These notes, scribbled in pencil, were peppered with small exclamations in schoolgirl French, the exact phrases, Selene noticed, that Octavia had so diligently committed to memory while attending Miss Cliff's. Clearly, it was her mother's blatant intent to insinuate both her daughters into this man's good graces—so that, surely, he would be inclined to marry one of them.

21 yards white silk veiling, highest quality, two yards wide and gauzy

wash fabric carefully in seven waters

while damp, work thoroughly and rapidly through a solution of 1 jar Balmain's Luminous Paint, half a pint of Demar varnish, one pint odourless benzine and 50 drops lavender oil

tack fabric to large wall space and let dry

wash with naptha soap until odour gone and material is soft and pliable

this silk fabric, upon exposure to light, will shine a great while in the dark, appearing as a soft and luminous vapour

I received this new recipe from Mr. Herne by post yesterday. I waited until Mother and Octavia had gone out shopping this afternoon, then Tot helped me to prepare material as Mr. Herne's instructions direct. Octavia and Mother are as confounded by my methods of materialisation as any—and eager to get at the secret. I've had to pay Tot to help me, but still, I think she rather enjoys herself. And I do trust her.

Mr. Herne adds in his note that a very similar recipe is being used in America with great success.

Though her head ached and her throat felt raw, Selene refused to miss her excursion to Paris. Who would be kinder to her, she trusted, than Charles Blackburn? There were, however, three aspects of his company she dreaded. First, when not drenched in his own food, for he ate with a smacking, wet-mouthed gusto, he was cocooned in a pall of tobacco smoke. Bad enough London's dismal choke of coal fog, a haze so palpable it drizzled a blackish grit over everything, leaving even the interiors of houses speckled and dingy. Linen handkerchiefs, touched to the nostrils, came away black. Not to mention the low-crawling yellow fogs...in the midst of these, a white, brumous tobacco smoke obscured her benefactor. Thirdly, he coughed incessantly, drawing up a copious phlegm he then seemed obligated to spit off to the side, a habit no doubt salutary for himself but quite sickening to herself.

Nonetheless, by his great fortune (secured in the cotton mills, her father liked very much to ruminate and reflect upon), Charles Blackburn had earned the privilege of an easy generosity. And though he paid heed to Octavia's received messages concerning Eliza, he absolutely doted on Selene. It was Selene he found most enchanting.

As their ship crossed the narrow passage between Dover and Le Havre, as they made their way to Paris by train, Selene slept a great deal. She woke once to see field upon field of harvested potatoes, like tumbled hills of greyish pearls. Charles Blackburn, in his sober frock coat and black trousers, wore an expensive top hat and a waistcoat of a deep rose brocade which argued with his ham-coloured complexion. He did not sleep but contented himself with reading his leather-bound edition of Emanuel Swedenborg's theological treatises. Frequently he looked up to study Selene, who slept, feet tucked under her skirts, head tipped lightly against the window. He noticed how her hair, in the depths of its brown coils, glinted with a greenish lustre. She wore a fawn-coloured travel suit and a chocolate-brown hat with fawn netting; on one side of the hat bobbed a rather dreadful cluster of artificial cherries. She would make a fine actress, he thought, admiring the translucent skin, the finely shaped dark brows. Quite comparable to Ellen Terry or even The Divine Sarah, both of whom he had seen perform in London. Poor exhausted creature. He was determined to spoil her until she recovered her vitality.

On the cab ride from the train station, they were, that first evening in Paris, driven toward the Rue de Rivoli. Before them loomed Le Grand Palais. Lit from within, it resembled nothing so much as a great, pale green crinoline. Gas lamps burned like jewels in ornate iron fixtures down the wide boulevard leading to the Hotel de Meurice, where they would stay. Selene, now awake and eager in her observation of the city as it passed by, was made suddenly witness to a terrible accident. Their cab slowed, then stopped. A great commotion ensued, pedestrians running, shouting, horse-driven traffic brought to an abrupt halt. Charles Blackburn signaled their own driver, sitting on a high seat behind them, to pull on the door lever so he could step down. Minutes later, he returned, and with solemn-faced effort and loud huffings, pulled himself back inside their carriage.

"Horse accident. Unusually bad."

Their cab began to roll forward. They passed by the scene and Selene, for it was all on her side, saw the hansom cab overturned, the grey horse collapsed on its side, entangled in pieces of the carriage, its broad chest punctured by one of the long shafts. The driver, who was weeping, sat on its frantic, half-lifted neck to prevent the horse, in its panic, from trying to rise. Its ribs were hideously visible, and as their cab passed by without seeming to move at all, Selene saw the shocked eye, rolling in its wide, bloodied socket. The passengers, two men, had managed to climb out and now stood haplessly to one side of the ruined carriage.

"What will happen to it?"

"It's throat will be cut, so it can die quickly."

She saw the satiny pad of blood pooling under the dying horse, saw the stain it would leave upon the brick street, a stain ridden over, blindly passed over by the churning wheels of countless carriages drawn by hundreds of horses who would smell it, and shy from that spot, aggravating their drivers to further abuse them.

"The horse feels nothing now." Selene looked at her benefactor. "I assure you, the animal feels nothing. Its spirit has passed beyond pain."

Charles Blackburn laughed aloud. "Horses with spirits? Souls like ours? Oh, that goes too far. We have more likely driven by what will soon become someone's stew of horsemeat. Now take my handkerchief and blot your eyes so you can see the Comédie

Française. And there, just beyond, is the Opera House. Splendid, aren't they?"

She looked at her benefactor's pink, kindly face. Around him she saw nothing. Still, the horse seemed to her an ominous prediction. She could not rid herself of the sensation that the one tragedy prefaced some second misfortune having directly to do with this man.

*

For five days, they toured—Versailles, Notre Dame, the Louvre, dining leisurely between shopping excursions where Selene was introduced to French fashion; she tried on hats, dresses, shoes, and jewelry. Indeed, a trunk of her old things would have to be shipped back to London to make room for all Mr. Blackburn purchased for her, including the latest French corsets and lace-trimmed nightclothes.

Elegant surroundings, a good deal of sleep and gifts lavished upon her by Mr. Blackburn cured her throat complaint. Admiring glances she drew from Parisians as she walked beside Mr. Blackburn further restored her. Her companion coughed as much as she'd dreaded, however, puffed on his cigars and ate with disgusting vigour. Selene scarcely touched her food, fascinated by her newly corseted eighteen-inch waist.

On the fourth day, an interview secured by Mr. Blackburn had a less salutary effect upon her. This was a consultation followed by luncheon at the home of Dr. Jean-Martin Charcot, renowned neurologist and director of the Salpêtrière Hospital for the Insane. At eleven o'clock, Selene and Mr. Blackburn arrived at 217 Boulevard St. Germain and were ushered by an assistant into Dr. Charcot's study. Floor to ceiling bookcases were divided by balustraded galleries with winding stairways, and long narrow windows of stained glass produced a tenebrous, churchlike gloom. His study, Dr. Charcot would tell them later, on their way to lunch, was modeled after the Library of the Medicis in the Convent of San Lorenzo in Florence. Now however, they saw him seated at the farthest end of the long room, a diminutive figure behind a large desk. Following some heated whispering between the Doctor and his assistant, Selene was asked to wait in the hallway. Dr.

Charcot's appointments, the assistant informed her while escorting her out, were always held in strictest confidence. She was led into a sepulchral hall with dark, melancholic alcoves crammed with medieval furnishings and tapestries whose subjects seemed mainly griffins, dragons and writhing serpents. Several patients waited there with their nurses; across from her, a corpulent young man in a black cape sat hunched on a Baroque prayer stool. Behind him a male nurse stood, impassive. An emaciated woman swept past on the arm of her physician, dressed in a low-cut, black velvet gown. The veins branching across her thin chest were painted blue—a current fashion among the French and English aristocracy. Moving haughtily past, she flung a curse at Selene over her skinny shoulder, "Whore! Pig! English Bitch!" The corpulent man stared at Selene, a fixed, rude stare that she escaped only when Mr. Blackburn and Dr. Charcot emerged from the study. The three of them made their way down the hall and into a pleasantly sunny dining room. Charcot stood at the head of the table, a short, taciturn man whose marmoreal, clean-shaven face (uncanny resemblance to Napoleon, Blackburn would later comment) was set in an impenetrable mask. Following an inaudible greeting and the slightest of bows in her direction, he never again looked at her or addressed her. To his immediate right sat a wiry, brown monkey in a child's chair, a white bib around its hairy neck. With its long, agile fingers, the monkey plucked bits of fruit tenderly cut and set on its tray by Dr. Charcot who murmured and spoke caressingly to it as he virtually ignored his human guests. At precisely twelve-thirty, the neurologist petted his mouth with his napkin, rose, bowed formally to Blackburn, and saying patients awaited him, left without even a glance at Selene.

They finished their luncheon, while the monkey, its bib untied, was carried off by the assistant. "The man is clearly a genius," Blackburn said. "The behavior of such people is often peculiar. I told him of Eliza's symptoms but he insists on seeing her personally. He tells me he has treated the Emperor of Brazil, the Queen of Spain, and the Grand Dukes of Russia. There is little doubt he is most brilliant, still, I may have placed too desperate a hope in him. I don't know. Dear girl, you haven't eaten a thing. I shouldn't have bought you that corset—you haven't eaten since. Tomorrow I should like you to accompany me to his Friday demonstration at the Salpêtrière. Quite the thing to see, I've been told. My god, I think I'll have another of those chops. Did you see how Charcot dined only upon fruit, like his monkey?"

*

They arrived early and were given front seats in the amphitheatre. The audience seemed composed equally of physicians and devoted curiosity seekers. These Friday demonstrations had become a favourite entertainment for Parisians. Selene sat directly in front of the raised platform with its cluttered array of charts, drawings, diagrams, statuettes, plaster casts, and a large blackboard marked with formulae. The first patient was lifted onto the platform on a stretcher. A girl around Selene's age, she was helped to stand upright by a matron of the Institution. The girl wore a bell-shaped skirt and plain white blouse. Her black hair was loosely caught in a bun at the nape of her neck.

Doctor Charcot, arriving from his office inside the hospital, stepped up on the platform, attired in a top hat, an apron around his middle and heavy galoshes on his feet. He bowed coldly to his audience and turning his back, stood before his exhibit, meekly seated in a wooden chair. This was, Blackburn whispered, Charcot's most popular subject. Audiences never tired of watching the young girl, hypnotized by Charcot, reenact the trauma of her rape. The hysterical gesturings, cries of resistance, the sobbing surrender, enthralled the onlookers. She presented herself as entirely pliant to the will of her Doctor. He helped her to stand, drew her backward against himself, her blouse coming slightly apart down the front, her head tipped back, neck arched—like a damaged lily embraced by cold, clinical arms. Selene saw how the girl savoured the theatrics of her performance. She saw the bond of power Charcot held over the girl and she over him, an intimate union having little to do with medicine or the diagnostic skills of a neurologist. This was a complex drama which gave pleasure to them both.

Six other patients, all of them women, were led to the platform. On the chalkboard, Dr. Charcot meticulously outlined the clinical manifestations of their various hysterical disturbances. Often these involved some impulse to disrobe. Precise in his diction, mysterious in his silence, Doctor Charcot commanded his patients, exhibiting them like rare, monstrous trophies. Selene studied the postures, often erotic, of these women, their highly ritualized pattern of back archings (the *arc en circle*), elaborate rocking motions, low, haunting cries. One woman named Marie, when touched repeatedly under the left breast, where Dr. Charcot wished, he said, to demonstrate an active hysterogenic zone, cried out sorrowfully, "*Mère! Oh, ma mère!*"

"Disgraceful," Blackburn chomped at his supper of oysters and fried eels. "Apologies, my dear. He is so famous. Hundreds. It is said he has cured hundreds of cases of insanity, more than anyone else in England or France. I wanted to see the possibilities, if any, for Eliza. What diagnosis, what hope of recovery. But I cannot subject her to this man's treatment, no matter what rate of cure he boasts."

"Surely his private clients are not put before the public? These are particular sorts of women whose class and symptoms lend themselves to such theatre?"

"But they are tragically unaware of themselves. Utterly innocent of the spectacle they put on."

Selene stopped cutting up her partridge, which was dry, laid her knife down with quiet emphasis. "They are perfectly aware. I distinctly saw how each one enjoyed the attention she received."

"You would suggest they have no desire to be cured. Why? Would a return to health mean loss of celebrity? Is that what you imply?"

"Doctor Charcot and his patients depend upon one another. He relies upon his half-clothed patients for effective advertisement, while the patients publicly submit to him to avoid their otherwise dull existence. I distinctly saw this."

"Certainly no place for my Eliza."

"I would think not."

"I carry a photograph, taken when she was just your age. Seventeen. Would you care to see it?"

He passed her the little gold-embossed *carte de visite*. Selene held it under the light of a candle burning near her.

"She turned twenty this past May. This was taken before her illness, while her mother was still alive."

"She is exquisite."

"L. Gordon tells us she would do well with you."

"What?"

"Octavia's spirit control, L. Gordon, states that Eliza would fully regain her emotional health under the care of your family. Under your care in particular."

"Oh," Selene returned the photograph. How perfectly optimistic of L. Gordon, she thought. How clever an appeal.

"Deuced hot in here." Blackburn wiped at his perspiring forehead. Selene stared at the widening patch of grease on his chin.

A new worry. The voices are beginning to return. Especially hers. Phoenicia's. Warning me. Of what I am uncertain, but I feel a new heaviness around me, a dread gathering in all my limbs. My success has never been greater, there is money enough for my family's happiness—my father no longer needs to work, and his health is improved thereby—but there is a constant sinking at the pit of my stomach, and a hearing of voices, not only hers, but a whole strange keening. Yesterday I nearly did not get out of bed, my exhaustion suggested sleepwalking, that I had been up during the night and did not know it. A gloominess settles over me.

And my sister? She thrives on L. Gordon's pencilled messages, is now cheerful enough for the both of us. Charles Blackburn is very positive about her new-found "abilities." Yet they are clever tricks—all learned from me.

Standing before him in a small twitching of doubt, Tot poked at her employer, who sat embedded in his favourite chair by the firelight, boots off, head tipped back onto the crocheted antimacassar, mouth agape, a stertorous snoring rumbling out of that cavern. A respectful calling by surname had not worked. Tot tried a second time.

"Mr. Cook, sir."

"Mr. Cook!" She trod gingerly on one of his big toes. Nothing. Then a vicious ding with her shoe. Denis Cook shuddered, shook himself, gazed about with sheep's eyes.

"Wha?"

"A gentleman, sir. In the hall."

She curtsied as Mrs. Cook had yesterday instructed her, stiff in the new black uniform and ribboned cap.

"…mistaken, I'm sure. It's Selene everyone wants now."

Tot leaned forward to whisper. "He's been waiting quite some time."

Thus did Rudyard Volkman find himself belatedly ushered in and seated across from a disheveled, shoeless fellow, no doubt the girl's father. Mrs. Guppy had warned him of the girl's quite contemptible family.

Volkman was a fastidious man possessed of a handsome profile which in no way matched the more ordinary frontal portion of his face. Acutely aware of this deficiency, Volkman addressed people sideways, making him most difficult to hear. In such a way, Mr. Volkman now addressed Mr. Cook, his head poised at a flattering angle. Hoping to appear more truly awake than he was, Denis Cook slid to the edge of his chair. A ring of macassar oil stood behind his head, an offensive halo.

"I'll drive my point home directly, Mr. Cook. I desire admittance to one of your daughter's seances."

Denis Cook sized up his visitor for hints of affluence.

"I have written numerous times over the past three months and received no reply."

"Selene's health is extremely delicate. The strain currently upon her would quite crack any man."

"No doubt. I understand there is a select circle. What must I do to qualify?"

"What are your qualifications?" Mr. Cook thought this quick-witted of himself.

"I am a dedicated spiritualist, a committee member of the London Dialectical Society appointed to investigate spiritual phenomena. I intend writing a book, already contracted, on the important English mediums of our time. I had hoped to include your daughter in my book. What might I do, Mr. Cook, to gain my admittance?"

"You understand, Mr...."

"Volkman."

"Right. Mrs. Cook and myself do not, under any conditions, accept money. I stress this. We take no money."

"A gift of jewelry then? I have in my possession a rare double strand of amber beads and a matching brooch. Originally the property of my deceased wife's mother. Certainly I have no need of them. Would such a gift do?"

Mr. Cook smoothed back his hair, rubbed one bare foot sideways over the other, then with a show of indifference, gave his consent.

Later that night, in bed beside Mrs. Cook, he chided himself on two counts: falling asleep by the fire since he hadn't slept a wink since and second, he hadn't demanded, as a condition of admittance to his daughter's seance, that his own name be somewhere put down in Mr. Volkman's book of famous English mediums. He wanted to see his name in a book, he wished to be admired by people he did not know. He would insist on this when he saw Volkman at tomorrow night's seance.

*

ON DECEMBER 9, 1873 AT 7:00 P.M., A SEANCE WAS HELD AT THE COOK HOUSEHOLD ON ELEANOR ROAD IN HACKNEY. SITTERS INCLUDED MR. AND MRS. COOK, OCTAVIA COOK, MRS. AMELIA CORNER, HER SON ELGERON, MR. THOMAS BOYNTON, MR. BALFOUR LODGE, MR. CHARLES BLACKBURN, MR. RUDYARD VOLKMAN AND ONE HOUSEMAID.

—Notice printed in *The Medium and the Daybreak*

*

(From a letter delivered anonymously and published in *The Spiritualist*, December 12, 1873.)

GROSS OUTRAGE AT A SPIRIT CIRCLE

I protest the recent outrage perpetrated on Miss Selene Cook, a seventeen-year-old medium, during a seance held for a select group of sitters in her home on this past December 9.

With Miss Cook enclosed in her spirit cabinet, the spirit of Florence King emerged to walk among the sitters, taking each one by the hand and speaking conversationally, a gesture customary for this particular spirit. As Florence approached Mr. Rudyard Volkman, kindly extending her hand to the new visitor, he grasped the hand, then extended his grasp until he had seized her by both arm and waist together, crying "FRAUD!", exclaiming he had got hold of none other than Selene Cook in his arms and in fact, could distinctly feel her corset. In the scuffle that ensued, Florence King's spirit person was rescued by the bold actions of Elgeron Corner and Thomas Boynton who managed to wrestle Mr. Volkman to the ground. Suffering superficial injuries to his nose and complaining over a partial loss of his beard, Mr. Volkman was then escorted by these gallant gentlemen from the house.

The indignity suffered by the spirit of Florence King as well as the shock to the frail system of Miss Cook as a consequence of this brutal seizure must be protested. The specious argument put forth by Mr. Volkman that a suspicious interval had lapsed between Florence King's seizure and the opening of the cabinet where Miss Cook was seated is easily resolved. The intolerable shock to Miss Cook's nervous system by this sudden manner in which she had to reabsorb the spirit matter of Florence King took a cruel toll. She was unable, for some minutes, to demand that the cabinet door be opened. When it was, by Mr. Cook, Selene was discovered in a frightful state of hysterics, the tape still around her waist and binding her as firmly to the chair as it had been when the door had first been shut upon her.

To satisfy his own crude curiosity, Mr. Volkman, who is known to be a close friend of the notoriously vicious Mrs. Guppy and dares call himself an investigator, has risked the well-being of an innocent young girl—inexcusable behavior for which I—and others—hold him most accountable. The thread of connection between feminine persons of the flesh and feminine persons of the spirit is a most fragile one; to treat it as Mr. Volkman most inexcusably did on the night of December 9, is to willfully endanger the integrity and health of both. Such gross outrages in the peaceful atmosphere of the spirit circle will not be tolerated.

*

(Reply from Rudyard Volkman, published in a rival newspaper, *The Medium and the Daybreak*, December 16, 1873.)

—Sir, under the heading "GROSS OUTRAGE AT SPIRIT CIRCLE," a charge was recently brought against me in a certain spiritualist journal. My letter of defense having been withheld by the journal in question, I beg permission to give it publicity through your own widely read columns. It is as follows—

Sir:

In the report which appears in your journal of a seance lately held at Mr. Cook's, I am accused of seizing the ghost, thereby breaking conditions by which the members of the circle were bound as surely as Miss Cook was bound with her pieces of tape.

In defense, I have to state that having for forty minutes observed and scrutinized the face, features, gestures, size, style and peculiarities of utterance of the so-called spirit, the conviction pressed itself upon me, irresistibly, that no ghost, but the medium Selene Cook was before the circle. I also perceived an occasional tiptoeing by Her Ghost-ship as if to alter her stature and was much struck by the utter puerility of her remarks during the seance. I remain confirmed in my conviction, as a spiritualist investigator, that this struggling ghost (whose corset I could most readily feel) forcibly extracted from my arms by several keepers of the peace was none other than Selene Cook.

She is, I am convinced of it, a FRAUD.

Yours truly,
Rudyard Volkman

Tot swept under the grate, relit the coal fire, trimmed the wicks, lighted the two kerosene lamps, emptied out stale water in the flowered washbasin along with the contents of the porcelain chamber pot, opened the drapes, then closed the drapes, pinched out a bit of seed for the poor bird which would otherwise starve...

Mr. Cook had just left, taking Rudyard Volkman's amber necklace and brooch to the pawn shop, in hopes of retrieving a small sum, enough, he gravely assured Mrs. Cook, to carry them a week or two more.

Mrs. Cook sat eating bacon, a residual craving from her old, impoverished life on Green Street in Southwark, in the galleried inn where she and Denis had once lived, tending a pen of pigs for their landlord in exchange for a regular supply of bacon to offset their fare of bread and tea. The slightly sweaty, rancid odour of cooked bacon which now pervaded the house somehow consoled her.

Octavia had gone out again. Through a church advertisement in the Hackney newspaper, she had taken up bell-ringing. She practiced with five other unmarried women, raising and lowering differently toned bells in the rendering of traditional, cautious melodies. They had already given three modest Christmas recitals, a thing Mrs. Cook found ridiculous but Mr. Cook said no, since her schooling had been stopped, it was beneficial for Octavia to have an innocent distraction—what harm could come of her dinging and donging a few bells?

By now, the Cooks had engraved upon their sorry hearts the contents of the anonymous letter, along with its barbed response by Mr. Volkman. They understood the calamity which had befallen them. Mr. Cook, who, in his enthusiasm for acting the idle gentleman, had quit his print shop job, stubbed out the last of his expensive cigars and returned to work. Mrs. Cook carped at Tot about what savage prices were fixed on everything now that it was Christmas. Octavia was told her old black velvet jacket with the balding cuffs could serve another winter. And Mrs. Cook pronounced at least twice a day that this would be a poor, pinched Christmas, though by God's grace they would manage a roast goose and a lighted plum pudding.

Selene occasionally rose from her bed to stand beside the window, seeing nothing. Tot had been ordered not to answer any brisk knocking at the door, for it was sure to be the street musicians, whose singing was traditionally rewarded with a distribution of alms. It's us who's in need of alms, muttered Mrs. Cook, the two times there was such knocking, in as ill and bacon-wrecked a temper as anyone had ever seen her. Both times the musicians waited, then moved on down the snowy street. From upstairs, Selene watched them.

In addition, the postman was waited for with no small trepidation. A letter from Manchester, anxiously expected, had not yet arrived. Then one morning, Tot retrieved the mail and stealthily extracted the thin, cream-coloured envelope with its familiar brownish scrawl, before giving the few Christmas cards and advertisements to Mrs. Cook.

She carried the letter which weighed like a stone in her pocket and stood a moment before the closed door. Then she knocked, went in and for the first time in days, found Selene seated at her dressing table, gathering the long, loose strands of hair from her brush and coiling them into the cut glass hair-catcher.

Tot approached, drew the letter from her pocket, let go of the missive as though it had scalded her hand, and fled the room. She shut the door then sank with some awkwardness beside the keyhole.

The letter lay untouched on the dressing table. Selene continued brushing her hair. Tot couldn't believe it. Then she heard Mrs. Cook bellowing for her from the kitchen. She was expected to go out that afternoon and pick out a small goose from the market. She dragged her eye reluctantly from the keyhole.

Selene yanked the door open to make sure Tot was gone. Then with a kind of grim hope, her heart beating hard, she took up her little brass opener and ripped the side of the envelope, drew out the single sheet of paper and unfolded it. Except for four words formed in bold, angry strokes, not even a signature, it was entirely, utterly, malignantly blank.

It is over.
My enemies have triumphed.
Tell me what to do.

Several hours later, Tot returned from the bird shop where she had gone to purchase a spindly goose only to discover the whole household in an uproar. Selene had disappeared, no one knew where. A letter lay on the floor of her bedroom torn to pieces. By carefully matching them, Mrs. Cook read the words I SHALL STOP PAYMENT. It was, as Tot could attest, dark as pitch out and snowing hard as well.

A child-like figure, queerly garbed in a too-large black cloak with a hood, stepped down from a carriage, paid the fare from Hackney to Regent's Park, climbed six steps to stand before a brick Georgian style house on Mornington Road, where, in keeping with the season, two evergreen wreaths hung on red ribbons on opposite sides of the plain black door. A black-mittened hand raised the brass knocker, hesitated, let it fall.

William Herapath, remembering it was the maid's afternoon off, shuffled out of his laboratory in worn-down leather slippers. Irritably shifting his pipe in his mouth, he cracked open the door. Before him, the snow falling thick and white around her, stood the schoolgirl medium.

"Mr. Herapath?" Her voice seemed to him exceedingly soft. "Might I come in?"

THE MORNINGTON ROAD EXPERIMENTS

William Herapath scarcely glanced at the two newspaper articles she had thrust into his hands. He knew them, had read them the previous day, concluding as he did so that here was one poor medium's career shot down. He also recalled attending a seance of hers some weeks before in the company of an American physician named Purdon, who had found her psychical talents decidedly less than spectacular. Now Miss Cook sat opposite him, plaintively whispering her great trouble. Her family's fate depended upon her income and now, with the angry withdrawal of Charles Blackburn's patronage, or stated more bluntly, his weekly cheque, she hardly knew what was to become of them. They had incurred debts, she managed to weep as she spoke, looking not at him but at the pocket handkerchief he had proffered, a gift from Mrs. Herapath, now entangled wetly upon itself in her lap. Looking at this young woman, remembering certain words she had uttered, fear, despair, doom...he felt a stirring of something within himself, pity he supposed. Charity inspired by the season. Or worse, something of the cruelty of advantage.

"And from me you desire what, Miss Cook? I regret your unfortunate circumstances, but how exactly do you envision me your Savior? I have no money to lend you, as I live entirely at the mercy of my wife's income. I would pose, I should think, one more threat to this game which has placed you and your family in such a desperate circumstance."

"I have not come for money, Mr. Herapath. And what I am about is no game!"

"Of course not. I misspoke."

"What I intend is to sacrifice my powers as a medium upon the altar of science. Under your...gaze, I shall be proved authentic."

"And should I find you...authentic?"

"Then you would compose an article refuting these sorts of slanderous articles. A validation, written and signed by you, stating that I am genuine. To be published in all the spiritualist newspapers in London."

"And if you are not?"

"Not?"

"Not genuine, Miss Cook. Not an authentic medium. What if I find you full of trickery, of false phenomena, what then?"

"Then I will stand disgraced and my family ruined."

"High stakes, indeed."

"What choice is left me? I have the highest regard for your abilities, Mr. Herapath, as well as an equal confidence in my own."

"Your confidence is persuasive."

"You will do it then? You are willing to test me?"

"I am intrigued, Miss Cook. That is, I suppose, a form of consent."

So it was done. Quickly, Herapath worked out a set of conditions to which Selene acquiesced. She was to move into his home directly after January 1 and cooperate with as many tests and experiments as were needed. Should these tests prove her validity, he agreed to write and publish an article stating so. He would also write directly to Charles Blackburn. And under his scientific authority, Selene would then resume public seances.

"I anticipate, Miss Cook, some satisfaction in working with you. As you may know, I have several years' experience with these kinds of tests—having worked with the great D.D. Home, the American, Kate Fox, and several others. But to have you established in my home, at my disposal, will be quite a unique circumstance."

"And I, Mr. Herapath, will be forever grateful. You had become my sole hope." So saying, the girl looked as if she might take up crying again and further demolish his handkerchief.

"No need, Miss Cook, no need."

"I shall return a fortnight from now and cooperate to the fullest extent of my abilities. Why this money, Mr. Herapath?"

"Cab fare, my dear child, both for going home this afternoon and for your safe return."

"This is a great deal more than cab fare. I cannot accept it."

"Nonsense. I remind you it is still Christmastime, Miss Cook. Mrs. Herapath and I desire that you and your family should enjoy a most excellent holiday."

3 January 1874

To the Editor of *The Spiritualist*, Balfour Lodge:

In my own history investigating the subject of spiritualism, I have kept deliberately clear of controversy. In light of the current speculation surrounding the case of Selene Cook, I feel compelled to depart from this previous history of caution and assist, if it can be done, in removing unjust suspicion from a woman so young and sensitive and innocent. It has become a duty for me to give the weight of testimony in favor of her whom I deem unjustly accused.

To date, no one claims to have observed Miss Cook secured in her cabinet while the ghost of Florence King walks in the room amongst the various sitters. In my opinion, *the burden of proof rests upon this narrow compass.* And proof must be absolute. In default of evidence not put forth by those who have attended her seances, let me, newly admitted at this eleventh hour, give testimony, beginning with an incident which came to my notice at a seance I attended this past December 30, at Mr. Thomas Boynton's home.

The cabinet was a back drawing room, separated from the front room where the company sat, by a curtain. Miss Cook entered this cabinet after the usual formalities of Mr. Boynton and myself searching the room and examining the fastenings. After a little time, the form of Florence King appeared at the side of this curtain, then retreated, saying her medium was unwell and could not be put into sufficiently deep sleep to make it safe for her to be left.

Sitting within a few feet of this curtain, I heard Miss Cook moan frequently and sob as if in pain. This uneasy condition persisted throughout almost the whole of the seance. And once, as the ghostly form of Florence stood directly before me in the drawing room, I most distinctly heard a sobbing moan, belonging most definitely to Miss Cook, come from behind the curtain, entirely separate from the figure standing before me. This figure, I do admit, was startlingly life-like, and in dim light, its features did closely resemble those of Miss Cook's. Still, undeniable evidence gave proof positive that the moan came from Miss Cook who was in the cabinet, whilst the spirit figure who stood outside the cabinet, Florence King, remained silent.

Your readers, sir, know me, and will, I hope, believe I would not come hastily to any opinion or ask them to be persuaded by too little evidence. This small incident I now describe is perhaps too little weighted to stand as much proof to those who did not witness, as I did, its occurrence. But this I do beg of them—let those inclined to judge Miss Cook hastily, suspend such judgement until I bring forth positive evidence and enough of it to settle the question.

As of today, Miss Cook is devoting herself exclusively to a series of seances with me. These are to extend over some weeks, and I have been promised by Miss Cook that every desirable test will be granted me. Persuaded by the integrity and honest nature of my young subject, I have every reason to expect that the promise given to me by Miss Selene Cook, that of scrupulous inquiry, will be so honored.

Yours,
William Herapath

*

Having been awake half the night in the tedious composition of this letter, William Herapath dropped his pen to observe the sun struggling above the silver netting of bare branched trees along Kensington Park. Rooks by the hundreds rose and circled the trees beyond his laboratory windows, then floated down, hunching upon the branches like winter's black fruit. The loathsome sight of them was too much like his own wife, fluttering about his home, settling, perching, then setting off restlessly with strange, shallow cries, always in her ashy black plumage, the mourning costume she wore even now, a year after their son's death. Guilt checked him. Would not any mother who had lost two of her children to cholera in half a year's time, then a third to poison be inclined to madness? Each child had drawn its last breath in her arms. And was he not changed by the recent death, in faraway Cuba, of his younger brother Philip? Had not both he and his wife been indelibly marked by their sufferings? He knew some of his colleagues in science considered him half mad, thinking his pursuit of spiritualism to be evidence of unresolved grief. Yet his wife, Maude, was tolerant of him where they were not. Lately she had taught herself, through the study of ladies' magazines, to preserve birds and squirrels, standing them in naturalistic settings beneath various sized bell jars. If this was a strange sort of hobby, at least, like his interest in the spirit world, it consoled. At times, though, he felt he could not bear their twin melancholies another hour. He physically ached for rejuvenation, for lightness of step and mood, but instead he daily watched Maude conduct herself as if life were an abhorrent accident and not a blessing. His own moods had shrunk of late to two: chilly detachment and a peevishness caused, he believed, by sexual stagnation.

Reviewing his letter, he reminded himself to send a published copy to Charles Blackburn along with a personal note, informing him of the intended series of tests on Miss Cook. In fact, just yesterday, a note from Miss Cook had arrived by post, saying she hoped to arrive in two days' time, being very nearly recovered from a mild case of the grippe. Again, he studied the ink's tracery, its bold but feminine hand.

Indeed, when Maude Herapath woke to find her husband still not in bed beside her, she went downstairs and found him, asleep at his laboratory desk, the letter from Miss Cook caught up in his hand.

*

Absolutely accurate what Boynton says, Herapath thought, sucking on his thumb, scorched from his failed attempts to regulate the nearest candle flame. A guest is a looking glass that points up the eccentricities of one's family.

To his right sat the medium, looking like a compliant child, her excessive politeness masking what? Amusement? Not shy, though...he would never think of her as timid.

"Is your dinner agreeable, Miss Cook?" This was himself speaking, as his wife's place at the table was vacant. The cook had left the room, having relayed the message that Mrs. Herapath was on her way up from her basement studio.

Indeed, before Miss Cook had occasion to reply, Maude Herapath swooped into the dining room and sat down with a great whooshing of her ashen skirts. Herapath's finger throbbed painfully as he held it under the drinking water in his goblet. My God, he thought, seeing his wife as through a stranger's eyes, as through his guest's eyes. Good God. Look at her.

As any connoisseur of wines, geologic specimens, artifacts or any other thing knows, one can find unexpectedly alluring the exception to the rule, the peculiar rarity. William Herapath had found Maude, among the young women of his acquaintance, to be (along with the high incentive of her wealth) most queerly memorable. Her wand-like, alabaster neck supported an oblong head with hair so pale and features so nearly washed away, she reminded him of nothing so much as a mutated white fish. Her hair was of a strange grey blonde, her skin and nearly lashless eyes the same. With his collector's fondness for minutiae as well as for any unique variation to the standard, he had overlooked, or misunderstood, her other qualities. Thus he found himself, not long after their marriage, severely disappointed. Where he had interpreted her silence as feminine virtue, he found a stammering girl terrified of life. Where he had seen her morbidity as an eccentric but still flattering ploy for his attention, he found a creature obsessed with death. The loss of three of their eight children had simply exacerbated these traits. This evening, across from him, sat a vague looking woman in an outdated mourning dress, her hair peeled back and so thin one could see the sallow scalp beneath it. Most repellent of all, his wife smelled of formaldehyde. With the same fascination she reserved for all forms of death, she pursued this newest pastime of taxidermy. It was a hobby in vogue among London housewives; a good many ladies' magazines devoted articles to it. But Maude had taken her skills beyond the dictates of fashion. In his opinion, she had become monomaniacal, and worse, he was wholly dependent upon her.

"Maude, will you extend a welcome to our guest? Miss Cook has come to reside with us for a few weeks. She was about to inform me as to whether or not her dinner is acceptable."

"My dinner is perfect," Selene began. "Thank you, and I..."

"You appear charming. I should like my children to meet you." Mrs. Herapath smiled showing broken, greyed teeth. Her trout's eyes were fixed, as if on a specimen, upon the young girl opposite her. She continued to stare, eating with furtive, distracted gestures.

"Where did you find this creature? What is she here for? If you ever told me, William, it's quite slipped my mind. The male jay I am working on is splendid. First rate. I am of a mind to have you photograph him for me."

"My wife preserves birds, Miss Cook. Mainly birds. It's a hobby with her."

"How fascinating, I suppose. At home I keep a finch in my room. I had thought to bring him this afternoon, but I was afraid the cold air in the cab might harm him. And I thought it might be impolite to bring a pet into someone else's home."

"Not so much impolite, Miss Cook, as dangerous, given my talents," Mrs. Herapath laughed, a small, dry malicious sound.

Just as it was needed, not because anyone was hungry, but because the silence at the table had grown heavy, dessert was brought in, a rice pudding studded with dark, muscatel raisins, each of which Selene fastidiously dredged up from her pudding and heaped to one side of her plate.

"I'll have those," Herapath stretched out an arm to seize a clammy handful and thrust them into his mouth.

"Oh." Maude pressed her large napkin to her temple.

Herapath did not look at her. "What is it?"

"My head. I have got another throbbing headache. Absolutely killing."

"Have you got a cold compress? My sister has success with that remedy," Selene offered helpfully. "Octavia reads a great deal and suffers eyestrain. My parents fear she will blind herself from so much study."

"Yes, that is much the same with me I think. Eyestrain..." Maude was animated now that her symptoms were being discussed. William refused to let her take advantage of the girl's innocent sympathy.

"Maude, I am going upstairs to set up the library for a seance."

"Will you be joining us?" Selene asked Mrs. Herapath, then looked at him as though he were heartless. What she did not know was that Maude was capable of embroidering upon her ailments for unholy lengths of time. Years ago he had decided she harboured some living and restless complaint that daily migrated from one organ to another, from one crevice of the body to another. By now the only surprise left was its location. Unwittingly, over the years of their marriage, Maude had instructed him in the tyranny of illness.

"I would be delighted, nothing less than charmed, Miss Cook. I confess I have never attended a seance. I have only heard of them through my husband's interest. I do have one question I would like to put to you."

"Yes?"

"Do you contact the recently dead?"

"Maude, I hardly think Miss Cook wishes…"

"Yes, Mrs. Herapath. Quite frequently I do."

"My son died May 7 last year, and I…"

"Maude."

"It's quite all right, Mr. Herapath. It is only natural for the living to ask after loved ones who have passed on."

"I simply wondered, Miss Cook, if you would be so kind while you are here in our home…"

"Yes, of course, Mrs. Herapath. I will attempt to contact your son if you wish."

"Where is this young woman staying, William? Where have you put her?"

"In the small room off my laboratory."

"Good lord, William. I cannot believe…" Mrs. Herapath turned to Selene. "My son died in that room."

"May I ask how?"

Herapath spoke up, though the question had been directed towards his wife. "He had gone into my laboratory, which it was expressly forbidden for him to do, and ingested a chemical used in my photography. He was poisoned instantly."

"I am terribly sorry. How old was your son?"

"William had just turned five."

As he said this, he felt a pressure that seemed to want to extinguish his breath. He watched his wife folding her napkin, gazing at the medium as though nothing at all weighed on her mind.

"The children are upstairs having supper with their governess. May they attend your seance? It might be educational for them."

"I don't know, Mrs. Herapath." Selene looked to her husband.

"Maude, they would have to be absolutely obedient."

"Well, of course. We can have Looie sit with them."

"Miss Cook, will you come upstairs to see that all is arranged to your satisfaction?"

"Yes, of course. And Mrs. Herapath, do try the wet compress for your headache. In combination with lying down in a darkened room, my sister claims it is nearly the best cure."

*

She started up the stairs ahead of him, pausing to admire the stained glass window on the landing. She examined, too, the water garden installed beneath it; never, she exclaimed, had she seen anything half so clever.

"Is this your wife's garden?" She glanced back at him.

"Yes."

"She seems immensely gifted."

"True, but..." He stood perplexed.

"What?"

Looking up, he could see her necklace, its three golden stars strung along the shadowy hollow of her neck. "She lacks joy."

Selene smiled. "Well, I've enough for the both of us, haven't I?" With that, she tripped gaily up the stairs. He followed, feeling how stodgy he was, how wanting in joy himself. Unlike the young woman nearly dashing up the stairs ahead of him, he took steady refuge in gravity, in silence. How he might attain such light-heartedness as hers he could not imagine.

Beside the mantle, upholstered in heavy, moss-green velvet, he found her studying the large brass mantle clock.

"There reclines the figure of Art, and on this other side, the figure of Commerce." He referred to the half-draped female figures posed on either side of the timepiece.

"And why does Art lie down and Commerce stand? I don't care for Commerce. She looks entirely too cool."

"And cool you might be, counting pounds and shillings, shillings and pence all day long. Better to be supple art, sensuous creation, lovely as yourself, Miss Cook."

She gave him a look over her shoulder which both checked and exhilarated him. He moved nervously away. "I've hung a curtain between the library and the morning room to serve as your cabinet. And here is a chair, tape, rope."

"A bell? Do you have a silver bell I might use?"

He went directly to a side table and got one.

"There is quite a strong fragrance in here, Mr. Herapath. What is it?"

"In here? No doubt you smell the white hyacinth from the morning room. Maude is forcing both the narcissus and hyacinth bulbs into bloom, something she does each winter."

"It is delicious."

"Do you think so? I've always found hyacinth to have a faintly corrupt odour. It is the flower of death, you know."

The governess had made the children grasp hands, sit in a semicircle upon the carpet, while she sat solemnly behind them. The children watched their father tie and tape a young woman to a chair. This oddness of what he was doing subdued them. Then Mrs. Herapath entered the library, clapping her hands briskly together.

"Wonders! Is this how it's done, William?"

"Quiet, Maude. Do go over and play a hymn for us on the piano."

"I know no hymns, do I? What about Grieg? Chopin?"

"For heaven's sakes. Anything will do. Anything that will raise the psychical energies in this room. Miss Cook, are you settled as comfortably as you would wish?" He distracted himself with checking seals and knots. With his hands moving so close around her, he could not bring himself to look at her.

"I am fine, thank you."

Dutifully, Mrs. Herapath played the piano. The children tried to remain still but eventually they fidgeted and nudged one another. The governess scolded them, so they tried again to be very good, to sit still and to concentrate, but upon what they didn't exactly know...on the lady fastened to their father's library chair and stuck behind a curtain which had begun to sag?

Obeying the signalings of his hands and the pursings of his lips, Mrs. Herapath ceased playing. All looked steadily at the curtain. Minutes passed between Lady Art and Lady Commerce. Mr. and Mrs. Herapath stared fixedly, the governess stifled a yawn, and the children tried, with increasing restlessness and mischief, to see behind the makeshift curtain.

"D'ya think there's a ghost back there?" The Herapath's oldest boy, Rupert, breathed into his little sister's ear.

"William's behind the curtain. Watch out! It's Willie! He's in the room!"

In answer to Rupert's mischievous shrieking, the little girl let out a terrifying squeal of her own, ran and butted her head into the heavy curtain. It collapsed over her, revealing Selene, still firmly tied to her chair. The sight proved too much for the children who grew uncontrollably merry.

"Stop!" Herapath roared. "Stop at once! Looie, get them out of here. What a debacle. They have destroyed my first experiment. My apologies, Miss Cook. Uncontrollable savages. I should never have let them in."

"William, calm yourself. It's beyond their bedtime, that's all. Besides, they do not know Miss Cook from a brick on the road and suddenly there she is, tied to one of our best chairs. It was simply too much for them."

Herapath scowled, an end of rope stuck between his teeth, impatiently freeing his unfortunate subject.

"Shall we try, once more, without the children?" Maude tinkled a few hopeful notes on the piano.

"No," he plucked the rope out of his mouth. "No. After this absurdity, I will carry out future tests in private. In my laboratory. Are you perfectly sure you're all right, Miss Cook. Your wrists are slightly chafed."

(Selene would later wonder if he had encouraged this whole slipshod seance, urged it to failure so he might have her to himself, claiming a necessary solitude in his laboratory. Without any proof, she felt this was precisely true.)

"Perfectly fine. I feel rather tired, actually."

"Of course. Well, an end to the evening then. Shall I escort you to your guest room or would you prefer that Mrs. Herapath go with you?"

"No, I shall be fine on my own, thank you. Mine is the room down the hall from your laboratory, am I correct?"

*

In those several moments before the Herapath children, their governess and Mrs. Herapath arrived, Selene and William Herapath had been most efficient, readying the room with one another's crisp cooperation. In an entirely new confusion, Selene had felt herself grow conscientious, nearly stern, all to conceal the fact that she found Mr. Herapath exceedingly attractive. Other gentlemen of her recent acquaintance, Thomas Boynton, Arthur Purdon, Charles

Blackburn, these were men whose admiration of her she had handled skillfully and to her advantage since her deeper feelings were not involved. But from the moment William Herapath had invited her into his home on Mornington Road, and especially this evening, his voice, his large, deepset grey eyes, his luxuriant dark hair and beard, all disturbed and strangely affected her. Indeed, on the landing, she had nearly placed her hand familiarly upon the sleeve of his brown velvet jacket. And during dinner, she had found herself glancing often at his hands, noting how large and finely shaped they were. The touch of them, as he had tied her to the chair, had quite shaken her.

Now she lay awake in a horridly small, windowless room that smelled faintly of chemicals. On the table beside her, a candle burned. That was because William, the Herapath's deceased son, was in the room. He had appeared directly before her as an elongated oval mist, then as a little upturned root of a child with great dark eyes and outstretched, pleading hands. She was not as startled as she thought she might be but simply closed her eyes against the apparition in order to better concentrate upon the success of tomorrow's experiment. Her whole happiness and that of her family depended on this man's unswerving judgment in her favour. She realized she would do nearly anything to make it so.

*

Where the deuce was Gimingham? Removing his glasses, William Herapath rubbed at his eyes. Either the cruel mix of sleet, rain and a bitter north wind had detained his assistant or else Love, that other inclement blast of weather. Educated like himself at the Royal College of Chemistry, Gimingham had been employed as Herapath's assistant for nearly two years. He was a lank greyhound of a youth with as punishing a twin affliction of pockmarks and stammer as Herapath had ever seen. Yet the boy was brilliant in the subjects of chemistry and electricity, and dedicated to whatever labour was set before him. Of late, however, Gimingham had altered. He had begun to whistle, a tuneless piping which drove Herapath nearly mad. He invented bad jokes, then laughed insanely over them. And he had taken to pomatum, arriving with his sandy tussock of hair so larded and reeking of orange flower water that Herapath could identify him, like some fatal jungle flower, from half a mile away. Found some girl to play the heavy swell to, eh? he had once teased, and Gimingham, turning a bright cherry hue, had nearly let slip the set of photographic plates he was holding.

Herapath drew out his gold pocket watch, a wedding gift from his wife. He was beginning to suspect Love not weather. Half past. He was fanatical about time, as lashed to the workings of his timepiece as a sea captain to his compass. Other people's indifference to the slipping away of irretrievable hours infuriated him. Where, for instance, was his medium? She was as tardy as Gimingham. And his tea, devil on a stick, had gone cold. Let those two squander their lives, he wouldn't. He pulled down his most recent issue of *Fowler's Phrenological Journal*, paging through to find and reread that excerpt from "Creative and Sexual Science" which continued to fascinate him:

> Let no sun set without a full, hearty, soul-inspiring love feast. Not a few days of courtship or honeymoon Love, but its complete life-long exercise alone should suffice... This Love making, this incessant delicious agitation of this nervous pitch in each, by the sexual electricity of the other, explains that *modus operandi* by means of which the action of all the physical and mental functions are thus wrought up, excited, exhilarated, intoxicated, disciplined, mobilized, thrilled in both... Celibacy is an outrage against nature. In everything exists a Loving or Creating agent. The voice, the walk, the handwriting, the blood itself indicate and are affected by sexual states. Even the rap at the door is sexed.

He studied his watch. Nearly ten and still as solitary as he had been at 7:30 when the housemaid had brought in his tea tray and re-lit the fire, a small blaze serving chiefly to remind him of how chilly his laboratory with its glass cabinets, wood countertops, work tables and glass rods and beakers, was.

His one companion all morning had been a preserved fox. Hunted, shot and presented to Maude by his younger brother, Philip, the animal had been her first attempt at taxidermy. Her errors, even to the untrained eye, were disconcerting. Cracking skin, odd bulges, a rigid pose. A young female with a russet coat, the glass eyes stared blankly, the right front paw raised to suggest imminent flight. Yet, she had eluded neither capture nor this humiliation, badly stuffed and set as a paperweight on one corner of his large oak desk.

"Sir."

Looking like a snowcapped persimmon, red-faced and half frozen, Gimingham shuffled in from the hall.

"Apologies, sir. I missed the train and had to walk."

"No matter, no matter. I'll ring for tea, you warm yourself while I go over what we will be doing today. Miss Cook should be down from her breakfast at any moment. And Gimingham?"

"Sir?"

"Employ a little less bear grease on your hair. Whoever she is, I guarantee she'll like you better for it."

"Thank you, Sir. I suppose I haven't got the knack just yet."

"Well, you will. Love is a man's swiftest tutor."

"Fine phrase, Sir."

"Yes, I suppose it is."

*

Having breakfasted leisurely and entirely alone, Selene now stood in the doorway of William Herapath's laboratory, unable to remember exactly what he was renowned for. Chemistry? Physics? Thomas Boynton had told her, naming a whole line of accomplishments and discoveries. He thought his friend a genius and often said that to know William Herapath was to know the likes of Sir Isaac Newton or Galileo. Most recently, he had discovered an element called thallium, though what an element was and why one would want to discover it, Selene had neither knowledge nor much curiosity. The first object she saw as she stood quietly unobserved, was a tatty looking animal on Herapath's cluttered desk, a red fox staring cross-eyed over the edge of an untidy heap of papers, stacked journals and books. Beside the fire, noisily sucking his tea out of a saucer, stood a tall, hunched fellow, no doubt the assistant. But where was he?

"There you are." He startled her, having appeared suddenly beside her. "I took the liberty of searching for you. Let me introduce you to my assistant, Gimingham. We are nearly ready to begin the day's tests. We will be performing the first series four times over. Repetition is the key to proof, you know. I performed a similar experiment on D. D. Home in May of 1872. Thus you are in illustrious company."

(Where had he been? He had traveled down the hall to her room. Finding the door closed, had softly knocked. *Even the rap at the door is sexed.* Hearing no response, he had turned the doorknob and stepped into the little space she had so recently slept in. Her things were everywhere, the room redolent with her odour, mixed with the scent of violet powder. A scarlet flannelette petticoat was flung over the chair. He reached out to it, a curious, pleading caress. There stood the willowware pot with the three stalks of white hyacinth he had had the housemaid bring down from the morning room after she had first admired them. Beside the flowers was her little beaded purse. Standing in the cream-coloured room his son had died so tragically in, William Herapath was entranced by the scent of violet and hyacinth, the odour of her clothing, the underlying fragrance of his deceased child, all mingled and caught as if under glass, as if in a dream of tremendous yearning. Then, from down the hall, issuing from his laboratory, came the bright sound of her laughter, mischievous as bells. And joining in, Gimingham's callow, foolish cackle.)

—FROM THE NOTEBOOK OF W. HERAPATH—
THE SELENE COOK EXPERIMENTS
1874

I seek the truth continually, but only now have I carried off the priestess from her shrine, and in my own home enjoy testing phenomena I have witnessed elsewhere under less conclusive conditions. The following is a list of phenomena I hope to encounter and document in the course of my investigations:

1. Movement of heavy bodies with contact, but without mechanical exertion
2. Percussive and other allied sounds
3. Alteration of the weight of bodies
4. Movement of heavy substances when at a distance from the medium

5. Rising of tables and chairs off the ground, without contact from any person
6. Luminous appearances
7. Movement of various small articles without contact with any person
8. Levitation of human beings
9. Appearance of hands, either self-luminous or visible by ordinary light
10. Direct writing
11. Phantom forms and faces
12. Special instances which seem to point to the agency of an exterior intelligence
13. Miscellaneous occurrences of a complex character

WEIGHTS AND MEASURES

On the first day of our undisturbed experimentation, I performed the following test with the spring-board apparatus which had been earlier set up by my chemical assistant. This consists of a long mahogany board, one end of which rests on a table, while the other end is supported on a spring balance and fastened to a strong tripod stand. At my direction, Miss Cook placed the tips of her fingers lightly on the extreme end of the mahogany board which was resting on the support, whilst Gimingham and myself sat, one on each side of it, watching for any effect which might be produced. Almost immediately the pointer of the balance was seen to descend. After a few seconds it rose again. This movement was repeated several times, as if by successive waves of the psychic force. The end of the board was observed to oscillate slowly up and down during the experiment. Gimingham now took up a small hand-bell and a little cardboard matchbox and placed one under each hand, to satisfy me that he was not producing any of the downward pressure. The very slow oscillation of the spring balance became more marked. Watching the index, I saw it descend to six and a half pounds. On looking immediately afterwards at the automatic register, we saw that the index had at one time descended as low as nine pounds, showing maximum pull of six pounds.

This demonstration with the spring board does much to prove the existence of an unknown force. I noticed in this first experiment (first in a series of four), that the force was exhibited in tremulous pulsations and not in the form of steady continuous pressure, the indicator rising and falling incessantly throughout the experiment. This fact tends to confirm that opinion which assigns this force to the nerve-organization, and goes far to establish Dr. Richardson's discovery of a nerve atmosphere of various intensity enveloping the human structure.

*

He could not sleep and found himself in his laboratory, reviewing his day's notes. The experiment had gone as perfectly as Homes's had. Miss Cook had been an ideal subject. Clearly, his calculations were in order. He would perform the same experiment tomorrow, three times in a row. Then why was he up, shivering in his long nightshirt? What kept him awake by the strength of its suggestion, a suggestion to which he finally succumbed, moving down the draughty, dark hallway until he stood directly outside her door? Could she be awake as well? A gold slip of light came from underneath her door. Could she have fallen asleep, the candle still burning? The danger of fire prompted him to knock.

"Miss Cook?" Knocked again.

He heard her stir, cross the room. The door opened. Her hair was in a soft storm, falling nearly to her waist. Her eyes were wide, pacific, utterly clear.

"Sir?"

Oh, spirit child. He could not, absolutely could not, breathe.

"I was awake, going over my notes. I saw your light, became concerned, was concerned..." Good god, if he sounded so like Gimingham, how idiotic must he look?

She was laughing at him.

"What are you laughing at?"

"My father wears precisely the same nightcap. They are out of fashion, Mr. Herapath. No one in England, except you and my father, wears a knitted nightcap anymore."

He inclined his head. "Take it off then, Miss Cook. Take the damned thing off."

Reaching up, she tugged it off, swung it delicately from her fingertips. "What shall we do with it?"

"Let your father have it. A second nightcap."

"Oh." The girl stood there, suddenly downcast.

"What is it, Miss Cook?"

"My little finch. Every evening when I am home, I let him out of his cage to sit on my shoulder."

"He must certainly miss such a treat as that."

"Yes, I suppose."

How Herapath found himself one moment in the hallway inquiring as to Miss Cook's welfare and the next standing fully inside her bedroom, awkwardly clamped onto his candle, while she sat with complete ease upon her bed, his nightcap in her lap, he really couldn't say—but there he gaped, as oafish and stumble-tongued as his young assistant. All he lacked was the reek of pomatum.

"Mr. Herapath, whatever can you be thinking? Do you wish to sit down?"

Desperately scanning the room for signs of a chair, he thought he glimpsed one beneath a huge heap of her underclothing, crinolines, petticoats, corsets.

"Here." She patted the bed beside her.

"Oh. No. I..."

"You have arrived to take the place of my finch, not on my shoulder, of course, but to keep me company a moment. There, I'll set your candle down beside mine. Now look, the room is twice as bright."

So began William Herapath's precipitous examination of a subject he had never before allowed himself to study. The schoolgirl medium would herself prove an able teacher that first night, employing a good deal of charm followed by a subtle retreat. As he sat beside her on the bed, brushing her dark brown, waist-length hair, which sparked with electricity between his hands, as they sat in their white nightclothes, the candlelight casting waves of gold around them, something in William Herapath's nature began again to take breath, instinctual root, to let go of sorrow, to let go time.

—FROM THE NOTEBOOK OF W. HERAPATH—
THE VARLEY ELECTRICAL EXPERIMENTS
1874

With the aid of a test devised by my colleague, Cromwell F. Varley (Fellow of the Royal Society), I did today attempt nothing less than to prove the literal truth of Christ's resurrection!

The object of the apparatus devised by Mr. Varley is to prove by electrical means that Selene Cook sits entranced behind the closed curtains of her cabinet while the materialized figure of Florence King moves and talks outside of that same cabinet, independent of her medium. The method devised by Mr. Varley and carried out to exact standards by myself is as follows:

The medium, Miss Cook, is placed in circuit with a two-cell battery, two sets of resistance coils and a reflecting galvanometer, an instrument visible and outside of the cabinet for the whole duration of the seance. Miss Cook seated in the armchair, is unbound and at liberty to move in what serves as her cabinet—my library—which is separated from my morning room by a thick curtain. Pieces of blotting paper, dampened with a nitrate of ammonia solution, are placed upon each of her bare arms and held in position by elastic bands. Platinum wires are then attached to the two sovereigns and led to the battery, to the resistance coils and to the galvanometer, all connected in a series and completing the electrical circuit.

By the drying of the blotting paper, the galvanometer showed a deflection of 220 divisions at the beginning of the seance at 7:10 p.m. and a decreased reading of 146 by 7:48 p.m. The decrease was regular and progressive. Throughout the reading, current flowed through the galvanometer demonstrating an unbroken circuit. Had the wires been removed in any way from Miss Cook's arms, moreover had the wires been joined by their ends together, the increased flow of electricity due to the removal of electrical resistance caused by the body of the medium would have increased the deflection significantly; instead, there was a decrease of deflection caused by the gradual drying of the blotting paper. While the apparition, Florence King, was fully out of the cabinet and the medium, Selene Cook, within, the galvanometer did not record any variation exceeding one division on the scale. Thus my statement as I have prepared it for future publication: <u>It will be impossible to put stronger language in my mouth when speaking of Miss Cook's perfect honesty, truthfulness and perfect willingness to submit to the severest tests I have devised for her; as far as experiments go, these prove conclusively that Miss Cook is INSIDE the cabinet while her spirit manifestation is OUTSIDE the same.</u>

*

(And discovered in the private papers of Sir William Herapath upon his death, 1912: *As to the Varley experiment performed on Miss Cook in 1874, two significant variations in the readings were recorded by my assistant, Charles Gimingham. Both of these occurred between 7:10 p.m. and 7:38 p.m. when the apparition was yet making preparations to emerge. As follows: At 7:22, my assistant and I heard from behind the curtain, some indistinct whisperings by Florence King. At 7:25 p.m., the galvanometer abruptly dropped from 191 to 155 divisions. A fall of 36 divisions in one minute. Evidently, Miss Cook had shifted her position within the cabinet and in so doing, had moved the sovereigns. There was, however, no break of circuit. After this, we noted an occasional hand or arm shown briefly through the curtains. Between 7:35 p.m. and 7:37 p.m., during one of these demonstrations, the galvanometer reading plunged from 152 to 135, then rose again to 156 divisions. As Florence King showed us her arm from behind the curtains, the galvanometer fell 17 divisions, indicating much movement on Miss Cook's part. I admit, here and most privately, the suspicious nature of that occurrence. However, once the apparition emerged entirely from the cabinet, the apparatus remained steady, not falling more than one division, thus neutralizing the doubt above engendered. This steady reading, as I stated in my published validation of Miss Cook's authenticity, clearly proves Miss Cook to have remained quiescent in the darkened cabinet whilst Florence moved, animate and visible, on the other side. The two abrupt drops in divisions I did, with great professional misgivings, withhold from my official validation of Miss Cook. While my own doubts were somewhat appeased by the steady reading of the galvanometer once Florence King was outside the cabinet, I did not desire to throw untoward suspicion upon her by publishing a detailed account of these two varied readings. How easily the variance might have been seized upon, misinterpreted and so nullify all I deemed to be Miss Cook's very real achievement of separation between herself and the apparition of Florence King. To protect Miss Cook, to defend her honor, I suppressed any publication of these variations.*)

*

The objects in her room were arranged as artfully as a bowl of ripening fruit. Selene herself was positioned in what she hoped would be an alluring posture when he came to her room as he had, punctually, at 10:30 p.m., the past two evenings. But this odalisque pose, now long sustained, had produced a numbness in her limbs; her neck, too, held a new murmur of stiffness to it. This pose, artful, alluring, and maintained for nearly an hour, had been exchanged for a new awareness of appearing vaguely ridiculous. To fix one's possessions and one's limbs in an attitude of innocence to convey a less than innocent message had been the crux of her challenge. Now Selene sat up, her plan defeated. The moment had passed, replaced by tedium and fresh anxiety. The past two nights he had rapped on her door, desired admittance which she had granted him. He had sat beside her and once, while brushing her hair, had grown so heated, that he had begun kissing her shoulders, until she took back the hairbrush and, with an affected yawn, showed him to the hall. But here it was, a quarter till midnight, her yawns genuine and her worry unabated. The day's experiment had gone badly. He had recorded a discrepancy in the electrical readings. He and his clammy assistant had behaved over-politely to her thereafter. Herapath had not dined with her, in fact, no one had. Realizing and resenting her exile, presented with yet another dish of mutton glazed with fat, Selene had half a mind to go up and eat her supper with the Herapath children. She feared his infatuation had been dampened by the outcome of his electrical experiments, that his suspicions and not his ardour were aroused. Obeying the sudden, shrill trumpeting of her nerves, Selene stood up and peevishly disarranged everything. If he didn't care, neither would she. Made petulant by the derailment of her plans, Selene opened the door and peered down the cold, dark hallway toward the laboratory. Nothing.

In the midst of more troubling speculation, as she lay awake and huddled beneath the covers, Selene heard all at once his distinctive knock.

"Miss Cook? Might I have a word with you?"

That night, and for the first time, Selene allowed William Herapath to kiss her, first on the cheek, then, as she gazed up with what she hoped was an irresistible winsomeness, full on the lips. What she could not have anticipated, in this premeditated surrender of morals, was the warm flare of response in herself from that first, deeply ardent kiss. When she broke from his embrace,

Selene Cook's dismay, her confusion were unfeigned. The ploy she had devised had turned on her. The effect his deepset grey eyes had upon hers, the heat of his mouth had weakened her limbs until full acquiescence, which was to have been confined to the borders of a single kiss, seemed inevitable. He knew it, too. Without a word exchanged, it was understood he would pursue her a short distance more to her fated end, and her capitulation would be complete. And because of this, the chase could be savoured—for the emotion of anticipation forever surpasses that of actual obtainment. The fall from grace, when it came, would be steep, would set them both on who knew what course of scandal. Thus, on both sides, there existed a natural impulse to balk, to gather up boldness, audacity, heedlessness, those backward attributes of passion.

After he had departed, Selene lay in her bed, the arrangement of herself unmeditated, her fingertips travelling over her lips, feeling their fullness at the center, their downward slope and corners, marvelling at their altered newness, how incomplete they felt by themselves.

William Herapath lay beside his wife, nearly ill with the abrupt deprivation of his senses. If Selene knew little what to imagine beyond the re-invention of that single, hot kiss, William Herapath, who knew well his own wife's flesh, by that study alone, aroused himself to near groaning by most rich speculation.

*

Gimingham pored over the text by J. E. Mayall on the making of albumen paper. Stupified by a bad head cold, he read aloud in a congested mutter, the icy laboratory provoking from his nose a steady drip which he continuously wiped away with one mittened hand.

Albumen derives its name from albumen ovi, the Latin name for white of egg. It exists most abundantly and in its purest natural state in eggs. It is one of the chief constituents of many animal solids and fluids. Its chief characteristic is its coagulability by heat. The albumen of the hen's egg is the easiest to access. The eggs must be fresh, not more than five days old. They ought to be kept in a cool place. Those from the country are better than town-laid eggs, and I advise, where practicable, that the hens should have carbonate and phosphate of lime strewn about to peck at. This enriches the albumen and renders it more limpid. Each egg must be broken separately into a shallow cup, and the yolk retained in the shell as well as the germ; then pour into a measure until the required quantity of limpid albumen is obtained.

With no small disgust, Gimingham regarded the glisteny smear, the clear albumen-like material he had just collected from under his nose onto his thin black mitten. Where Herapath's eggs came from, whether they were laid in London or Kent or the farthest reaches of Nottingham he had no idea, much less whether the hens who laid them pecked at phosphate of lime. Crikey, he was at death's door. He wanted to be home in bed with his mother petting and soothing him. No doubt he had caught cold while carrying in the four new cameras delivered two days before. Herapath had owned two, now he possessed six, all wet-plate collodion cameras, each slightly varied in design and technique of use. The laboratory was overrun by three-legged black boxes with black cloth tents or hoods at their backs. From where he sat at William Herapath's littered desk, they appeared to Gimingham like square-headed black herons or stick-legged beetles of grotesque, almost brutal size.

Gimingham believed Selene Cook to be an utter fraud. As far as he was concerned, all spiritualists were frauds and cheats, but it was pathetically clear William Herapath was infatuated by this particular trumpetess for the spirit world. Trumpet strumpet. Gimingham was unimpressed with the girl, not far from his own age and too slender, too languishing, too tragic. She made him think of some cheap, ill-wrought tomb ornament. Touching her, and he had spent considerable time in the privacy of his bed at night imagining just such a thing, would be like bumping into a marble post in an unheated cathedral. He preferred his dance hall girls with their painted cheeks and pouty lips. He kissed them whenever he liked, releasing the scent hidden in the artificial flowers pinned against their warm breasts. Selene Cook—ha!—a gelid thing with chemicals for blood, all too calculated in her parlour tricks. Herapath's monotonous experiments, meant to prove the separation of space and time between the medium and her apparition (who to Gimingham looked an exact twin to Selene Cook) were absurd. When Florence King was wafting about, why not simply draw back the curtain and see if Selene was still fastened to her chair? The measurement device, the galvanometer, and now his having to make albumen print paper to be fed to six cameras, these were over-reactions to the obvious. He guessed why of course, and wisely kept silent. As a young chemist, he was steadily employed (though he had, weekly, to remind his employer to pay him), and it would do him no harm, Gimingham realized, to be able to say he had once studied with the eminent scientist, William Herapath.

This Mayall text was of small use—he had no way of controlling the diets of hens. Swiping at his bothersome nose, Gimingham turned to the book by Le Gray for the exact formula he needed:

Take the white of eggs, to which add the fifth part, by volume of saturated solution of chloride of sodium, or what is still better, hydrochloride of ammonia, beat it into a froth, and decant the clear liquid after it has settled for one night.

Pour the liquid into a basin and prepare your positive paper on one side only...dry it and pass the hot iron over it...

The paper thus prepared is very highly varnished. If you desire to obtain less gloss, add, before beating the eggs, the half or more of distilled water containing equally a fifth of water saturated with hydrochlorate ammonia. You may thus modify the degree of brilliancy of the proof. The mixture of half albumen and half water is excellent, it gives much fineness and firmness without giving the proof a varnished appearance.

You may keep this paper some time before you apply the nitrate of silver to it, as it does not spoil.

When you desire to use it, put the albumen side on a bath of nitrate of silver, containing one part of nitrate by weight, to four of distilled water, and let it imbibe four or five minutes; then hang it by the corner to dry, and finish it as I have already described.

This paper gives much depth to the blacks, and great brilliancy to the whites. In leaving it a shorter time in the nitrate bath and using Whatman's paper, you may obtain a reddish-purple tint that is very harmonious. Carson's papers, and usually all those which contain admine, give black tints.

Gimingham sighed dejectedly. Why could they not simply buy photographic paper already prepared, as they had always done? Because of Selene Cook, that's why, because lust inspired, in his employer, a corresponding fastidiousness.

*

William Herapath sat dumbfounded on the girl's bed, a length of diaphanous cloth trailing from his hands. Three nights in a row he had taken photographs of Florence King by magnesium flash, twelve photographs of a luminous spirit manifestation. Now he grasped the very substance of its trickery in his hands. A few flimsy yards of silk conjured up the whole spirit world. Selene Cook, or at least the apparition manifested by her, was counterfeit, and William Herapath had been as gulled as any child at a county fair. Beside him, on the bed, lay a pair of Selene's ribbon-trimmed pantalets.

He knew where she was. Upstairs at breakfast with Mrs. Herapath. He had overheard them conversing, had then snuck down to her room to search among her things, not search precisely, for he had had no suspicion, none at all—he had merely wanted to be among her things, to caress them and so grow more familiar with her, perhaps smell them and so come nearer that divine flesh her garments housed. He had stood beside the dark blue dress she had worn the night before, tenderly lifting the abandoned petticoat with its half hoop in the back. The pantalets had fallen out from underneath the petticoat. He had thought to hold them close to his face, bring himself to the edge of a very bliss at the sweetish odour emanating from them—when a gauzy length of cloth drifted out from the slit between the legs. Only for a moment was he perplexed. Then he identified the pale, gossamer material worn by the ethereal Florence King.

William Herapath was a man of science. He did not do what the average man, hoodwinked and betrayed, might have done. He did not rush upstairs and confront her with the evidence before pitching her into the road. No, the magnitude of the girl's ambition quite impressed him. He left the room quickly so as not to be discovered (and had he not come there because her coy seductions had so goaded him?), careful to leave all, well, nearly all, exactly as it had been. He would use this traitorous cloth to his advantage, if not as a scientist then as a man. If she was no authentic medium, if he now saw, for the first time, her intent to charm him, her tender, dewy-eyed looks all contrived to seduce him—to gain her advantage—well, poor creature, now he was onto her, and what he could obtain in terms of that awareness gave him superior, incontestable, thrilling advantage.

*

"I seem unable to summon Florence to us tonight. I am feeling poorly, strangely so. May we not forgo this evening's experiments?"

True, she did look unwell. Not unwell like his assistant, who was hoarse and hacking, but some less physical, more complex strife had produced in her a greenish pallor.

"Everything is in place, Miss Cook. We must keep to our agreed-upon schedule. I cannot waste expensive chemicals and solutions prepared by Mr. Gimingham. Besides, they are difficult to maintain properly and remain sensitive for only the briefest time. Gimingham has been hard at work all day, and I do not know if he will be well enough to come in tomorrow. Regrettably, Miss Cook, I must insist we proceed."

She stood in his laboratory, the same height as his various cameras. At his refusal to cancel the evening's experiment, Selene seemed to droop within her voluminous skirts. His grip upon her forearm was not gentle as he led her behind the black curtain and tied her to the chair with his usual deft fashioning of knots and seals.

She said nothing, but bit down on her lower lip, looking like a small, trapped animal. He could not resist.

"You look exceedingly slender this evening, Miss Cook. Are you without some usual bit of apparel?"

She did not answer. He bustled about, appearing to set up lenses on cameras, tripods, hoods, solutions, exactly as he had the previous three nights, except for these differences: he had dismissed Gimingham hours before, and he would waste no paper, no chemicals, no solutions, no collodion-treated plates, he had only made her think so. He would, in fact, use nothing. Behind his inoperative camera, on one knee, his head tucked beneath the black hood, he waited.

After some minutes, in a small, strained voice, Selene called out to him. "I do not know why, but Florence refuses to come to us tonight. I do not understand."

For the first time, he heard the deceit in her voice, the theatric sob. Little cheat, he thought.

When the curtains snapped wide, Selene, bound in her chair, gasped at William Herapath's sudden, thunderous appearance. "Could this be the impediment to Florence King's appearance, Miss Cook?" Herapath produced the gauzy material from behind his back with a flourish.

He actually hadn't thought beyond this moment of ambush. The effect was more gratifying than he could have predicted. She whitened, fainted. Clumsily, he unfastened the ropes, undid the seals, lifted her up into his arms. He felt like a villain in some lady's novel, of the sort Maude used to read. Panting a little from her unexpected weight, he bore his little counterfeit down the hallway to her room.

The first swoon had been genuine. But as he watched over her, he observed how each time her eyes opened, and she reassessed her dire situation, she most conveniently fainted away again. The helpless posture, eyes closed, the slack mouth and limp form, all these suggested acquiescence and roused him beyond neutral observation. As she lay in her real or feigned third swoon, what did it matter, he no longer cared, he began touching her, kissing her, taking full liberty with what was soon to be his—her hair, her supple throat, and, pressing his chemical-stained hand over her dress, the racing heart.

He had purchased her silence. She must, out of a desperate hope not to lose his validation, surrender to him. As if hearing his thoughts, Selene stirred slightly, opened her eyes, and when he bent down to gather her once more in his arms, this time she did not protest, no longer having authority to distance him. Her sole remaining power, and they both knew it, was in carnal surrender.

Yet even surrender requires patience. The dozens of cloth-covered buttons, the loosing of stays, the hooks and fastenings everywhere. As each layer fell away, less substantial and more fragranced than the last, as he came nearer her naked core, as he knelt beside the bed unlacing then removing each of her small white boots, Selene saw, over his shoulder, the poignant mist of William Herapath's son, a pleading shape, its innocent features blurred, crossing between worlds.

*

Gimingham, ignorant of what had transpired the evening before and, blind to all but what lay drearily before him, prepared a steady stream of the albumen papers, while William Herapath prepared to finish out his series of pictures, his supposed proofs of Florence King. He would instruct Selene to don her bit of flummery and assume wraithlike postures. In the last photograph, he had her pose naked beneath the sheer drapery in order to give, he said, Florence King an ethereal advantage. He hastened through these photographs, shortening exposure times from 45 to 15 seconds, ironically remembering as he did so, the Pre-Raphaelite photographer's injunction—that only by repression of detail could divine revelation be found. And each night, long after Gimingham had left, after these rushed sessions in his laboratory, he seized Florence King by the spirit-draperies in order to better embrace Selene Cook, fleshly and warm inside them. That he had been hoodwinked by so young a woman was bad enough—but that he had hoped to prove the resurrection of Christ and beyond that, reinforce the empirically threatened existence of God, only to be made a mockery of, a fool of, was a foul draught of truth bearable only in one way, through the passion he now exerted upon the object of his betrayal.

William Herapath was a superbly disciplined scientist, and upon his youthful subject he now exercised those skills which had brought him and would continue, all his life, to yield him discovery upon discovery. Curiosity, care, repetition, variety, study of the object at hand, experimentation, utmost care and a single-minded concentration on the best result. In short, he produced, after tireless nights of testing, a marvelous series of low continuous sounds and cryings out which satisfied him in the correctness of his procedure. He had produced in his test subject a sustained sexual bliss.

*

Meanwhile, Gimingham recovered his health, and Mrs. Herapath fell to diligent dissection of yet more specimens. With morbid zest, she sliced the throats of blue jays, holding each until its life floated into the air of her studio, already thickly engraved with the souls of slain birds. In the midst of this, Octavia Cook, along with Tot who carried by one weary arm, a familiar tole bird cage with a pale yellow finch inside it, arrived at Mornington Road. They appeared, uninvited, for five o'clock tea. Mrs. Herapath managed, though spottily, to serve them in the morning room. Selene was present, but Mr. Herapath was not, attending yet another of his gentlemen's clubs.

"Well," Octavia was explaining, "you lift each bell, though not easily, for they are made of the heaviest brass, lifting the leather loop straps quickly so as not to show the clapper, straight up and with a flicking of your wrist. Each bell is one note, the largest has the deepest tone, the smallest the higher tone. Most recently we have practised Hayden's 'Sheep May Safely Graze.' Do you know that particular piece of music, Mrs. Herapath?"

She did not, Maude replied. Octavia shifted in her chair, anxiously awaiting Tot who had transported the bird downstairs to Selene's room, no doubt an elegant space, brimming over with luxuries and gifts. In fact, Octavia scarcely knew what she was saying to this queer-looking woman, so preoccupied was she with observing the state of comfort and well-being her sister had settled into. While the burden of caring for her parents had fallen upon her, Selene was, well, *here*. While the Cooks scrimped and despaired over their next meal, Selene shared nothing of her privilege with her own family. Octavia had noticed the new, striped mauve and black dress Selene wore, its black silk fringe around the bodice, and a fine crapestone brooch she had not seen before. She observed the langour, the complacency her sister appeared bathed in, while Octavia's meagre earnings from her bell concerts seemed, since Mr. Cook had again fallen ill, all that kept a leaky roof over their heads and a bit of bread on their plates. Selene had promised that when Mr. Herapath's experiments were complete and with her abilities validated and made public, she would return home, take up her seances again and share all she had with them.

Octavia glanced around as she sipped her too-bitter tea. Everything done up in gold and dark green, the air with its odd chilly scent, perhaps the way a scientist's house would smell. Still, the quality of everything was high, there was no want or lack here. Selene was flourishing like a hothouse plant, heedless of her family's difficulties. Octavia had not yet had the opportunity to press her sister as to when she would return to their home in Hackney. Feeling self-conscious and ungainly in her mended dress, Octavia set down her teacup and rose to leave.

"Thank you, Mrs. Herapath. I apologize if my unexpected visit has inconvenienced you."

*

"Dearest Tot!" Selene seized hold of both her servant's hands. "Swear you won't tell. I cannot keep this to myself. If I confide in you, you must swear to tell no one."

Tot nodded, if only to encourage Selene to release the pressure upon her hands.

"It is Mr. Herapath. He does not love his wife. He says, though he is most indebted to her, he says she is half-mad, and that I am..." From here, Selene whispered in her servant's ear.

Tot did not care to hear any more. It was like grasping a flaming torch in one's hand and then being told to pretend it didn't burn. This sinful news, this damning confession set itself like a stone in Tot's conscience. She felt neither grateful nor closer to Selene because of it.

"Thank you for bringing my poor darling bird. I shall tend to him day and night until he is well. He's missed me, that's why he's weak. Oh, my life alters from one moment to the next, and I am as lost to its outcome as anyone could ever be. Tot, forgive me. And *swear* you will tell no one."

*

In the chilly foyer, Octavia confronted her sister. Tot stood nearby, heavy and flushed, trying to appear ignorant of what she had just heard.

"You must come home, Selie. Things are dreadful. You cannot know how awful. You have not written or visited us."

"Tell Mamma and Pappa I will be home as soon as I can. Mr. Herapath is nearly done with his testing, and has promised to publish his vindication of me in all London's spiritualist papers. Then I shall return home and, having convinced Mr. Blackburn of the trueness of my nature, I will take up my seances again. Octavia, I do not live in whatever splendour you imagine. This dress has been given, or rather lent to me, by Mrs. Herapath. My room is an icy coffin. Worse, it is frequented by a ghost. I only stay on here to help you, to help my family. Be patient, I beg you."

But when the two women left Mornington Road, Octavia remained suspicious, for on the omnibus back to Hackney, Tot looked glum, her face clouded, and Octavia could only worry what that might mean.

*

That evening, returning to the confinement of her small room, Selene occupied herself trying to feed the little finch. As it refused to take more than half-hearted pecks at the seed in her hand, a peculiar, acrid odour filled the room, no doubt the chemical which had poisoned the Herapath's child. He was here, then. Behind her. Gently, she returned her finch to its cage, latched the tiny door. Turning, she spoke to the child about the need for him to go to heaven, to allow himself to leave this place. She could not see him this time, only felt the spot of chill where he was, smelled the chemical odour. Words came and she spoke them softly, until both the chill and the odour dissipated and the child's spirit withdrew, was finally gone.

A short while later, waiting for William (impossible, any longer, to call him Mr. Herapath) to come to her again, Selene thought to take her finch out from its cage once more. This time he pecked avidly, capturing each pale grain hilled in her upturned hand.

February 17, 1874

Eliza, Chère Enfant,

Of late, I am strangely pinned to a line of Swedenborg's—
"The whole of heaven is a Grand Man (Maximus Homo); and it
is called a Grand Man because it corresponds to the Lord's Divine
Human"—this travels like an illumined melody through my
other sundry, colourless thoughts. I begin to be persuaded, Eliza,
this world is colonized entirely by GHOSTS. A community of
spirits who daily arrange, mitigate and dismiss our pitiful, urgent
concerns.

Oh, but it is February, the month most melancholic and least
pleasing to me. We have had here in Didsbury six days of
gloomiest, blackest-seeming rain and it has made of me, in my
cold study, a dyspeptic philosopher. I rave, Eliza. Perhaps I
should reside with you at Clapham. Would that not be a fine
thing, father and daughter shuffling our black decks to the last
lunatic end of time, inhabiting the same mad, interior space?
Eliza, an extraordinary event has occurred. An extraordinary
possibility has come up. I begin first with the event, then the
possibility.

I have been in correspondence with the scientist, William
Herapath, who, as you may recall, agreed to perform a rigorous
series of tests upon Selene Cook, including the Varley experiment
which I knew of and had specifically requested he perform. By
his judgement, Florence King is indeed a non-corporeal essence
divided from Miss Cook. Wednesday last, he invited me, along
with a small number of other regular sitters, to Miss Cook's first
seance following the conclusion of his series of experiments.

I went, my skepticism rather well grouted in. All this has
reversed. Miss Cook proved her mediumistic nature to be so
authentic, so true, that I now continue my financial support of
her. I can think of no more useful way to dispense with the
wealth I have amassed over a lifetime than to encourage those
who labour in the vineyards of spiritual growth. As for you
and I, hourly suffering the loss of a loved one, we gain hope
from the surety that we will, one day, be re-united. The veil
will be rent. There will be no blindness. All will be a radiant
communion of joined souls.

I promised to tell you a second thing. I have twice weekly
been receiving pencilled messages from L. Gordon, spirit control

of Octavia Cook. She says you are not to stay where you are, dear one. In spirit form she has visited you at Brooke Asylum and observed your conditions. She has seen you endure mistreatment and urges that you live with the Cooks in their good care. She particularly commends you to the care of Selene. The pragmatic means to this is unclear, but the directive from L. G. has come twice now and so I wait for instruction in how to carry out such a plan.

I am glad, Eliza, for your new interest in art. As I sit here, I have your little watercolour before me. From its faerie-like subject, I derive a most consoling sense of you near me.

The rain here in Didsbury renders everything cold, glossy, indistinct. Thank you for the bright colours in your little art work, a jewel in an otherwise dark universe of rain.

My nibful of ink has run itself dry. I have much business to attend to here in Manchester, at the mills, so will remain here in Didsbury for some time to come. I shall write often and look to see more of your pictures, dear girl, for you are all I have left of family in this, let us emphasize *this*, world.

Your Loving Pappa

February, 1874

To the Editor of *The Medium and The Daybreak*:

The editor of *The Spiritualist*, Balfour Lodge, has declined, for reasons best kept to himself but easily guessed at, knowing his relation to Charles Blackburn, to publish any of my recent letters, so I submit this newest one, in the form of a direct Challenge, to my old friend and colleague, William Herapath: I put forth two pragmatic suggestions, which, if carried out by him, would prove beyond any suspicion that Florence King is a non-corporeal spirit entity and not Miss Selene Cook scantily and thrillingly costumed as a ghost.

1. Place a drop of India ink upon any of Miss Cook's fingers. While Florence King moves among the sitters outside the cabinet, examine her hands for the indelible spot of ink.
2. Draw open the curtains and unwind the red shawl from about Miss Cook's head. She will moan a little no doubt of it, for I have heard the figure, its head swaddled in red, sob

considerably when lightly touched by either Mr. Herapath or Mr. Blackburn, thus far the only two sitters permitted near her.

Nothing can be proved while Miss Cook's head is unidentifiable. Any one could be approximating her form and figure lying there, disguised by a shawl while Miss Cook herself moves about as Florence King. This concealment of the face, weakly justified as protection from the bright magnesium flash of the camera, raises a strong presumption of fraud. No photographs were taken during the three seances I attended in February, and my observation of Florence King, admittedly hampered by the dimness of lowered gaslight in the parlour, was that she seemed a facsimile of Selene Cook. The shape of the eyebrows was exactly similar, the hands identical too, small, oval tipped and slender. The movements of the body were precisely alike, girlish and playful.

I challenge Mr. Herapath: If Florence King is not made of solid flesh and blood and bone as I believe she is, if she is not simply pretty young Selene Cook in a white headdress and a white cotton robe playing semi-skillfully the character of a ghost, prove it by these two useful suggestions: the use of India ink and the removal of the shawl. If in his confidence, William Herapath would oblige me with these two proofs, simpler and more useful than all those complex and, frankly, suspect experiments he has been describing in his lengthy letters to *The Spiritualist*, I will publically and enthusiastically withdraw my doubts. Remove, old friend, those prescribed conditions of your seance which facilitate trickery—the hymn singing, the holding of hands, the darkness, the distance held firm between sitters and cabinet, the shawl—remove these theatric obfuscations and let common sense persuade us of Miss Cook's and Miss King's separate identities!

I have known William Herapath and his dedication to the empirical truth for over twenty-five years. This new coyness over conditions, this penchant for theatric effect troubles me. It is inconsistent with the disciplined nature and scrupulous methods of the man I once knew. I ask him to indulge me by carrying out these two simple suggestions. Any refusal will confirm my mounting suspicion of grossest fraud.

Yours Sincerely,
William B. Cox

I grow confused by how I deceive and yet do not deceive. I have, in this business, provoked much envy and skepticism and the basest sort of curiosity. At first, when Thomas Boynton gave me the idea, I thought to provide the figure manifestations of Florence King as a means to exceed my sister's counterfeit mediumship. (And I know well how to counterfeit.) But the spirit of this woman who calls herself "Florrie," a woman who I <u>do not</u>, from what I am told of her, <u>even like</u>, has found its way into me, has stubbornly affixed itself to my flesh, and I fear I will not ever rid myself of her. So I am glad of William's decision, upon reading Mr. Cox's letter and several like it, written in the same mocking and skeptical tone, to take leave of these manifestations. William thinks they are now dangerous, that our little fraud will be uncovered. If only he knew how truly dangerous they are to me—that at times I grow uncertain of who I am—I have taken to burning a great many candles in my room at night. To keep <u>her</u> at a distance. To keep <u>her</u> away.

What a little fool Octavia is—envying me!

(I have read this over and feel it is wisest to consign what I have just written and confessed into the fire.)

"Octavia! Is that odious woman here?"

"Miss Marryat? Of course she is, and you should be pleased. She's certain to write you a favourable report."

"Where does she sit?"

"I saw her go to the far right end of the circle. Her face is absolutely painted on. Mr. Herapath is going to invite her inside the curtain. The one you need to be cautious of is that Mr. Cox. He's here, I saw him, though thankfully without a bottle of India ink in his hand. Supposedly he's present as a neutral observer. He sits at the opposite end from Miss Marryat. You must observe him closely yet not get over-near. I feel certain he will try to expose you."

"Who else? I'm all nerves tonight and cannot think. My head throbs, and I feel hot, but then my hands, feel, they are freezing."

"Mr. Cox is your one wasp in the nest. Then there's Balfour Lodge, the Corners, all the usual who warmly endorse Florence King."

"Where is Tot? What can be keeping her?"

The two sisters whispered in the draughty, unlit hall. A crooked stairway led up from the basement kitchen to the rooms off the hall where the seances were now held. Octavia held the wig with its long, auburn ringlets in her hands, while Selene paced about looking, if not ill, certainly sick with apprehension. This was to be, as announced two evenings ago, Florence King's final earthly appearance. After tonight, she would be whisked, forever, back to the spirit world, and Selene would again produce face manifestations in the cabinet, the rappings and flickerings of light and ringings of bells, all dull in comparison, but safer, much safer.

When the challenge from his old colleague William Cox appeared in *The Medium and The Daybreak*, William Herapath decided the best course to follow was not blots of India ink and unwrappings of red shawls, but to have Florence King be suddenly called home, summoned back into that atmosphere from which she had mysteriously emanated. After all, Selene's most urgent goal had been accomplished—Charles Blackburn was home in Didsbury, his generous cheques once again arriving weekly. There was no reason Selene could not simply resume her older, safer seances. These manifestations of Florence King were risky, too many people disbelieved, making the possibility of a fiasco, a debacle of exposure, a danger to Selene and especially, to himself.

So two evenings ago, with practically the same group of sitters, Florence King had, with fading gesture and sinking voice, declared her intent to leave them forever. The sitters were invited to say their good-byes this evening at seven o'clock.

Selene was nervous about the wig. She had never before worn one, though she had practised in her room that afternoon. She and Octavia, who had become affectionate again, had taken turns wearing it backwards and forwards, then plopping it onto Tot's head when she came in with their tea.

Now Tot appeared at the top of the stairs, holding the red knitted shawl and wearing a rough-made replica of Florence's dark blue dress.

"Likely, she mislaid the shawl," Octavia hissed. "I saw it in my room. The girl is half-blind as well as ugly. She's a fool."

Octavia took hold of her sister's moist, clammy hands. "Have you got everything? Are you certain?"

Selene nodded. Octavia kissed her on the cheek.

"Have her say good-bye specially to me, Selene? I fear I shall miss your Florence King." Hardly true, still Octavia sensed some advantage in saying so. Perhaps it was mainly relief. Seeing Selene become more equal to herself.

They could hear the hymn-singing, dominated by William Herapath's stubborn baritone:

> *With a slow and noiseless footstep*
> *Comes that messenger divine*
> *Takes the vacant chair beside me,*
> *Lays her gentle hand in mine.*

"I'd better go in. I'll be sitting in my usual place beside mother."

Tot loathed doing this impersonation. True, all she had been asked and paid by Mr. Herapath to do, was to lie face down on cushions on the floor and not move, her head and face bundled up in a red shawl. But each time, she became terrified she might smother or sneeze, or in some other horrible way ruin everything. She had been five times to confession because of her five deceptions. Each time, the priest advised her to quit these unholy impersonations. Each time, she was persuaded by the coins Herapath pressed into her hand. This was to be the last time. The risk of discovery had become too great. Should anyone attempt to touch her, Selene had advised Tot at least fifty times, she was to begin moaning or sob a bit. Should anyone try to remove the shawl from around her head, she was to shriek wildly, kick, do whatever she could to foil the attempted exposure.

As Octavia opened the door, the singing of hymns grew louder, and for a few moments, Tot and Selene plainly heard Mrs. Marryat's quaver meet Herapath's monotonous bass, and the other voices rising in a not unpleasant unison. Then the door closed and the sound again became faint.

Selene glanced at her confederate. The poor girl's face was flushed with dread. Selene jounced the wig on one finger, winking mischievously at her.

"How do you suppose my William would look in such a fixture?"

Tot giggled a little, then Selene let them into the "cabinet" through a small, low servant's door off the hall. Selene went first, then, in her identical dress, Tot slipped in close behind. Stealthily they assumed their rehearsed places, Tot concealed behind a three-panelled screen, and Selene at the curtain, ready to step out as herself, the schoolgirl medium, Selene Cook.

The curtain opened. Solemnly, Mr. Herapath extended his arm to Miss Cook, they bowed to the sitters and then, in full view of those assembled, he assisted her in lying down upon a set of cushions, her little boots sticking up from under her skirts, the shawl loosely turbaned about her face and head. Stepping back, he drew the curtains shut and began to speak in an overloud voice as Tot and Selene stealthily switched places. Selene went behind the screen, emerging a minute later in her white diaphanous robe. On this final evening, instead of the white headdress she was accustomed to wearing, she had on the wig. With her head prickling beneath the long, auburn tresses, Selene took her place behind the curtain, waiting for Tot, as rehearsed, to begin her groaning sounds, followed by a dramatic silence during which Florence King would waft gracefully out from the confines of her cabinet to the great and gasping pleasure of the audience.

EXCERPTS AND ACCOUNTS
OF THAT DEBATABLE FAREWELL

I.

"The farewell seance was held on Thursday last. Florence King had emphatically stated that she intended to give it only to the few tried friends now in London, who for a long time had been fighting her medium's battles with the public. She made but two exceptions, inviting Mrs. A. Marryat Ross-Church and Mr. Cox. The other spectators were Mr. William Herapath, Mrs. Amelia Corner, Mr. T. Boynton, Mr. G. R. Tapp, Mr. and Mrs. Cook and daughter Octavia Cook."

—from *The Spiritualist*
April, 1874

II.

"...on that occasion, we had the benefit of mutual sight also, as the whole company were invited to crowd round the door whilst the curtain was withdrawn and the gas turned up to the full in order that we might see the medium, in her blue dress and scarlet shawl, lying in a trance on the floor, whilst the white-robed spirit stood beside her. On this occasion of Florence's last appearance amongst us, she was good enough to give me what I consider a still more infallible proof (if one could be needed) of the distinction of her identity from that of her medium. When she summoned me in my turn to say a few words to her behind the curtain, I again saw and touched the warm breathing body of Selene Cook lying on the floor, and then stood upright by the side of Florence, who desired me to place my hands inside the loose single garment which she wore and feel her nude body. I did so thoroughly. I felt her heart beating rapidly beneath my hand; and passed my fingers through her long hair to satisfy myself that it grew from her head. I can testify that if she be of psychic force, psychic force is very like a woman.

"Florence was very busy that evening. To each of her friends, assembled to say good-bye, she gave a lock of her hair (long hair of a light auburn colour which hung in ringlets down her back, reaching nearly her waist) and a note which she wrote with her pencil. Mine was as follows: 'From Florence King to her friend

Augusta Marryat Ross-Church, with love. *Pensez à moi.*
April…1874.'"

—Augusta Marryat Ross-Church
April, 1874

III.

"Florence exacted no conditions from me, but gave me
permission to move about, look into the cabinet and touch her
as I liked, except when she especially asked me not. I occupied
my usual position standing close to the side of the curtain where
she appeared. The rest of the sitters were arranged round the
room, holding hands.

"For about an hour and a half Florence was coming out at
frequent intervals. Several times, she walked into the room
resting on my arm. Once, as she hesitated to come away from
the curtain, I put my arms round her and gently drew her some
paces forward. During this time I had many opportunities of
looking into the cabinet and I saw Selene lying on the floor each
time. Several times I opened the curtain sufficiently to let the
gas light shine full on Selene and Florence when they were both
in the cabinet together.

"I was very desirous that this should be seen by all the others,
and when Florence was standing at the side talking to me, I drew
the curtain away and called attention to the fact that Selene could
be seen lying down. Florence stood rather in the light so I asked
her to move a little to one side so as to let the others get a better
view. This she did, but soon asked me to close the curtain.

"Selene's head was tied up in a red shawl, so I asked Florence
to go and arrange her dress so that one foot and one hand should
be visible. Florence at once complied, and I looked in the whole
time she was doing this. When she had arranged Selene's dress
as I had requested, Florence came to the curtain. Asking me to
hold it to one side, she invited the sitters to look in, allowing
those at the side to move forward, so as to get a better view of
Selene and herself.

"Florence then walked up to Selene's side and leaned over her,
in full view of all present. She touched Selene on the head, and I
then heard Selene make one of her sobbing, moaning noises; at
the same time I saw her foot and hand move. I was leaning right

in the cabinet at this time, and, being within a few feet of Selene, could not have been mistaken."

—excerpted from William Herapath's letter to
The Spiritualist, April 1874,
one copy delivered to Charles Blackburn

IV.

"Last night the medium was in her bedroom, unbound, and entranced, lying on the floor. The leader, William Herapath, stood in front of the awning, and made himself very active each time 'Florence' appeared; stooping down with his face almost touching the face of 'Florence'; physically and unscientifically hampering all her movements, so as in several instances to compel the spirit with her hand to knock the face away from her, though done in a playful manner. He reminded me of a fussy mesmeriser, who desires to show himself off to the audience. The result of the mannerisms of the awning keeper, and the crowded state of the room, reduced the whole seance to principally that of 'Florence' showing herself at the awning, and busying herself with cutting off souvenirs of her hair and distributing them to each visitor. I trust that at future seances the leader, whoever he may be, may not be a familiar half-showman and half-playactor, on more than respectful terms with the ghost; but let the spirit have 'sea-room,' for her own advantage and that of the visitors.

"I was much struck with the strong resemblance the spirit had to the medium last night, even to the colour of the face; the mannerism of action also was the same, the voice was similar when joining with the sitters while singing in the bedroom behind the awning. To those who had not seen 'Florence' under other and test conditions the impression must have been that 'Florence' was Miss Cook, and Miss Cook 'Florence' in a state of undress."

—Mr. William B. Cox
The Medium and the Daybreak
April, 1874

V.

"...and I have a most absolute certainty that Miss Cook and Florence are two separate individuals so far as their bodies are concerned. Several little marks on Miss Cook's face are absent on Florence's. Miss Cook's hair is so dark a brown as to appear almost black; a lock of Florence's which is now before me and which she allowed me to cut from her luxuriant tresses, having first traced it up to the scalp and satisfied myself that it actually grew there, is a rich golden auburn.

"On this last evening, as on others, I timed Florence's pulse. It beat steadily at 75, whilst Miss Cook's pulse a little time after, was going at its usual rate of 90. On applying my ear to Florence's chest I could hear a heart beating rhythmically inside, pulsing even more steadily than Miss Cook's heart when she allowed me to try a similar experiment after the seance. Tested in the same way, Florence's lungs were found to be sounder than her medium's, for at the time of this farewell seance, Miss Cook was under medical treatment for a severe cough.

"When the time came for Florence to take her farewell, I asked that she would let me see the last of her. Accordingly when she had called each of the company up to her and had spoken to them a few words in private, she gave some general directions for the future guidance and protection of Miss Cook. From these, which were taken down in shorthand, I quote the following: 'Mr. Herapath has done very well throughout, and I leave Selene with the greatest confidence in his hands, feeling perfectly sure he will not abuse the trust I place in him. He can act in any emergency better than I can myself, for he has more strength.' Having concluded her directions, Florence invited me into the cabinet with her, and allowed me to remain there to the end.

"After closing the curtain she conversed with me for some time, and then walked across the room to where Miss Cook was lying senseless on the floor. Stooping over her, Florence touched her and said, 'Wake up, Selie, wake up! I must leave you now.' Miss Cook then woke and tearfully entreated Florence to stay a little longer. 'My dear, I can't. My work is done. God bless you,' Florence replied, and then continued speaking to Miss Cook. For several minutes the two were conversing with each other, till at last Miss Cook's tears prevented her speaking. Following Florence's instructions, I then came forward to support Miss Cook, who was falling onto the floor, sobbing hysterically. I looked round, but the white-robed Florence had vanished. As soon as Miss Cook was sufficiently calmed, a light was procured and I led her out of the cabinet."

—excerpt from a second letter of
William Herapath's, printed in
The Spiritualist
April, 1874

*

"Dearest, what has become of your hairpiece? You looked impossibly fetching."

They had ridden by hired coach out into the darkness. The flickerings of the gas-lamps looked like summer's fireflies evenly strung, he thought, kissing the top of her head, her hair still flattened by the weight of the now absent wig.

"I bequeathed it to Tot. Even with half its curls cut off for souvenirs, she seemed pleased."

"You think she will wear it?"

"Lord, she may. Octavia and I popped it on her head yesterday and prattled on about how elegant she appeared in red ringlets. What if she believes us?"

Laughing, Selene then began violently to cough. She must, he worried for the twentieth time, have picked up the same chest cold Gimingham had barely rid himself of.

"Do you feel well enough to travel, dearest? We can delay our trip."

"No." She coughed into the handkerchief he produced out of his top pocket. "I want only to be with you." She sat looking out the dirty little window. "Besides, I have a feeling."

"What do you mean?"

"Octavia knows far more than I would have wished her to."

"How? How do you mean?"

"The letter I left for her implied what I have always told her, that you and I are friends and no more. But tonight after everyone had left, when we embraced, I distinctly saw her, half-concealed in the hallway. She was watching us, William. I didn't tell you. I didn't wish to upset you."

"What might she do?"

"What she has always done. Sulk. Weep. Brood. Punish. You cannot know the long and tiresome history I have had with my sister. She lives entirely through me and yet resents me."

"Do you think this time she will be moved to more deeply harm you in some way?"

Selene turned to William. "Perhaps if we buy her a gift? That might soften her temper. She loves things that are French."

"Is she so easily bribed, your sister? Fine, then. I'll pay for whatever you choose." He sometimes wondered at Selene's naiveté. Or was it an over-confidence in her ability to charm people? She had certainly succeeded in bewitching him. But then he was a man. A sister might be different. Still, he thought, they had triumphed. Florence King's existence, while doubted by some, had not been disproved. The farewell seance had proved flawless in its execution. Selene's reputation as a spiritualist was restored to its former lustre, Charles Blackburn fed once more from the palm of her hand, and now they were off for a week's fugitive rest in Paris. Maude's complacent acceptance of his need to attend a conference in Paris made him feel indulgent toward her; he should buy her, too, a gift of some sort. Before him lay an illicit wealth of days and nights in which to do exactly as he pleased, and what pleased William Herapath was to be in Selene's presence every moment.

"But we must take care of your health. I see, my darling, how terribly depleted you are by the strain of these past weeks. I must make certain you recover your vitality while we are there."

"Oh, why am I always sick when I go to Paris?" she said, cheerfully enough, before she began once more to cough.

She rested, leaning against him, his arm tenderly encompassing her slight form. Herapath tried to reason away an anxiety, provoked by the wheezing he could hear in her chest as she breathed. The best cure, he persuaded himself, would be time away from London where he would be able to care for her, attend to her every need, breathe for her if need be. The jealous sister could be placated when they returned.

*

Octavia ripped up the pencilled scrawl addressed to her from Florence King, bits of which drifted indifferently to the carpet. Now she paced, waiting distraught for Tot whom she had just ordered down from the attic.

"You knew didn't you? You knew!" Octavia seized Tot by one ear and pulled fiercely.

"Deceitful, wretched girl! You knew didn't you? She yanked harder until Tot yelped and nodded, her promise to one sister breached by the other's cruelty.

"You've known since we went to Mornington Road. You went with her to her room. That's when she told you, wasn't it?"

In a last effort of loyalty, Tot kept silent. Octavia slapped her. "Wasn't it?"

"Yes, m'am."

"Do you know where they've gone—Paris! To Paris! Oh, they've fooled everyone haven't they, and now sneaking off to Paris! Well I saw them, do you know I saw them this evening, in the parlour. It was disgusting what I saw. I am still sick from it. I wanted to think it a kiss of friendship but any fool could see what disgusting sort of kiss it was. They are more than friends, and I have been deliberately kept from any knowledge of it. Look at you. The guilt of your face condemns you. *Why?* Why does she get all of it, success, admiration, gifts, trips to Paris, oh and not just one, but two in a single year! Because of her selfishness, I was forced to leave Miss Cliff's, to give up my preparations for teaching. I have been wandering about in her shadow ever since. Oh, the bell choir. I have that. And my French studies which dwindle from lack of practice. How I should have liked to have gone to Paris! I, at least, would know how to speak properly to people. I am trained to carry on intelligent foreign conversation with people, while she, she will merely simper and point. Oh, the outrage! And while she is in Paris, being indulged, being beautiful, being charming, being *stupid*, I am but one in a dismal row of spinsters, raising and lowering a line of bells. Oh."

Octavia turned cool, self-possessed, eerily subdued.

"That will do, Tot. Go to bed. I am sorry for hurting you. It was not you I wished to hurt. But you should have told me. I should have known. My sister has jeopardized not only her own life but destroyed my happiness as well. She connives to willfully ruin me, and I shall correct that. I shall decide what course of action to take."

Her ear reddened and throbbing, Tot left without curtseying. She felt wretched for having confessed. She could see, by Octavia Cook's vengeful expression, that some sort of calamity would surely befall Selene. Meanwhile, Octavia stood, bits of ripped paper around her feet, her face set in a cold, vengeful glare.

*

On the recommendation of a colleague recently returned from a tour of Paris, William Herapath had reserved a room in a small, second-class hotel on the Isle de la Cité, near the Cathedral of Notre Dame. Beyond securing a place for them, he had no other itinerary. He could not afford one. Instead, he envisioned them strolling the waterfront, browsing among bookstalls, the bird and animal markets, perhaps visiting the Louvre or any of the more economical tourist sights should she care to see them. What he had most clearly imagined was their hotel room—claret-coloured wallpaper, velvet upholstered furniture, damask drapes with gold tassels, an ornate bed similar to the one he and Maude had slept in on their honeymoon. And what he had most craved was unguarded sexual union with her.

But the hotel room, as he now stood in the center of it, was cramped and dull. The nearest claret colour could be found in the inferior quality Turkish carpet. A brass bed supported a small and lumpy mattress covered over by a slightly soiled white counterpane. The wallpaper consisted of a purple floral design upon a bilious yellow ground. The eight-foot windows were dirty and opened inward; beyond these was a small ornamental balcony of iron grillwork washed over with pigeon droppings. This overlooked not Notre Dame, but tenement housing, St. John des Pauves, with its broken mansarded roofs and sad bloom of greyish laundry. The depressing sight underscored his failure, his inability to provide Selene the elegance and luxury she deserved; jealously, he recalled her enthusiastic accounting of her trip to Paris with Charles Blackburn—the Hotel de Meurice, L'Opéra, the Comédie Française. He had hoped to replace such impossible demonstrations of wealth with a romantic, dare he admit it, a poetic setting. Perhaps his colleague had had a more appealing room. He should inquire as to moving, the possibility. He could not stay here a full week. This fell too hideously short of what he had wanted for her.

He turned from the squalid view and looked at Selene, still asleep at half past ten in the morning, the dark brown nest of her hair tumbling out from the top of the coverlet. He worried about her fever, had scarcely slept himself, feeling the unnatural heat of her all night. Asleep, she had breathed noisily due to congestion in her lungs. Even with the clear weather, he thought the temperature too brisk for her to go outside. He would have someone bring her a cup of chocolate and some bread. He could no longer sit here, trapped in this dour, hideously blossomed room.

Equipped and outfitted with a silver-headed cane, compass, telescope, map of the city, and engraved brandy flask (all, except for the map, gifts from his wife), William Herapath less than boldly set out, thinking first to tour Notre Dame, then cross the Pont Neuf, have a light meal before returning to see how she was. The whole prospect seemed pointless and depressing without her.

*

"Tot! Are you listening? Should you choose not to help me in this matter, I assure and promise you, I will march directly to that church of yours and inform whatever priest is currently on duty how you have abetted an immoral situation between a young girl and a married man three times her age. How in full knowledge of what was taking place over on Mornington Road, you said nothing and did nothing. Now. Take this downstairs and put it out for the postman. It's a most crucial letter."

21 April 1874

Mr. Blackburn—dire news! Your "little nightingale" as you sometimes call my sister, is compromised.

Two evenings ago, following Florence King's farewell seance in our home, which you will no doubt read various accountings of in "The Spiritualist," etc. I came, by sheerest accident, upon my sister and William Herapath, at a moment they believed themselves to be alone. I cannot be more specific, but what I saw shocked me in the extreme. My sister and Mr. Herapath were together in the parlour, to one side of the fire, oblivious to my presence in the hallway. I was able to observe them for certainty's sake, in hope, in what vain hope! I can put no better interpretation on what I saw.

This, Mr. Blackburn, was no demonstration of friendship or congratulation or esteem or anything other than what I plainly witnessed: the frankest display of bodily passion and emotional abandon by both parties. I thought better of letting my presence be known, and swiftly made my way upstairs to my room where, as you can imagine, I gave way to a very tumult of emotion. Scarcely had I recovered my wits from this first shock when a second was then delivered. In my room, on my desk, a most peculiar and ill-thought-out letter from Selene swearing me to secrecy. She and William Herapath were to be gone, it said, that very night, most likely to Paris. I was to tell our parents she had returned to Mornington Road with Mr. Herapath for a final week of conclusive tests. Incredibly, she asked me to deceive those (including myself) who have done nothing but support and defend her through all trials. I am in a rage, Mr. Blackburn, and in some part jealous as well, for I have long desired to visit Paris. (My grasp of the French *vocabulaire* is quite strong.) Recalling the strained look on our servant's face after accompanying me to the Herapath home while Selene resided there, I called her to me. Under most gentle prodding, the kind of smooth manner that works best with servants, she did confess knowledge of this secret *liaison de cœur* between William Herapath and my sister as long as one month ago!

As you see, those of us closest to Selene have been tricked and gulled and lied to. I admit to puzzling over William Herapath's lavish attentions to my sister. Particularly in seance, he would hover about her and fuss so, but he was <u>married</u>, I assured myself, bound by laws of man and God.

An obligation to the truth, combined with the highest regard for your intelligent and sensitive nature, barely overcomes my natural disinclination to tell you this unfortunate, this frankly scandalous news. As I write, I think how we might better have been served by Mr. Herapath and my sister had they maintained integrity and not succumbed to this immense deceit. Due to the length of time his experiments went on, a most troubling light is now thrown upon what was said to be an objective investigation by a reputable man of science.

I know well this news will tear down your faith in my sister and transform your opinion of her. It has deeply damaged mine. And I am shamed she would ask me to sanction her immorality, be accomplice to her illicit union.

Oh, Mr. Blackburn, I am broken down. My one consolation is the certainty you will, when you receive this letter, be as deeply stricken as I am. And were I a better instrument for her fine voice and not this current creature bowed down by shame and anguishment, L. Gordon would most surely send her spirit greetings to you.

> *Vôtre Petite Amie,*
> Octavia Elizabeth Cook

*

Selene lay gazing awhile at the watery green reflection of the Seine upon the ceiling, at its marble floating light. She looked toward the tall windows, the narrow catch of sky like a bright enamelled brooch. She looked at the room, its charming wallpaper, the one wooden chair, the plain wardrobe. She slid out of the deep warmth of the bed, set her bare feet down upon the rough carpet, crossed the room to look behind the purple Chinese screen. There was a porcelain bathtub and fastened to the wall beside it, a brass spigot shaped like a swan's head, its neck downturned as if searching wistfully for its reflection.

She was reaching to turn on the water, when a sharp rap at the door startled her. Slipping back into bed, Selene feigned sleep, as the chambermaid carried in a large pot of hot chocolate and fresh brioche, chatting gaily in a French which due to the poor quality of language classes at Miss Cliff's, Selene could make little sense of. After the woman left, she ate the soft center of the bread, greedily drank the chocolate, moved the tray off her lap, slid down and overcome with weariness, closed her eyes again.

When she awoke, the light in the hotel room was a honeyed amber which made her think it was late afternoon. Where was he? She saw no new note, only the old one, propped against the washstand. She considered how she felt. Better, she thought. She would go out for an hour or so, and when she returned, surely he would have returned too.

In her travel coat, forgetting her hat, Selene walked and walked, asking directions then not understanding them. She felt dizzy numerous times and had to sit down. Finally, at the hazy, green-violet hour when all the gas globes, the ornate lamps measured strictly along the waterfront and across the bridges, were lit one after another like flaring opalescent gems, Selene happened upon the street which contained their small hotel.

He was pacing, had been frantic for more than an hour, not knowing whether to go look for her or stay, as he was now, a caged fool. She was ill. She should not have ventured out alone. What was she thinking? She should have waited. He had worried himself to death, my god how he had worried. He embraced her, nearly hurting her in his angry relief. All of this tired Selene. She sank, a little woozily, onto the single chair. Beside the bed stood white carnations in a vase, beside the vase, three boxes of robin's-egg blue, each tied with white ribbon.

After a long and muddled debate over what they should now do, Herapath became frantic in his wish that everything retrievable of their time together should be perfect. Selene, wanting mainly to sleep, tried to decide if they should dine out, dine in, what should they do next, could decide nothing until he put his hand to her cheek and felt how feverish she was. Let me hear you cough, he demanded gently. She coughed, obedient, coughed again. To him, it sounded neither better nor worse than the day before.

"I think I would enjoy a bath," she said.

While the water spilled into the tub, Selene sat on the edge of their bed and untied the ribbons, lifted the lids off each of the three boxes. A green pear-shaped bottle of French perfume, a pair of tortoise-shell haircombs, a book of poems by Baudelaire. Out of worry for her, he had spent recklessly. He didn't care.

"This hotel room is so much shabbier than I had intended, Selene. I tried to procure us a better room. When you were with Mr. Blackburn..."

"Shh." Her hand floated down upon his. "Everything is as lovely as I could ever want."

He went to order a private dinner for them. Coming back upstairs, he opened the door with his ornately worked key. In the gold-shot aura of gaslight from the ceiling fixture, the room seemed improved over its earlier, unrelieved ugliness. The purple screen lay folded against the wall, and Selene, wearing only her camisole and drawers, lay in bathwater up to her shoulders. Her eyes were shut, her neck rested against the porcelain lip of the tub. Her dark hair was caught in a loose chignon, the tendrils wetted, dragging dark signatures in the water. One arm lay draped along the edge of the tub, in her hand was clasped loosely one of the carnations. The chair beside the tub held a robe on it. On top of the robe, the book he had just given her lay open as though she had been reading. Her body in the pale green water, the tub with its rolled edges glinting like gold. She turned her blue, feverish eyes upon him, smiled, picked up the book and began to read aloud in a charming schoolgirl French.

*

It was as they ate, sitting opposite one another on the bed, Selene wrapped in his patterned dressing gown, that she began to tremble, first lightly, then her teeth hitting together, then an uncontrolled shaking of all her limbs, along with paroxysms of coughing which ended in the spitting up of bloody phlegm, all of which caused her great shame and embarrassment. I'm sorry, she kept saying until he told her to stop, whereupon she began to say other things, words which made little sense, forged of delirium and fever. He put her to bed, covered her and went downstairs to have a doctor called.

Though he nearly shouted at the stony faced concierge, still, a doctor did not arrive until nearly midnight. After a cursory examination, he pronounced her gravely ill with pneumonia. There was nothing to do, the doctor said, but let her sleep and give her light broth. She will either die or take weeks, perhaps months, to recover. *Vôtre fille?* Your daughter? Mortified by the question, Herapath nodded yes, yes this was his daughter.

After two days and nights of sitting beside her, spooning into her mouth a host of elixirs and syrups and teas and small bits of toast (the chambermaid brought him a steady supply of home remedies, so kind, he could have wept for the goodness of human nature as evidenced in this woman). It was while Selene slept, her chest humming with water, that he decided to walk the short distance to Notre Dame.

He sat at the back of the great Cathedral, his head bowed, until he was roused by British voices near him. A tour was being led by an English-speaking Frenchman. About a dozen English tourists stood gazing rapturously up at one of the massive panels of stained glass. Gazing upward with them, he came to a decision. He would take her home now. She would recover more surely in the familiar surroundings of her family. The possibility of her dying here, in a second-rate Parisian hotel, terrified him. Not only the tragedy of it, but the unthinkable botch it would make of their lives. Well, his life. The only sensible course of action was to get her home.

That Selene would refuse to go, refuse to leave their hotel room, that he would be forced to dress her himself, that she would cry out, call him a coward, abandoning her to the wrath of her family, that she would cease either to speak to him or to look at him on their hastily arranged journey back to London—none of these things had occurred to him, nor did he anticipate them—so William Herapath had no reason to believe his plan anything other than expedient, sensible, and only coincidentally, protective of himself.

*

Octavia lay in bed, reviewing her French grammar book, bitterly aware that her sister was, at this very moment, on French soil. She repeated aloud the subjunctive imperfect tense... *je parlasse, tu parlasse, il parlât, nous parlassions, vous parlassiez, ils parlassent.* She had lately thought to teach the language, for after he read her letter, there would be no more money from Mr. Blackburn. It was past eleven o'clock when she heard the sound of a coach and horses pull up beneath her window. She got out of bed, her grammar book dropping to the floor and held her candle close to the window. A man stepped down from the coach, gave money up to the driver, then half climbing back, emerged from the coach with a small figure, only a little larger than a child, in his arms. Octavia wiped at the glass with the sleeve of her nightdress, until she gained full confirmation of what she thought she saw... William Herapath with Selene! Octavia thought he glanced directly up at her window, but she was not certain. She dashed about the room, locating both slippers and sticking them on her feet, grabbing up her heavy shawl, glancing in the looking glass, unreconciled, as usual, to her plain features. Taking up her candle, Octavia hastened downstairs and found her mother and father in the front hall, gathered around Selene, who, in Herapath's arms, seemed scarcely conscious. The truth was given out and unlike her youngest daughter, Mrs. Cook was not the least naive and Mr. Cook, though on his feet and still mainly asleep, understood enough. Harriet dismissed any abstract moral emergency in favour of the physical health of her eldest child, and within minutes, had Tot putting up a good fire in Selene's room, getting the bed ready with hot foot bricks, and securing Mr. Herapath's promise to fetch the family surgeon at the address Mr. Cook yawningly scratched down for him. She ordered Octavia back to bed, having no use, she said, for two corpses on her hands.

Upstairs, Octavia lay once more in bed, the fire in the grate lapsed to three or four dimly glowing coals. She could hear, down the hall, her sister's cough, a watery rumble, as ominous a sound as she had ever heard.

No doubt Charles Blackburn had received her letter or would receive it soon. And yesterday, she had made her way alone to the house on Mornington Road. What a tea and saucer drama that had been! Taking the omnibus back to Hackney afterward, Octavia realized that a letter to Mrs. Herapath might have done just as well. Instead, she had been shown into the parlour and after half an hour's wait, ushered downstairs to Mrs. Herapath's private laboratory beside the kitchen.

As Maude Herapath apologized (she simply could not, she said, interrupt the gutting process or it would ruin the outcome), Octavia's nerve came close to failing. If Miss Cook did not object, she would continue her work. Tea, if she wished any, could be brought directly to the laboratory.

Octavia's resolve wavered. She considered inventing some other, spurious reason for her visit. She could inquire as to the health of Selene's finch, but as if divining her thought, Mrs. Herapath turned toward her, "Oh, by the way, your sister's little bird is splendid, simply thriving. I have transported him upstairs to the morning room and am amused by how diligently he works at getting the other birds in the room to sing. He chirps night and day as if to break the glassed-in silence of the others. It is a tribute less to his intelligence than to his stubbornness."

"What is it you are doing?" Octavia asked thinly, though it was plain enough the woman was dissecting a large rook, its blue-black plumage pinned, the throat and belly slit open, its entrails deftly prised out and heaped like ugly, discarded ribbons into a wide-mouthed green glass jar. Mrs. Herapath answered in a straightforward, convivial manner, spoke of "recipes" for preserving the skins of birds in what she called a relaxing box, of her own intent to write a craft book on the subject—she had made several unique chemical discoveries, methods of hastening the drying process from the usual fortnight to under ten days. Then, without looking up from her work, which involved lifting the brain from its cranial cavity, followed by a delicate gouging out of each eye, asked sharply, "Where is she, your sister? I have not seen Selene since Mr. Herapath left for his conference in Paris. It seems she's evaporated like one of her notorious spirits. I really thought she would care better for her finch, she professed such devotion to it."

"Mrs. Herapath," Octavia smoothed out her brown leather gloves. She felt a strange triumph. "It is your husband she is devoted to. I believe by now the finch has been entirely forgotten." There. She had said it.

"Miss Cook, what do you imply?" Mrs. Herapath faced her, wielding a scalpel, scarlet limning its edge, her friendly manner replaced by an accusatory one that both intimidated and irked Octavia. After all, she was the one who had summoned courage enough to confront and disclose the truth.

"Mr. Herapath and my sister are lovers. They have been so since she moved into your home this last January. I anticipate your question—how do I know, what is my proof? I've seen them. Also my sister has confided in our house servant. I have full acknowledgement of this from Tot, though Selene swore her to silence. Worst of all, Mrs. Herapath, my sister is this very day and hour with your husband in Paris. There is no conference, unless it be a private one between the two of them. My sister left a letter foolishly asking that I conceal her trip abroad, let our parents believe she was here in your home for a week's concluding tests." Octavia drew forth the letter from her coat pocket. Mrs. Herapath made no move to accept it. "I cannot understand what led her to ask such a thing of me."

"Miss Cook. Tell me. Why did you come all this way? And it must be raining, I see your shoes are soaked through. Surely you must have considered the effect your news would have upon me. But what of your sister? Why would you wish to so thoroughly expose her in this way? I am merely curious."

Octavia had not anticipated this turning of the question upon herself. Truth, she thought to reply, but that was not it. Integrity then? Betrayal of loyalties, ideals? Octavia grasped for reasons to exonerate herself but could not. Perhaps because I hate her, she thought. This felt nearer the truth but was unspeakable, almost unthinkable. Octavia kept silent. She folded the letter, pushed it back into the hip pocket of her coat, drew on her gloves.

"I wished you to know. I thought you should know. My deeper motives, Mrs. Herapath, are obscure, even to myself."

"Oh well, child. I appreciate your concern. How kind a person you must be, to have come all this way for such a slender purpose." Mrs. Herapath smiled too vaguely, a smile which, Octavia would later decide upon reviewing it in her mind, was more a grimace related to the circumstance, to the shock.

Mrs. Herapath turned back to her laboratory table, wiping glossy bits of entrail off the scalpel and onto a linen towel. She began rubbing the raw, scraped skin with a whitish preservative of arsenic. For a moment, blood glistening on the discarded scalpel transfixed Octavia with its secretive properties.

"I assume, Miss Cook, you are capable of finding your own way out."

Octavia shifted irritably about in her bed, covering her ears with her pillow so as not to hear her sister's coughing. Mrs. Herapath had gone too still, too calm, and that had seemed to Octavia more satisfyingly ominous than any other sort of reaction.

June, 1874
Sydenham Park

He had waited nearly an hour. The small, rented skiff was moored under an enormous willow whose pliant branches hung in a cool, green-tasselled fountain over the lake's edge. He had brought cushions and a light blanket, a small hamper of fruits and cheeses, bread he hoped wasn't yet stale. These were now stowed in the boat.

William Herapath had kept himself from complete despair by maintaining the most tenuous of connections to her. Having told Maude he was taking up Sunday walks through Regent's Park, and instead, waiting for Tot on the church steps, in this circuitous way, he learned she had recovered. He also learned she rarely went out, that confined to her bed, she read a great many books, had gone through all of Octavia's, all her own from Miss Cliff's, and was now reading the books Mr. Boynton had delivered to her house (some of these coming not from Boynton but from himself, giving them through his friend, the same books he himself read). What he could not learn from Tot, but hopefully surmised, was that she was at least as miserable as himself. With Tot he was careful to reveal nothing of his own life, nothing of Mrs. Herapath's two recent attempts to take her own life in the very room Selene had stayed in, the same room in which their son had died. He disclosed nothing of his remaining children's grief and confusion, nothing of his own depression that blackly enveloped him no matter where he went.

His habit of meeting Tot outside St. Jerome's went on well into late May. On one particularly warm Sunday, the notion seized him that perhaps he and Selene could meet, if only once, for an afternoon. The following week he gave his letter to Tot, along with the promise of a bit of money if she managed to bring him a reply by the next Sunday.

Now he waited, nervousness making him one moment forget himself, the next feel a sickish knotting in his stomach. He was made anxious, remembering how wretchedly they had quarreled that last night. When she was so ill and he was panicking. She despised him. Of course she did. She had called him a coward, which he probably was. Still, he feebly assured himself, she had agreed to meet him. Yet she was late, by an hour or more. Perhaps she had agreed only to spite him by not showing up. He felt suddenly old and foolish, his romantic outing in a rented skiff a puerile, asinine plot. He was a dolt, an idiot. She was making a fool of him, and he, no doubt, deserved it.

"William?"

He rose up from the long grass and turned to face her.

"You look well," he said. But she didn't, didn't at all. He had said it only to conceal his shock. In her eyes, the youthful mischievous light he had so loved was gone. And how, he bitterly wondered, did she perceive him? Surely he looked as ill-used by fate as she. He felt ridiculous, far too tired and too old to play the part of tragic lover.

"Is this to be our yacht?" A trace of her former playfulness, for which he felt grateful. Perhaps she did not loathe him altogether.

"Yes. I've had it rented since early this morning." He helped her step into it, arranging cushions for her, climbing in himself, untying the boat and beginning, a bit clumsily, to row. He looked backward over his shoulder, deciding what path they would take across the small lake.

She lowered her white cutwork parasol as the boat glided out from under the long green-arrowing branches of willow, and passed into a sunlight that skimmed the water's surface.

"This is a lovely surprise, William."

"Yes, I hoped it might be."

"I've recovered, you know."

"I know." They both laughed. There had sprung up between them a constrained politeness, mainly hers, a sort of implacable courtesy which nettled him as he had no idea what coolness or warmth lay beneath it.

"Recovered, yes. But strangely, I have had no more of my visions, I hear no more voices. It is as if the fever burned all spiritual matter out of me. Isn't that peculiar? I read a bit now."

"What is it you read?"

"Everything. Shakespeare, Emerson, Swedenborg, Donne, Coleridge, Tennyson, oh and the Brownings of whom I find I am deeply fond, particularly her poetry. Mrs. Browning's. And Mr. Boynton has kindly lent me dozens of his own books."

"Selene? You are familiar with Byron's canto from *Don Juan...* *Round her she made an atmosphere of light/ The very air seemed lighter from her eyes,/ They were so soft and beautiful, and rife/ With all we can imagine of the skies."*

"Yes, of course." She looked down into the water, as if to avoid his worshipful gaze. "My mother and father and Octavia are all going to live with Mr. Blackburn."

"In London?"

"Yes. He's purchased a home in the new Ladbrooke Grove estates, and they have agreed to stay there with him. He's been gravely ill and has become entirely attached to Octavia's spirit guide, L. Gordon. From what I understand, he depends upon her daily for pencilled messages of false hope."

"And what of you?" The strained artifice of this conversation was nearly killing him. He wanted only to know if she still, in the least, loved him.

"I'm to be married this July, the twenty-fourth."

"Good god—to whom?" He could not comprehend what he had just heard her say. As if in a dream, he noticed the haircombs he had purchased for her in Paris. She was wearing them.

"I think you may have met him. Elgeron Corner."

"That great swell! Whatever for? Forgive me, I cannot tolerate him."

"Understandable and forgiveable, William. The reasons for my decision, and I assure you, it is *my* decision, are complex. Directly after the marriage, I shall be moving to Wales."

"This becomes unbearable. My own life, groaning in its same stale wheel, while you, you have sped from event to event. Why Wales? And why, may I ask, Elgeron Corner?" He tried to keep calm, to match her queer serenity. It seemed imperative she not guess the depth of his feeling for her. It was acutely clear how little she had ever cared for him. As he had always feared, she had mainly used him for his reputation.

"I did agree, under conditions set forth in Mr. Blackburn's most recent will, to care for his daughter, Eliza, at the home he has purchased for her in Usk Vale. Elgeron has just been made a sea captain and so will scarcely ever be there. I have come to care for him, William. In my illness, he has been a constant visitor."

And here he felt her reproach, felt her punishing him for his decision in Paris. "You exile yourself to care for a madwoman? Marry a man who will not be with you? No, Selene. This cannot be the path your life now takes."

"Actually, I rather anticipate the novelty and peace of it. I've heard she is docile. There, in desolate country, we shall live, a disgraced medium and a gentle lunatic. Look round that clump of trees along the bank, a pair of swans, black ones, can you row us over? What of yourself, William? I do not for a moment believe your claim of stale monotony or whatever it was you just said. No one with a mind as inquisitive as yours can leave it unoccupied or vacant of interest for long."

She was right, of course. He was deeply intrigued by a new series of experiments on electricity, also his development of the cathode ray tube was very nearly complete. The monotony he referred to was emotional, a vacuity of feeling, a painfully scraped out cavern where his heart used to beat. And now, with such bitter news, pain itself took the place of his heart.

"Well. Things go on. One doesn't fall down and die."

"That's wonderfully inspecific. How are your children?"

"Eager to go on any outing they can convince me to take them on. They all show keen minds."

"And what of Gimingham, your assistant?"

"He's gone off to Brazil to work."

"There's something I've never told you, William, and of late it bothers me you did not know. While at your house last winter, I shared my room with your son's spirit."

"You saw my son?"

"I felt his presence many times, and on three occasions saw him. On the last night he left us, his spirit at peace. I thought you should know."

"So you truly believe there are spirits? You believe this?"

"I have seen them and more than once. Often I will see a living person's future as well. Or I did. Without willing it, I could perceive the details of someone's destiny."

"Would you tell them?"

"Usually not."

"And mine. Have you ever glimpsed my destiny?"

"Strangely, never. Desire, any partiality of emotion, can block the reading of a fate."

"A kind of interference?"

"Precisely. My spirit abilities often frustrate me. They are so frequently unreliable."

"Unpredictable predictions?"

"Yes, something like that."

He rowed, and they were silent. The boat skimmed the surface of the black-green water. Behind Selene, who sat still in her white dress with her white parasol, the sun scarcely moved, endowing her motionless figure with a great, languid aura.

"You look ethereal."

"Do I?" She laughed. "I'm too thin. When I pass myself in the looking glass, what a frightful twig she has become, I always say."

"The weight will come back."

"Not if you neglect to feed me. What have you brought?" She began to tug the hamper out from under the seat.

"Careful, the boat!"

The afternoon passed into the lightest of spring evenings, a lilac-scented dusk with mild green skies. He rowed them back to their meeting place. The melancholy between them had an almost palpable weight, for their whole history, as he considered it, had been suppressed. Not allowed to live. First at his behest and now at hers.

As they stood beside the dusty road awaiting her carriage, Selene, again seeing the black swans, reached down and dug about in the hamper for a last bit of bread. At the lake's edge, she tossed pieces of torn bread onto the lapping surface. The female swan, either more industrious or simply hungrier, retrieved them all. William came up beside her.

"May I write you?"

"When I am in Wales? If you'd like."

"You will let me know your address?"

"Of course."

From her tone, he did not believe her and felt desperate. "Perhaps I will come out for a photography excursion. It's the fashion, in my Photographer's Club, to travel to Wales and attempt mystical photographs of Tintern Abbey, of haunted castles, waterfalls, cliffs being eaten by ivy..."

"I hope you will come visit ... my husband, Eliza and myself."

It was strange relief seeing the carriage approach. Selene extended her gloved hand which he kissed formally. She kissed him in return, upon the lips, before turning to step up into the coach.

He handed money up to the driver and came over to the open window. "I've paid your fare."

Her gloved hand lifted in a small, white flashing wave.

Standing in the road's center, watching her carriage disappear around the curve, thin dust veiling it, William Herapath looked to anyone who might have observed him, calmly resigned.

He managed to wait until he was well out upon the lake, rowing the skiff back to its docking place, made himself wait until the lake's surface and the darkening overhead sky corresponded to that place without light in himself. He wept then a long time, wept until whatever water traversed on his way to the opposite shore was made colder, less penetrable by the bitter chemicals of his grief.

As for Selene, she was past such display. She sat quietly enough on the ride back to Hackney, her hands clasped over their new-forming child. She had found the courage to tell him about the spectre of his son, but none to reveal this new in-coming soul as the single, joyless reason for her impending marriage to Elgeron Corner who had agreed, only grudgingly and for a price, to shield her with his name from further disgrace.

USK, WALES

Pwy wyt, Ddfodwr?
Os cyfaill, gresan calon i ti;
Os diether, lleteu garwch a'th erys;
Os gelyn, addfwyuder q'th garchara.

(Who art thou, comes?
If stranger, hospitality shall meet thee;
If enemy, courtesy shall imprison thee;
If friend, the welcome of the heart to thee.)

—from a stone tablet
Llanover, Gwent
South Wales

Oakdale House
Llanbadoch
near Usk, South Wales
July, 1874

Having unpacked her trunk of clothes, Selene moved between the tall cherrywood armoire and dresser, putting up her several dresses, folding linens, untangling her bits of jewelry in their several caskets, arranging them on the dresser's slightly warped surface. A second black trunk, unopened in the doorway, contained books, toilet articles, William Herapath's gifts as well as several elaborate dresses bought for her in Paris by Charles Blackburn, and three feathered, beribboned hats, not one, she realized, suitable for the place she now found herself exiled in.

Walking into each of the vacant second-floor bedrooms, she chose this room overlooking the gravelled, circular drive beyond which shone the river Usk, winking behind a green fretwork of trees. Oakdale House faced southeast, so here she would have benefit of both morning and afternoon sunlight. Later, Selene would realize her old room in Hackney had faced the same direction and more than any view of the river, this explained her choice; the flood of light was familiar to her senses.

Though the house itself was stately, a small-scale Georgian mansion built of pale gold terra cotta, most likely by some minor English industrialist made wealthy by his investment in the coal fields of Cardiff and Black Mountain, it was sparsely appointed with ill-used bits of furniture and frayed carpeting, as if the industrialist's dream had lacked power to go beyond its primary architecture to any detail more fully realized. Perhaps he had died, and Charles Blackburn had then picked up the property at auction. In any case, what was here could not be much improved upon as Selene had no money of her own. She was entirely dependent upon what little of his seaman's wage Elgeron chose to send her and whatever allowance Charles Blackburn thought sufficient for the care of his daughter. Accompanied by a nurse from Brooke Asylum, Eliza Blackburn was to arrive in four day's time, taking, as had Selene, the train from Paddington Station to Newport, then travelling the twenty or so remaining miles by hired coach.

Oakdale was lushly, verdantly situated, but the nearest town, that of Usk, lay more than two miles north. The unbroken solitude, the ringing core of silence, made Selene uneasy. She discovered a piano in the dining room, badly out of tune, which might offer the opportunity, she tried cheering herself, to improve upon whatever rudimentary skills she had learned at Miss Cliff's. Accustomed (at least before her recent illness) to lively activity and admiration in London's spirit circles, Selene now found herself so isolated she began anticipating, with a kind a pithy eagerness, the arrival of a lunatic for companionship.

Her own fault, too, she supposed. Had she been less arrogant about her powers, more cautious of her performance, had she somehow resisted William Herapath's advances, she might still be in London, accepting gifts, invitations, meeting titled personages, or travelling to Italy like Mrs. Guppy. She had not, she realized, been wise. She had overestimated her own cleverness and underestimated that of others. And in her rivalry with Octavia, in her attempt to outwit L. Gordon's influence over Charles Blackburn, she had been forced to retire the figure manifestations of Florence King, her most spectacular success; they had been made to recede, vanish in defeat. In forcing her powers, she had lost them. In her gamble with William Herapath, in loving him, she had come to this.

Her marriage to Elgeron Corner scarcely one week earlier had been a cool and unsentimental civil ceremony, left unconsummated before Elgeron received orders to set sail for the Orient. She could, he told her, expect to see him three to four times a year. Though there was really no need, he said, given the nature of their union.

Octavia, still vengefully jealous, had attended her sister's wedding ceremony. Not enough to have betrayed Selene, now she appeared even to covet this fraud of a wedding where Mrs. Cook had wept on cue, and Mr. Cook had stumbled in his boots, inebriated beyond the measure of his weak health. The whole occasion, from its miserable little inception to its mercifully short finish, seemed hardly a thing for Octavia to lavish envy on. What it had been was travesty, a cheap bit of barter—Selene's reputation in exchange for Elgeron's future monetary gain. Or, as she was soon to discover, her reputation for the safeguarding of his. In their hotel room, Elgeron had proved impotent, a bewilderment at first attributed to his impending voyage, then as Selene was to discover, because he could not suppress a lusty affection for persons of his own sex and an equally entrenched aversion for persons of hers. Truly, a hasty bargain had been struck between her desperate parents and Mrs. Corner (no matter her mother's dislike of Elgeron, Selene thought bitterly, for her, reputation overruled affection). Becoming Mrs. Elgeron Corner would throw a mantle of respectability, however thin and specious, over Selene, give legitimacy to her unborn child. So it was with a perfunctory kiss and no small relief that the nominal Mrs. Corner waved Elgeron off to his ship, while he mainly hoped for profit from his noble, if coerced, gesture. For when Selene resumed her seances, her income, he was assured by Mrs. Cook, would become his.

In the meantime, Octavia's ravenous envy had been temporarily checked by two triumphs. First, Mr. Blackburn had, through a scribbled message to L. Gordon, proposed. Second, her adjunct plan, to have Eliza removed from the expensive asylum and placed in the much cheaper care of her sister in Wales, had also succeeded. Octavia's invention of L. Gordon had secured her a wealthy husband who, it was clear, had not long to live. And thus Octavia decided her education at Miss Cliff's, though interrupted, had not gone to waste. Incredibly, Charles Blackburn had even granted her permission, as his fiancée, to purchase a home in the privileged district of Arundel Gardens, so they could all of them, her parents as well, dwell harmoniously together. I am a lonely man and tired of being so, he had written to L. Gordon in one of his many tedious, ridiculously ardent missives. He knew how gravely ill he was and had, he said, no wish to die alone.

*

That first afternoon at Oakdale House, compelled by the anxiety of isolation as well as by a desire to explore her new surroundings, Selene walked north toward the market town of Usk, thinking to purchase food, some sundry supplies, and a quantity of candles. There were too few lamps in the house, she thought, scarcely one to a room.

She walked along the straightaway road, engineered centuries ago, the coachman had told her in his thick Welsh accent, by Roman soldiers who had first conquered Britain and then kept coming until they reached Wales, establishing it as a frontier outpost. They had left behind well-built roads and stone fortresses. Small villages had been built upon the remains of such forts. Burrium, the Romans had called the fortress now known as Usk. "You'll find us courteous enough to visitors," he had said. "It is our duty to be hospitable. Still, we're suspicious of new neighbors, slow to warm to the English and it's said we're secretive in our ways."

"Then I shall keep myself a constant visitor so you will be forced to remain courteous," Selene had laughed and caused her driver to laugh as well. "When I am a hundred years old, I shall still insist I am just passing through."

When she finally reached Usk, the town square, except for a yellow hen pecking about in the dirt outside the one hotel, appeared deserted. But stepping inside the dark, close shops, she found people willing enough to wait upon her so they could more easily gape. She grew quickly conscious of how English she appeared. Her dress, light blue with magenta stripes, ordinary in London, seemed extravagant. And her accent, she realized, represented all the industrial and political superiority inflicted upon these people by England. Though being perceived as superior, she decided on her solitary walk back to Oakdale, was not an entirely unwelcome sensation. She had answered polite inquiries as to which house she had moved into. Ah, the Oakdale place, and with that, the impression of her privilege increased. She told no one that first day, and no one thereafter, of her marriage. That she was expecting a child (and Selene estimated that it would be born in approximately five months time) they would see very well for themselves, as time passed.

As she waited over the next several days for Eliza Blackburn to arrive, Selene found herself, for someone living in a remote area, besieged by local people coming to her door, mostly on foot, offering to cook, to chop wood, to bring peat for burning, to clean up the property, to polish the inside of the house, to paint the outside, to start a vegetable garden for her, to bring in a flock of sheep and tend them, to fish—it seemed all of Usk had turned out, one by one, to offer help for a small fee. Selene rather suddenly understood the vast power of English credit. She hired nearly everyone who came to her, for was it not necessary to secure Eliza Blackburn's comfort? She would forward the receipts to her sister, turn her own exile into a welcome source of income for a great many people around Llanbadoch, and transform Octavia's meanness into charity. For it was clear that even if Selene Cook, a young Englishwoman, was to be awarded only the coolest of receptions, her sister's money would be taken in warmly enough.

By the Saturday Eliza Blackburn was to arrive, Selene had bread and meat in the kitchen, heat for cooking, and an old man named Gwyn Jones out behind the house in a scarlet cap, digging up a large vegetable garden for her. Perhaps, if her patient, the *aliéné*, proved tolerable, then her new existence as an exile and a recluse might prove the same.

When at last I hear it, the carriage from Newport, it is late afternoon and I am walking beside the riverbank, my only company an unexpected and sudden wish to remain concealed, to stay hidden until the occupants of that coach grow discouraged and leave, return to London. I had thought I desired company but when I heard the wheels turning fast, then slowed by the drag of gravel, heard the whinny of exhausted horses, I became jealous of my peace. I waited beside the river as the driver, the same who had delivered me here, called out, called louder, nearly shouting. Curiosity finally brought me forward into the open. His expression of relief changed to one of dismay, and following his gaze, I was made conscious of the soiled and now muddied condition of my pale blue dress, the same one I had arrived in, worn each of the days I had been here. Who will see me, who is there to care, I think, but quickly invent for him a story of tripping clumsily over a tree root beside the river while walking. That bit of lie appeased him so I then went up to the coach, stepped upon the runner and looked within. A dour face clamped inside a flat, grey bonnet loomed so close I could smell its mean breath. Beyond that, I saw a pale, shimmering face, large eyes turned beseeching toward mine and a great, dark bramble of hair. I say what I have rehearsed, welcome to Wales, but she is, this nurse, a horrid character full of complaint and opinion, and I want her gone. And when she demands to take her patient immediately to the third floor of what has become my home and lock her into a room before anything else, I feel sick with dislike for her. I want her gone and say so. During all this, the aliéné sits quietly enough on a red-painted bench beside the front door. Her wrists are manacled.

"Why is she forced to wear such restraint? She appears gentle enough."

"So she could not attack me on the journey here. One never knows the effect of an unfamiliar surrounding upon the insane."

"Did she attack you?"

"No. I am not well-acquainted with this particular patient at the Asylum and would not give her liberty to do so."

"Well, you may give me the key then and be relieved of your responsibility. Miss Blackburn is my patient now. The driver will return you directly to Newport where you may stay overnight before taking the train back to Paddington. Have you enough money for such a trip? Good. Be assured my sister will reimburse you for your expense."

*Within the hour, she, the coach and its driver were gone. Miss
Blackburn and I were enclosed in our new solitude formed all of
breath and curiosity and some thin, picture-border of fear. She is
sitting where I left her last, still on the red bench, her face clean of
all expression, her eyes unfocused. Her face looks like a sterile white
orb and her hair a greatly overgrown auburn thicket or hedgerow.
Since I have no training like that horrid Pindy or whatever she was
called, I determine to act according to instinct. Manners, protocol,
the social order of things mean nothing to this creature before me.
The last manacle of social expectation, the last link of propriety is
useless, foolish in the face of this. All on instinct, I leave her wrists
locked together a little while longer, until she might get more used to
me and her new surroundings.*

*I lead her down to the river, holding her by one arm, which is
thin and pliant as grass. It is dusk, all violet and gold, a twilight
bordered by green, charged with black. A delicate linen softness is in
the cooling air. We move past the brassbound trunk and the one
wooden crate taken down off the coach and left hastily in the
driveway. Our feet make soft sounds crossing the gravel. She wears
a plain lavender muslin dress, with neither stays nor corsets nor
petticoats nor any sort of adornment at all. Her dress smells bitter,
and I consider what a picture we must create together, drifting in
our dirty clothing toward the river. When she sees the flowing line
of river, she startles me with her response, a low-pitched torrent of
sound, half singing, half chanting, a babble in which I hear an
occasional word of French or is it Latin or even perhaps English,
then it is all washed over with sounds I cannot identify as anything
but gibberish. Her face is struck open with pleasure in the failing
light. We gaze together at the river's swift running current, the
richly blackened trees on the opposite bank, and I sense a kind of
accord or agreement between us.*

*That first evening she would not look at me directly. In the days
following, I sometimes felt her stare, when my back was turned or
my attention deflected. She acted curious about the objects around
her. But that first evening, we sat a long while upon the soft river-
earth until the air surrounding us had grown impenetrably dark. She
stood up, her fearsome thicket of hair sticking out from her great,
round planet-face, and in the moist humid darkness, stumbled back
toward the house. I followed. That was how we began, the pattern
we set together. I followed her. I spoke normally, always explaining*

what I was about to do, having no idea what she heard or understood. And when she spoke her peculiar tongue, I listened, acting as if I understood, and sometimes I believe I did.

Strangely true, my spiritual powers have narrowed since my illness, but I saw plainly enough how this woman though living to an advanced age, would never recover her sanity. And I saw, most curiously of all, that she preferred and chose it so, that her madness purchased some freedom for herself, some release from the burdensome yoke of propriety that befitted the handsome daughter of a wealthy English industrialist. In some manner she had sought out madness, and now madness was habit to her, unexpungeable because it so deeply pleased and satisfied her. It seemed perverse to me and I mistrusted it. I still do, but yet, it was clear, with the return of my old vision, what I saw.

That first night at Oakdale House, Miss Blackburn wandered freely about—though still manacled, for I retained some fear based on my lack of knowledge. We were so entirely isolated, if she chose to murder me, she could do so. I set about carrying in the trunk, so lightweight I almost thought it empty. Remembering the crate, I went out to retrieve it as well. As I picked it up, I realized, by the rustling and movement within, something living was inside. I carried it, nearly tripping with eager curiosity, into the candlelit parlour. Cautiously I peered between the wooden slats. Bedded down in straw was a pair of young white peacocks, eyes glittering, shards of gold candleflame wavering in their blackness. Only once before had I seen white peacocks—at the zoo in Regent's Park, and I had thought them magnificent, otherworldly creatures. I prised open the crate and let these two step out onto the dark blue carpeting. They ruffled themselves, then began to step boldly about the parlour, keeping close together, talking softly to one another. I sat beside the crate, sucking out a splinter I had got in my clumsy haste to release them, enchanted by the sight of their long feathers, like bridal veils, washing lacily over the carpet. I was afraid to let them outside for fear of predators or of losing them, so from that night I kept them inside the house where they soon grew tame and would feed from my hand and stand still to be petted.

Another decision was quickly come to that first night. I carried Miss Blackburn's trunk up the narrow stairs to the third floor and stood in the doorway of the cold and ugly attic room, the room I had been instructed by Octavia to keep my patient locked up in "for my own peace of mind." As easily as I had dismissed the nurse, I rejected any notion of Charles Blackburn's daughter living imprisoned in an attic. I carried the trunk back down to the second floor and chose for her the bedroom which overlooked a peaceable field, a meadowy expanse bordered by low stone walls. Finding me there, Miss Blackburn slumped like a tired-out child on the bed while I undid the clasps of her trunk. Inside were more lavender dresses exactly like the one she now wore, two heavy black shawls, an old-fashioned black silk bonnet, a packet of letters bound up with scarlet cord (from her father, I recognized his handwriting), other necessary items of clothing, and a faded length of blue ribbon wound tightly up. At the bottom of the trunk was an envelope addressed to me, from Dr. Munro at Brooke Asylum. I would read it later that night in my room, read directives as to how to care for her, what she liked and didn't like, a formidable list which I chose to ignore, for I believed it based upon prejudice and false understanding. That first night, I had all the courage of the ignorant, all the faith of the untried and gladly, with a sort of sly exhiliration, I watched the doctor's letter burn to nothing in my fireplace. I would let Miss Blackburn roam as freely as she liked, and the manacles which I had already unlocked from her chafed and reddened wrists, I placed high, out of sight, along with their key, on top of the armoire in my bedroom. In the time Eliza Blackburn and I lived together, I would never need or use them, proof to me of how foolish the world often is in its perception of danger.

5 August 1874

Octavia,

As of yesterday evening, Miss Blackburn is safely arrived here at Oakdale. As you know, I have no experience with persons considered "mad," but thus far, and it has been less than two days, I find the *aliéné* to be sweet-natured if mute. She is very pleasant to look upon, a thing I did not anticipate. It seems unjust of nature to bestow uncommon beauty on someone so utterly indifferent. I say mute though she does utter infrequent sounds which I can neither translate nor interpret. In time, I persuade myself, in time.

This is to assure you and Mr. Blackburn that life for Eliza (and myself) unfolds thus far to your design. My love to Mother and to Father. I trust I have got your newest address, in Arundel Gardens, right.

Your sister,
Selene

postscript:

Please ask Mr. Blackburn to send a cheque to cover cost of the enclosed receipts. There was much to be done before she arrived. Also, I have sent to Newport for two sturdier pairs of boots. I expect both Eliza and myself will be taking long daily walks. There is little to do here but walk. I feel rather like Napoleon tethered to his little isle of Elba. Or is this a prolonged honeymoon, minus the husband and the concealed horrors of husbands? It is very desolate here and the local Welsh so guarded, I sometimes fear I shall join ranks with Miss Blackburn, take refuge in some sort of lunatic behaviour.

I dismissed the nurse sent from Brooke Asylum. She was a detriment, a cold and crabbed thing, worse than any gaoler. I sent her back straightaway, receipt enclosed for that expense as well. Pindy, or whatever she was called, seemed not unpleased by my decision. I deduced this by the swift manner with which she drank off her tea and then nearly raced back to the coach which had not yet put down any of her luggage.

Wish your nurse well then, poor *moi*. Wish her well indeed.

S.

She gave this letter to Gwyn to post in Usk. He returned the following day with a letter for her, the first she had received since her arrival at Oakdale House. Selene recognized the handwriting at once, and while Eliza sat on the floor of the kitchen, twisting and untwining her piece of ribbon about her bare arm, Selene sat down at the table nearby and opened the envelope.

Dear Mrs. Corner,

May I offer my congratulations on the occasion of your marriage. I apologize for my initial graceless reaction. I extend both you and your fortunate husband my wishes for a long and prosperous union.

William Herapath

—Please let me know if you receive this as I am doubtful as to the address.

Selene read his words silently, then aloud, trying to ascertain the emotion behind them. Was he relieved to be rid of her, was he truly congratulating her, did he feel no love for her whatsoever? The letter was so brief as to be nonexistent, yet she struggled for optimism—if he cared nothing for her, he need not have bothered writing. Still, he could have said anything he wanted, could have spoken his heart. Or was he being cautious? Careful not to offend her husband if he were here? What did it mean that he had somehow sought out her address? Should she reply? What should she say? In an almost pleasant agony, Selene carried this enigmatic note with her for days, slipping it out from the pocket of her dress to read and re-read, as if to uncover its true meaning. She was determined to write him, but what to reveal, how truthful to be, perplexed her. Their afternoon at Sydenham Pond had been disastrous. She had planned to tell him about her pregnancy. As soon as he openly expressed his love for her, she would have found the strength to tell him. Instead, he had acted nervous, evasive, even coldly distant. He had expressed nothing. At some point, a shadowy thought had seemed to pass over his face, and this convinced her to stay silent, convinced her he did not love her. This was precisely what she felt the night he made her return sick to her family. Oh, he had claimed concern, had asked her for patience, had promised he would bring her to Paris another time, but she saw the anxiety in his face, the dismay, and did not believe him. So that afternoon on the lake, she told him instead about Elgeron Corner, lied about the nature of her impending marriage. She erected that barrier and it loomed, implacably, between them. And now, in her hands, this dry piece of courtesy. Still, it occurred to her to reply, yes, and in her reply, to test him. Try for a clever, arch, independent tone. Deliberately not mention Elgeron, achieve as charming an overall effect as possible. Then, when he wrote back, she should, she reasoned, be able to tell from the tone of his letter (as she could not from this formal note), if he still cared. Once certain of that, she would boldly confess the whole counterfeit nature of her marriage. She would invite, no, implore him, to come to her. He would see her as she was. And then her life might not be, as she now feared it was, entirely over.

As Selene composed her letter, labored over it, rewriting it until she was satisfied it had the proper tone, she next agonized over how to deliver it safely to him. How to circumvent Maude Herapath. Finally, she wrote a note to Thomas Boynton, enclosing the sealed letter, asking her friend to please make sure Mr. Herapath received it into his own hands. She said nothing about Mrs. Herapath and hoped that such a specific request would be enough to keep this letter out of harm's way. She loved him, had always loved him. This letter was all that remained to her by way of hope.

August, 1874

My Dearest William,

Yes, I have received your note of congratulation. How clever, to have in some secret way, divined my new address! I would accuse Tot of being your informant but she has, I learn from Octavia, been dismissed. My sister never could abide in her presence anything she adjudged ugly. Poor, gentle Tot was always to her an unsightly rebuke. Oh, how I would like her here with me! Or should I wish that she and your chemist, Gimingham, had fallen violently in love and run off to India? What I fear is that she is still drudging away, the only servant in some other middle-class home, sending sparse packets of money to an elderly parent somewhere in Kent.

(Perhaps in your next letter you will confess how you obtained my address?)

You ask how I fare but say little of yourself, an old and may I say irritating habit of yours. Very well then. I will reveal only the stingiest bits about myself until you agree to disclose more, in your next letter, about your feelings, your thoughts, your work. Perhaps you think me too stupid or too shallow or too little trained in the sciences to comprehend what it is you study, how you pursue your "truth" through the accumulation of empirical fact. In my own defense, William, I urge you not to underestimate me. Before those early fits and trances and visions came upon me, before my training in the art of seance, <u>before you ever knew me</u>, I was considered of a lively enough intelligence to be one of Miss Cliff's better teachers.

You have asked how I am. Picture a bit of quartz compressed beneath tons of coal and slate and peat, then dug up, washed off and held up to the sun, looking deceptively the same as before its dark, weighted interment. That is how I am. Should you unearth and clean me off I would be much the same as you saw me that last afternoon in Sydenham. (Though I have gained weight, I am happy to tell you, and have acquired a kind of country colouration from being so much outdoors. My cough seems entirely cured.) In other words, I survive.

What I have stumbled across in this region of south Wales, is <u>Nature</u>. That is all that exists here, <u>Nature</u>. Two days straight I sat at the piano, practising, stubbornly imagining myself still in London, before I gave up and stepped outdoors. I mean I went walking. Walked miles, came home spent, muddied, bristling like a hedgehog with twigs and thorns and yet thoroughly happy, as though I had striven for and accomplished some significant thing. My whole life in London, I had no idea nature so potently reigned elsewhere. Even the Isle of Wight is a spot tamed down for people. I have thought to send away for a number of books on botany and nature identification, wildflowers, birds, small animals, but it is really quite lovely to have no scientific name at all for what I see, no history or other authority to cloud my discoveries. It is all fresh, unnamed and I am free (or constrained it could be argued) to interpret as I please. Wales seems to possess a mystical landscape. Already, on my solitary walks, I have had several remarkable experiences, that of having glimpsed shadowy other-worlds, older histories still ongoing or perhaps

repeating, dimly heard, not as wind but beneath wind, the clear
rising and falling of ghostly noises. Do I test your patience, never
strong, with my claims?

Octavia tells me (and how proudly!) that you are thinking of
testing her spirit-authenticity much as you did mine. For heaven's
sakes, William, she is a fraud. Whatever she does she copied from
me. She has no powers of perception beyond the taught "game"
of the spirit circle. She is all cold parlour knowledge. She tells me,
too, how Charles Blackburn, weakened by cancer, is entirely under
the influence of L. Gordon, who, no doubt, advises him daily as
to how to amend his will in her favour. Forgive me. I know my
sister and am too often sorry for what I know.

As for Miss Blackburn's presence here at Oakdale, she is less
trouble to me than a housecat. In the beginning, I naively hoped
for a sort of companionship, however crippled, thinking it might
alleviate the loneliness so prevalent here, but after several weeks,
I can no longer deny her complete withdrawal from life. It is as
if she moves always under an enormous bell jar, in some glass
confinement of her own architecture and emotion. Though
harmless, she is inaccessible. I do not intend this cruelly but I
care for Miss Blackburn in the same way one might care,
indifferently, for a valuable but passive piece of art. She is
beautiful, though, which continues to fascinate me.

The weather is unceasingly hot, the day's light lasts long.
Violets bloom everywhere and in profusion, and I never tire of
gathering them into small jars of water and putting them
throughout the house. Chopin's favourite flower! Swarms of
gnats have recently come out, encircling my head in a kind of
gauzy orb. I grow used to it, used to everything.

Selene

—Though if you should choose to reply, I would be less lonely
and most pleased.

Maude Herapath paced back and forth in her basement laboratory, reading and re-reading the letter from Wales. A Mr. Boynton had come to the house earlier that morning, and finding Mr. Herapath out, had introduced himself and asked that Maude deliver the letter directly to her husband when he returned.

There was, and it puzzled her, no passion: the letter was cheerful, brimming with charm, it could have been a letter from a friend and nothing more. Still, William must never see it, must never be reminded of her, must not know where the girl was. Maude peered inside the envelope, shook out the few dried violets that had been enclosed. A message of love after all, in those faded violets.

She sat down at her bench. Choosing one of her scalpels, Maude sliced the letter, both its pages, into small, insignificant pieces. Next, as she went about the art of preserving yet another rook—frankly she was growing quite sick of them, this would be the last—she thoroughly wet bits of the letter in a prepared bath of formaldehyde, and along with the dead violets, deftly scooped the whole mess in, tamping it down in the glistening cavity of the darkly plumaged bird. Here was pain buried, transformed, made useful. In several days' time, Maude would show off this newest specimen to her husband, who would scarcely notice or comment, so lifeless had he become, so preserved in a dark mixture of his own gloom. Ignoring him and declaring it one of her best works, she would set the rook in the morning room among her favourites. A queer source of joy, knowing Selene's message was forever buried inside the stiff, black shape. Such covert revenge was all she had and, because it made her glad, she embraced it.

Untrue, false and again false! I no longer feel buried alive in the open, green sarcophagus of Wales. Gladly now, I leave my books undisturbed, unread, and ramble freely about the countryside, convinced that though there are seasons and rhythms to nature, there is no thing such as time. Space is a liquid wherein objects float transparent, all-endowed with a kind of ethereal light. The history of Wales is not first this event happened, then that, followed by this war and because of that treaty, no. As I climb the craggy hills, cross boglands crisscrossed with wide and shallow running streams, I deepen old paths, invent new ones, sit on the same rock for hours (and what are hours), feel myself travelling swiftly and everywhere at once. I see them, the Celtic peoples, Roman soldiers, Norman invaders, wandering pagans and saints of the church—even those of us who, like particles blown in by industry, by the English—who have built their coal labyrinths and the mining towns which rise up from those underground veins crawled through by naked men and women, by naked children, pale grubs choking on black dust, made to crawl on rough hands and torn knees, then blown to bits by explosions, turned into blackened bits indistinguishable from the very substance they are paid so little to bring to the surface of the earth by the pull of their rotting teeth. I heard last week of yet another explosion over in Black Mountain. Sixty miners, half of them women and children, all dead. The vision of it passed as a horrible waking dream before my eyes a full day before I heard news of it in Usk. Histories, the lives which make up those histories, occur all at once, all at one time. I have walked to abandoned cloisters and the ruins of castles, stood before the priory gatehouse outside Usk, an arrow's flight from the ruined castle where, local legend says, Norman ladies came to heal their hearts from broken romance. The prioress, in love with the local swancel of the castle Usk, often I hear their lovemaking cry out from the very stones that compose and fortify the walls.

Some evenings, I attempt telling her what I know, but Eliza is removed from thought, from idea, her security exists in repetition. Madness has its eloquent discourse, yet even eloquence, unvaried, proved monotonous. Her malady did fascinate me, but now I pity Eliza her endless retracing of what looks to be an invented order, but is more truly, a malady of dullest poetry. The peacocks trail her like white aspects of herself. They remain, as she does, within the house or within a strictly defined boundary outside the house. Though I am fond of Eliza and often filled with sweet melancholy at the sight of her, I am freshly eager, each day, to strike out alone on foot.

The first time I climbed the Usk castle steps which are thickly overgrown with wild ivy and moss, I grew dizzy, not from the height of it, but from realms too easily pierced. Too quickly I heard the Celt's death-agony, the cries of wounded and condemned soldiers, the hundreds put brutally to death, massacred. Just as I had in the green copse of larch near the old priory, I distinctly heard Norman ladies laughing among themselves as they played at some game. Here in Wales, time is permeable. I float through centuries and generations, events, loves and deaths, fevers, plagues and miracles. I travel where I am taken, see what I see, free of all linear constraint. What I cannot do is alter anyone's fate past or present, not even my own. What wisdom is it that sees the destinies of others, yet is helpless to amend or to save? Strange to say, I am most blind to my own fate. And what of the creature forming within me? What of its fate? I fear I am blinder still.

We are odd relations, Miss Blackburn and myself, strange-formed creatures soaring at different levels of the sky, each unable to speak of what she sees. I understand better that profound isolation animals must sometimes feel and thus their touching ways. It is how I exist here, in Llanbadoch, without language. For what breathes all around me are ghosts by the thousands, lives finished yet condemned or is it attached, as Miss Blackburn is to her madness, forced to repeat and repeat violent, brief lives, undeviating, yet ever the same.

History a fabrication.
Time as we know it, falser still.

The French portrait painter, Jules Bois, ripped off a hunk of oatbread and slathered it with butter, a fleck of which glistened near his mouth. Selene watched the yellow gem of butter melt into his lustrous, reddish-brown beard. By candlelight, the young Frenchman's beard reminded her of William's, how it had gently traversed her face, moved over her breasts like a softly scented, persistent animal... Weeks had passed, and she'd heard no reply. Nothing. Clearly he no longer cared for her.

"...and here I have stumbled upon the greatest of fortunes...two magnificent women. I have found Wales a unique water country, river goddesses forever rising up from its landscape. The ancient Celts, it is said, adored their women, along with everything else in nature. You are both immensely beautiful. When may I begin to paint you?"

While he chewed and spoke, Selene dipped the edge of her napkin into the water pitcher and blotted the front of her dress where a freckling of gravy had stained its white fabric. As her belly increased, so, it seemed, did her clumsiness. She shrugged. She had already learned a good deal about Jules Bois. Of his nature, which was just like Elgeron's. Of his quarrel with his lover, who had stayed on in Cardiff. "Whenever you like. Tomorrow? I cannot say about her." With a wave of her damp napkin, she indicated Eliza, seated at the foot of the stairs, a blue bowl in her lap. In front of her, the peacocks strutted, white necks straining, eyes tracking, waiting for bits of food to drop to the floor. "She does what she likes. There. They are out. The stains."

"*Tant pis.* Too bad. I would paint that one with her white, moon face and that coppery blaze of hair, and you, I would paint against the river's skin, a moth's wing dissolving in the cold, green water. Can you not persuade her?"

Another bit of butter clung stubbornly near his red, full lips.

"I cannot persuade Eliza of anything. And I do not swim, you know. You would end up putting a drowned woman on your canvas."

"Then I shall teach you. A woman like you, *enceinte*, must enter the water. Must be baptized."

*

Seated on the grassy river bank, Selene watched Jules Bois plunge into the deepest section of the river, then in a rushing of water, stand. His broad, white thighs and womanish hips were concealed by the water, his long hair tangled, gleaming darkly about his shoulders. She was astonished by his lack of bodily inhibitions, his boundless enjoyment of himself, of her, of anything that came his way. He was like some giant's child, in possession of all the unfettered eagerness and impetuous curiosity of a child. As he splashed noisily downstream toward the arched, stonework bridge, Selene began impulsively to unlace and tug off her shoes, roll down her stockings. She stood to remove her dress, sat down again, wearing only her chemise and camisole. "*Fantastique!*" he bellowed, striding out of the shining, bark-coloured water, his arms outstretched, his whole body glazed, his face alight, his eyes admiring her broad, rounded belly. At his coaxing, she grasped his hand and, after some protest, lay on her back in the mild current. His hands cupped her shoulders, then he moved to her side, supporting her lightly under the waist. Let go, he said, let go. Life comes from water. And you are now the source of life. I baptize you *la mer. Notre mère.*"

He then taught her to put her face under the water, to not be afraid. To swim, he told her, was to surrender. Like any great artist, like any wise lover, he said, one must sense when to surrender, when to control. These lessons came after Jules had worked hours at painting her. He would first set a fishing pole in the river near his easel, then move easily from one to the other. Sometimes he caught a trout, often nothing at all, once a salmon. Whatever he caught, they ate that same day, all three of them, the fish still nearly alive in their mouths.

*

In a sunlit clearing, Selene stood where he had persuaded her to pose for him, unclothed. Jules had never touched her, had no wish to, desired nothing of her. She had begun giving up her walks in order to pose for him, to drift in the mild currents of river limning her skin like air. Like him, she began swimming naked. She could unfold in his presence with no hindrance or shame, could contemplate the mystery of her changing body in the late summer light, listen to him describe its shifting beauties and creations. She stared at her stomach a great deal, for William's child had begun to turn, as if restless, and the thinning skin across her stomach rippled in response. Jules laughed often and in great splendid bursts, or he would sing, while she floated content in his massive currents of energy. She studied her breasts, touched the darkening nipples, their slightly raised, starry flecks. Goddess of life, he called her, and she began to feel, yes, and with some new pride, looking at herself, perhaps this could be so.

*

Because of Jules, Selene had nearly stopped counting how many days had passed since she had mailed her letter to London. In the calm, rosy dusk, she would walk with him back up to the house. Selene would play the piano or lie down to rest while he prepared dinner for the three of them, using what he could from Gywn Jones's half-wild garden behind the kitchen. Eliza sensed something of joy from Jules, too, for she very nearly clung to him, the peacocks devotedly trailing her. Jules whistled, joked, told stories, filled their days with his exuberance. One morning as he swept and washed the kitchen floor, it suddenly struck Selene that this was no man, not as she had ever known men to be. His untrammeled energy which asked for nothing, took nothing, his kindness, his lack of shame. She sat on the kitchen chair, gazing at this man, the baby shifting gently beneath her folded hands. Without wanting to, she saw how these were to be among the happiest weeks of his life. She saw that his paintings would be misunderstood and rejected, again and again, his spirit defeated, his vision overlooked or criticized by an unappreciative world, and when he asked, she would not tell him, and when he begged, she refused to tell him why she wept.

*

The floorboards creaked as she plodded past Eliza's room and climbed, short of breath, up the dark stairs. Jules lay asleep beneath an open window. He lay on his side, naked, his hands tucked under him. She stood above her friend for a long while as if by studying him she might absorb something of what he knew or was. Then she knelt down. His shoulders smelled humid, he smelled like the river. He woke, sat up and embraced her. He whispered he was thirsty—was she? yes, she said—so they crept past Eliza's bedroom and down to the kitchen. Here, he tipped the cup to her mouth, cool water sluicing down her chin and spilling onto her chest. Selene, *mère*, let us search for those goddesses who come up from the river each night.

In the river's current, they drifted slightly apart then back together. Above them, fireflies winked on and off, the black cloth of the night richly embroidered with their gold, threadlike dartings. Selene and Jules rode the river on their backs, mostly silent, sometimes whispering, the tiny fires clicking above their faces, their bodies bathed in the moon and the high, silver raining of stars.

*

"Down! Off!" Selene nudged the peacock off the kitchen table. "Silly beggar!" Above the wooden table where she and Jules were sitting, braids of white onion and chaplets of garlic hung like strands of rough pearls from the wooden crossbeams. Blue and white dishes were strewn everywhere, along with remains from a breakfast of eggs, tomatoes, bacon, sausage, bread. Jules, awake since dawn, had just finished making a pie for their lunch. Thick, gluey stalks of green leek, shells of eggs, limp scraps of dough lay scattered everywhere. They decided not to wash dishes, not to clean up, not to do any predictable thing, but to find Eliza and wash her instead. After all, she smelled like garbage, Jules complained as he shouldered the tin tub up from the cellar and set it in sunlight by the open back door. Even her hair had grown a tough skin of oil over its unbrushed, rootlike twistings. When it was half full of heated water, and a greyed block of soap sat ready on the wood floor, they searched and came upon Eliza curled in a corner of her room on a piece of old red flannel, toying with the now filthy blue satin ribbon her father had once kept tied around her wrist. She was humming like a piece of broken factory machinery, a repetitive sound not pleasant to hear. Jules crept up behind her and loudly slapped his hands together, startling her. He chased her all over the house, Selene followed, out of breath, fetching up the dropped blue ribbon, yes, that too must get scrubbed... the chase, she heard it downstairs now, full of wild yelpings, even the peacocks squawked and swooped about. At last Jules seized hold of Eliza and hauled her like a sack of wheat over his shoulder into the kitchen.

Selene worked the lavender dress, badly stained, off her shoulders and slipped it off. She wore no underwear. Nothing.

"What an odor, my dear girl. You smell not much better than a rotten onion. Worse than a dead vole by the roadside. Since you won't learn to swim with us, Jules and I are forced to put you in this tinny old tub. Peeled potato in a stew."

Eliza held her fingers to her face, studying the play of water off her fingers. The bath was a slow business where she sat inert while they worked at scrubbing her skin and untangling her hair. Selene sat back on her heels to rest. Feathers of soap rolled down the ivory ladder of Eliza's spine. "And now," Jules spoke with mock gravity. "We approach the breasts. What roses," he roared in an operatic baritone. "What heroic nipples! Oh worship! Most holy mad one, we clamour for your milk, we wash your great strong legs, what saplings, their thick hairs like the needles of pine, oh belly of a lunatic, overruled by the moon, we are on our knees to you! We come to be drowned and drenched by you, oh irresistible one!"

Selene watched as Eliza, oblivious, strung her beads of water and soap, water and soap. Then glancing up, she saw Octavia in the doorway, a second figure standing directly behind her. Selene scrambled to stand, to conceal the girl's nakedness, but it was impossible. Eliza stuck out in every direction.

Suddenly the figures vanished, and Selene grasped at the possibility, the slender hope, they were figments of some waking nightmare.

"Good God, who was that?" Jules looked toward the doorway. He set down the wet block of soap, picked up the wood bucket of clear water and poured it over Eliza's shoulders in a long tender sluicing.

Selene wiped at her forehead with her sleeve. "I'd better go see."

They stood outside, conferring excitedly. Her sister, stylishly dressed, turned when she heard Selene's footsteps on the gravel.

"Have you gone mad along with her? Who is that man in the kitchen?"

"That is Jules Bois, an art student from Paris. He has, until recently, been travelling with his companion through Wales. He is currently staying with us, just until he hears from his friend."

"And so Mr. Blackburn's property has been turned into a wayside hostelry?"

"He simply wished an opportunity to paint and offered to assist me in exchange."

"And you call bathin g a naked woman, putting his hands all over her, assistance?"

"Eliza can be diffic ult to manage, especially cleaning her. She...resists."

"From what I saw, no one was resisting much of anything. I really have not recove red. I feel positively faint with disgust."

"I suppose I am so rry for that. Who is this with you?"

"Apologies, Mrs. Corner. This seems to be rather a shock to us all." The man in question extended his hand. "Dr. Munro, Eliza's physician at Brooke Asylum. I have accompanied Mrs. Blackburn in order to make m y report on Eliza's condition. It seems to me we are off to a bit of an awkward start."

Octavia was biting her lip, almost chewing on it. "We must say nothing of this to Charles. It might kill him."

"Shall I simply say I found her very well scrubbed?" Doctor Munro's attempt at wit was ignored.

"Good lord, the scandal. I cannot breathe. What can he still be doing in there? If he hasn't done so already, no doubt taking advantage of her weak mind."

"I doubt that, Octavia." Selene spoke cooly, though she was unpleasantly conscious of the stained, wet apron covering the front of her dress. "I can see Jules back by the garden, emptying out the wash tub. Eliza's probably dressing herself, she's quite capable of that."

"I must sit. This beastly sun is killing me. I understood Wales to be a countryside of mist and rolling emerald hills. And so late in September! This is nothing short of torrid."

Octavia had wilted down into one corner of the sofa, eyes closed, one hand placed on her temple. Doctor Munro, having shambled back from the kitchen, held out a glassful of water to her. Selene watched the water pulse greedily down her sister's throat, some spilling down the silk front of her dress.

"Charles and I returned last week from Paris. I had this dress made for me while I was there."

"It suits you." It was an ugly purple with puce fringe. Tucked into the corner of the couch, Octavia looked like a rotten little plum.

"Thank you. Your own clothing is completely wet through. No doubt you'll catch a chill."

"Actually, in this heat, it feels refreshing."

"We had no intent to steal upon you like this, Mrs. Corner." The doctor's voice was unctuous. "Our driver appeared inebriated, and he drove recklessly which made Mrs. Blackburn agitated. I merely suggested we walk the remainder of the distance. I believe your sister is feeling the effects of her walk as well as the shock of the other."

As if to contradict him Octavia snapped upright, restored to her former bad temper. "Doctor Munro and I should like to see the house. Charles is most anxious to hear how she fares under your authority."

She stood up and stepped, unaware, into a grey crenellated tower of peacock manure. "I cannot understand how you maintain such a place by yourself. And in your...condition. You look seedy, if I may say so. Terribly tired. Black rings beneath your eyes. Have you no help at all?"

"A gardener. Occasionally someone from town. I don't mind."

"Well from what I see, no one could accuse you of overexertion. How long has he been here?"

"You refer to Jules? Nearly three weeks."

"And his paintings? If he is an artist, as you claim, and not merely the opportunist I am certain he is, I should like to see his artwork. His subjects."

"Here they are. I believe I've located them." Doctor Munro stood in the next room, facing a wall against which several canvases were propped, drying. Octavia walked in and without a word, gazed a long while upon various images of an unclothed woman, grotesque, white belly huge with child, standing in a river, lying on the grass...clearly her own sister. With a lurching, unsteady gait, Octavia left the room on the arm of Doctor Munro. Selene next heard them upstairs, invading her home with their heavy, offended tread.

She found Jules in the kitchen, cheerfully clearing up all the dishes. She was busy helping him when they both heard it, a shrill shrieking from upstairs. "Peacocks," he said, raising his eyes in the direction the noise was coming from.

Within minutes, lunch was laid out on the dining room table, thick wedges of the leek pie, cold ham, fresh oatbread, cold well water, all ready by the time Octavia and Dr. Munro made their aggrieved way back downstairs.

The meal, at its beginning, was largely silent.

"Where is she? Doesn't the creature eat with you?"

"I allow her to eat whenever and however she wishes. Sometimes she eats with us, Octavia. I believe today she is out in the garden."

"Why are those repugnant birds allowed to roam the house as if it were a zoological park? It is disgusting and unhealthful. They should be outdoors. They have soiled Mr. Blackburn's carpet, and I'm sure they would be much happier, or whatever it is birds feel, outdoors."

"They are pets," Jules spoke up. "Eliza's. They keep her contented."

Octavia ignored him. "It seems to me, Selene, you have made an egregious error. Your judgement is poor. You have permitted a mad woman, a creature who has lived a good portion of her days in an asylum, you have permitted her to dictate the conditions of your life. Conditions that, if I may speak frankly, are deplorable."

"It is my life, and I am content with it. Eliza is doing very well. She requires no restraint and even if she is odd, I find her agreeable enough."

"And your so-called paintings... Monsieur Bois, you have taken advantage of my sister. Those depictions of her are obscene."

"*Merci, madame.*" Jules bowed deeply then vanished into the kitchen with the remains of the leek pie.

"I have news, Selene, as you may have guessed. Mr. Blackburn and I were married a fortnight ago."

"Well, I must offer congratulations."

"Thank you. We are quite content. And you? Have you heard from your husband, from Elgeron?" Octavia said this looking pointedly at Jules who had come back in, feigned shock, then winked at Selene.

"Not one letter. If I am fortunate, he will have been ship-wrecked."

"Really, Selene, what a cold and puzzling attitude. You have disgraced yourself once, and are about to bring forth the result of that disgrace. Out of the charity of my heart and because you are my sister, I have tried my best to help you. You have a lovely house with a good allowance, and had you retained Nurse Pindy, who says, by the way, that you behaved abominably toward her, you might now be spared a great deal of work. You seem determined to destroy your life. Doctor Munro and I find you on a great moral declension, determined to ruin yourself at every turn. Posing nude. Birds soiling up the house. It is much more dire than we could possibly have envisioned. Not only that, the coachman says rumours are rampant in Usk about what goes on here. You, a pregnant woman with no husband, living with a lunatic and a degenerate Frenchman. Even here you quickly become a source of gossip and scandal. Even here you bring disgrace upon yourself."

"*Au contraire*, Octavia. I feel perfectly well. I have been taught by my friend Jules to swim and to fish. I am learning the natural history of this region. I have good relationships with those people who do come here on an infrequent basis to help me. And Charles's daughter is thriving, actually. She is at liberty to choose her forms of expression. I do not believe she will ever be fully recovered, but I believe her to be, in her own way, content. I have no desire to punish her with locks and chains for being other than what society expects her to be."

"Yet you allowed that young man to fondle her in the bath. I saw with clear eyes, Selene!"

"We were playing. It was all innocent."

"My god, drag innocence into this to justify your immorality. Shame!"

"There is no shame here. None except as you impose it upon me. Octavia, I must insist you leave. I am sorry if you are made so ill by what you have seen, but what you have seen is coloured by your own prejudice, your need always to see the worst in me. You claim to be offended, but I have seen how you sniff out scandal. You have a long nose for it. We were once close, Octavia, but it seems you have never forgiven me my dismissal at Miss Cliff's which cost you your schooling. I have apologized for that. I apologize again. But I could not help what happened to me any more than it seems you can help doing what you now do."

"What do you mean? What do you insinuate?"

"Cheating Charles Blackburn out of his fortune. Manipulating him with the fictitious 'spirit guidance' of L. Gordon. There is no L. Gordon. Only yourself. You are a thief, Octavia. No devoted wife, but a common thief."

Selene dodged the slap her sister aimed at her.

"I will not forgive you. I shall make you pay for that accusation. Dr. Munro! I wish us to leave this instant!"

At the first hint of caterwauling, Dr. Munro had quietly excused himself and slipped into the room where the young Frenchman's paintings were. He himself found them most stimulating, so much so, he did not immediately hear Mr. Blackburn's young wife shouting for him.

*

Throughout early October, as they waited, expecting Dr. Munro or perhaps a nurse, to return and take Eliza back to Brooke Asylum, first one of the peacocks fell mysteriously ill, then the other. They died within hours of one another. Using Gywn Jones's garden spade, Jules made a grave for them behind the house. Eliza seemed not to notice anything had altered or changed, seemed unaware any source of affection or attachment had been removed from her life. This imperviousness to sorrow tempted Selene to envy such detachment, to very nearly covet those who were declared mad in this world. Jules had just told her he needed to return to Cardiff. His companion had at last written to him and wanted him to go to Italy, to Florence, to study the Renaissance masters. Before Jules left, Selene reassured him, each time he asked, that yes, she planned on returning to London to have her parents assist with the birth of the child. The morning he left, she told an even sadder lie—Octavia, she said, had written a letter. Despite their quarrel, she had offered to return to Selene and the child at Oakdale House and care for them both until Selene was fully recovered and strong again.

*

Late in November, a succinctly phrased, formal letter arrived from William Herapath, so devoid of emotion (mainly news of his own accomplishments, along with a slight mention of his possibly coming to Wales on a photography expedition), she decided she would rather not have received it at all. Eventually, she did not bother to reply. She had already received one brief and cheerful letter from Jules mentioning his students, one in particular, and his own renewed love of absinthe. He did not mention his friend, nor could she make out the address he had scribbled on the envelope. He had not, it seemed, gone on to Italy.

Eliza had been taken away by a contemptuous Nurse Pindy two weeks before.

With the child moving restlessly inside her, keeping her strange, unseen company, Selene would walk to the river, swim down to the stone bridge, then float back, her arms languid in the cool water, her eyes closed or gazing through the leafy scrim to the sky beyond. She imagined herself a butterfly, her arms unfurling into wings of silken yellow marked with gleaming blue. When she got out, she would sit beneath an ancient oak and wait for the river otter, who lived beneath it, to slip noiselessly out from under his nest of roots along the bank, watch his dark shape glide into the river. Sometimes, she sat watching a grey heron or a cormorant come to fish for the salmon and trout that shot through the brown river like silver seed.

*

7 Arundel Gardens
Ladbrooke Estates, London
November, 1874

Sister,

I write to inform you that Eliza is safely returned to Brooke Asylum. Dr. Munro tells us she has, after some "protest," adjusted. He even managed to give her her old rooms, which I thought unnecessarily considerate. His fees have become exorbitant, and he intends raising them again. Mother and I have informed Charles that we feel forced to locate some less costly place in which to keep her. Unaware as the creature seems to be, I hardly think she would care. A simple roof over her head is all that is required.

As you know, Charles has been unwell for quite some time. He rarely leaves his bed (though he insists you stay on at Oakdale, no matter that the reason for your being there has been removed ... Charles retains a fondness for you which I find quite inexplicable). The fact is, Selene, my husband will not live much longer, and he has been your strongest protector.

I trust you have been delivered by now of Mr. Herapath's child. I spoke last week with Mrs. Corner. She says Elgeron writes to her faithfully, once a fortnight. Though she is mortified, she says, by his deliberate failure to inquire after you.

Au Revoir,
Octavia

*

Before consigning this newest piece of malice to the fire, Selene read the letter once more. She continued to be puzzled by her sister's spite. It seemed disproportionate. If Octavia could see the target of her hatred now, huddled miserably before a peat fire in the kitchen, great as a cow, ankles swollen and feet raised on a stool, awaiting the birth of William Herapath's bastard child. A birth which she must somehow endure alone.

Though not entirely, she thought, watching the flames take Octavia's expensive, monogrammed stationery and blacken it to ash. Gwyn Jones stopped by twice each week to see how she was. He brought whatever supplies she requested, and made sure she had fuel to keep warm and enough food to live on. Once his wife had sent a round loaf of brown bread, another time some fruit jam. His wife would be glad, he said, to help when the time came.

Rain had fallen all week, sometimes a soft mist, then grey hostile peltings of rain, smacking the roof and windows. She told Gwyn she thought the baby would likely come sometime the next week, so yes, she would be grateful for his wife's help. The thought of an old Welsh country woman taking care of her, knowing what to do, helped to keep Selene calm and unafraid. Though it was always Tot she envisioned plodding about on her splayed feet, helping deliver the baby, bringing Selene broth, brushing out her hair. She would daydream in this comforting way, then remember she had never seen the gardener's wife and scarcely knew Gwyn Jones, except as his employer.

When Selene woke to warmth spreading beneath her, she lay still a moment, then felt with one hand to see if it was true. As she struggled to sit and then light the candle beside her bed, a massive pain rolled through her belly. When it subsided, she managed, her hands shaking, to raise the candle above her bed. By its light, she saw a stain of watery mucus mixed with blood, bright as a rose. And Gwyn not here, his wife not here, not for three more days. A second wave of pain crashed through her, greater than the first. *I have never seen anything be born before, not even a cat.* She thought of Jules Bois, teaching her how to swim. To be unafraid. *Mère.* Goddess. Another wave took her and she cursed such facile romance, her teeth chattering.

One day and most of another went by. She neither ate nor slept, pain her constant attendant, pain and the mercy of semi-consciousness. Outside, rain kept on. She had made a mess trying to keep the fire going, dragging whole bricks of peat and stuffing them into the fireplace, as many as she could at one time. Still she was cold, her teeth shook like dice, her legs, too, tremored, would not keep still. From time to time, she heard herself cry out.

When it finally came, she raised up to see it lying still and scarcely breathing between her thighs, its little clenched face perfectly formed, its eyes closed. Staring at it, she remembered nothing. Felt nothing at all.

Gwyn's wife had had a premonition, then a dream. She told her husband they could not wait another two days, as they had planned, to go to Oakdale House. They were needed now.

hide, burn, get rid of it. no one must know. she thought to lay it down in the smouldering fire, this sin thing, but could not. she wrapped it in a striped dress of hers, kissed it, this perfect issue of her flesh. rain had churned the earth wet as blood. she dug with her bare hands where Jules had buried the peacocks. no. she carried it to the riverbank and thought to set it down in the blessed water. no. it felt blissful, cradled in her arms, against breasts which had begun, already, to ache.

The rain drenched Selene as she stood, the bundle in her arms, not knowing what to do.

Gwyn found the young Englishwoman leaning against the broad trunk of an oak tree by the brown, swollen river, with what looked like an old dress rolled and bunched in her arms. She gazed up, not recognizing him, her eyes glistening with fever. As he helped her to her feet and led her gently up the slope to the house, the bundle still clutched to her chest, she made no sense, the things she was saying, and he was glad for his wife, waiting inside the house.

Together they unwrapped the child from the blue striped dress, washed and secretly baptized it. Gwyn's wife stayed with Selene until she seemed well enough to leave on her own a bit. The young woman asked for nothing. She nursed the child the same way she accepted their help, indifferently. Before they left, and whenever they returned, Selene thanked them, her eyes vacant of expression, her voice scarcely audible. For a time, Gwyn came by faithfully every day to check on her. Always, his wife sent gifts. Bread. Cheese. A scarf knit of the same red wool as his cap. They worried the child had no name and no father to claim it. But they did what they could for the poor woman. The rest, including the child's fate, was God's concern.

*

William Herapath allowed his whole foolish idea seven more minutes. If she did not return from wherever she was, he would depart as precipitously as he had arrived, leaving behind him a ruinous, romantic obsession with a girl too young and too ignorant for his intellectual needs. The coach from Newport waited, its driver no doubt asleep. This entire excursion had already cost him far more than he could comfortably afford. He had left his photography companions because of an obligation, he had said, to visit an old friend. He had departed from the Inn of Three Salmons, asking his hired driver to go toward the village of Usk. Once there, he had inquired as to the whereabouts of a residence known as Oakdale. He had been met with evasive answers and sharp, sly looks until one woman, the owner of a tobacconist's shop, declared it was exactly two miles south. Following her instructions, he travelled by coach down a wide, Roman-built road which took itself rather naturally between the grey-green Usk river and a thickish row of woods. Through a late afternoon's obscuring mist, he finally spotted a large house of dusty yellow block. He paid his driver to wait and went up to the front door. No one answered, so he walked round the back and after a moment's hesitation, entered an open door into the silent kitchen where he now sat, checking and re-checking his pocket watch, as if it were a pulse. When at last, he heard a sound at the kitchen door, the rustling of material and a light bootstep, he turned and stared.

This could not be her. Could not be the delicate, impeccably dressed, doll-like girl he remembered, had thought of each day, could not sleep for the seductive vision of. He would not have recognized this creature on any street in London. In truth, he might have pitied it, would have stepped slightly and distastefully away if they were made to pass one another. He would never have said it was her. Not this creature, standing before him in a shapeless green shift, torn and muddied at the hem, her familiar dark hair now tangled around her shoulders. The plain complexion—still a woman, yes, but with chapped lips and wind-burned skin. In serene contrast to this dishevelment, she now lifted up by a small shank of yellow rope two silver trout, their scales rippling in the light at her back. He was a fool to have come.

"William. I have felt you near me all day. I was fishing when several of my neighbor's black cattle came and stood in the river. And later, as I rested, a brown-speckled owl flew out from a chink under the bridge and rushed past my face with its great brown wings. Thus was I told you would come."

Herapath remained dumbstruck by the sight of her, darkened with rain and river water. A mossy spectre, she frightened him. She looked what—uncivilized, as if she had forgotten who she had been and was now. Had he seen her walking down the road from Usk, he might have photographed such a strange bit of Welsh colour, half-peasant, half-faerie. He would have been pleased to catch such a queer, regional specimen on his camera. Just then, at that moment, he distinctly heard a soft mewling cry. An infant's.

"She is alive, William."

"Alive? Who? What on earth are you talking about?"

"She has been alive for three weeks. Is this why you have come? To see her?"

"Selene, I am simply on a camera expedition and thought it might be pleasant for us to see one another again."

"You are aware of her birth?"

"For God's sake, who are you referring to?"

"Your daughter. I have borne you a child, William."

"Yes, well, Selene, I honestly have no inkling what you might be talking about. And I have taken up my driver's time long enough. He has been patiently waiting—I arrived quite some time ago..." For the first time in his life, William Herapath considered that he might faint. The baby, he heard it, cried out again.

"First you stood at the front door, then you came round to the back." She laid down the trout like a wide glittering ribbon on the table before him. The stench quite overwhelmed him. "Will you stay?"

William Herapath cursed himself for his stupid notions, stupid remembrances. She seemed to mock him, to rebuke his sentimental expectation of finding her seated at the piano in a pretty dress, her violet-scented hair in a chignon, of himself bending down to kiss the downy back of her white neck, of staying the night with her, of having her as he had once had her, an exquisite animal at his passionate command. Not this unkempt, ruddy-faced creature in a torn green dress, her heavy boots pasted over with mud— smelling of fish, rain, mud, corruption.

"How is your research? Your science?" Why did she now regard him with such chilly, impolite clarity?

He stood and walked to the door, making a great fuss of looking at his watch in the dying light. "Fine, thank you. Within the month I am to be awarded an honorary degree for my recent findings in chemistry, and I have been, as I may have mentioned in my most recent letter, invited to join the Royal Society of Fellows. My work engages me. Selene, I must apologize, I am late meeting my companions for supper. Again, I congratulate you and your husband upon your marriage and now, it seems, upon the birth of your child." Then he was striding, practically sprinting, toward the high black shape of the coach, the thing that could take him away from her.

A cool damp hand caught up one of his. He shuddered violently. How soundlessly she had kept pace with him.

"William."

He was safer now, near the coach. He half-turned to look at her. "What is it? Do you have need of money? If it is money you need I can easily..." His own lie, the ease of its utterance surprised him.

"What I have learned in my time here, my exile as you once called it, what I have been shown and come to believe, is unprovable by scientific measurement. Three weeks ago, I gave birth to our daughter. She is a perfect child. Tonight this stands as a dark knowledge all around you. I observed you awhile from the doorway, then made some small noise so you would become aware of me. It was just then, in that moment, that I saw you will outlive me by a great many years. Your fame as a scientist will be as great as my failure as a medium, though both fame and disgrace are fleeting, they are dreams, neither one lasts or is remembered long. The child is yours, William. I swear it."

He could no longer see her face in a night which was grown dank and heavy with mist. Her voice terrified him, the feel of her hand upon his arm.

"Let go of me, Mrs. Corner. I scarcely think this is you talking. You have obviously gone shockingly mad, and I am truly sorry for that. I am sorry if I have in any way injured you. I must go."

As he stepped then into the carriage and leaned out to pull shut the door, he heard it again, that eerie, pale voice.

"William?"

He did not answer. He could not.

"Let me bring her to you so that you may see."

"Driver!" He rapped on the ceiling. The carriage wheels spun abruptly, the horses stretched out their legs and pulled hard, as if being pursued.

Not possible. She would have told him. At Sydenham. He would have noticed. No. The poor girl was lost, deranged, she spoke utter nonsense.

*

He arrived back at the Inn of Three Salmons, walked up the muddied path and into the dining room where he was given a table beside the large peat fire and served a bowl of Welsh cawys, what in London would be called a plain stew of cabbage, onions, carrots and mutton. He forced himself, for distraction's sake, to eat. Good lord. To think he had considered sending the coach away until the next morning. He might have had to spend an entire night with her. Perhaps it was best he had seen her so, not in the way he had hoped or imagined, but as she now was, quite obviously mad. He would excise her from his life, an error, a terrible experiment, good god, a wretched sin. She no longer existed. Some bewitchment had worked to destroy her. He could no longer write to her, certainly never see her again. Instead, by the great power of his will, he would return to his laboratory and there wrest from nature the secrets of her finite, physical world.

*

Following a miserable, sleepless night, William Herapath, simply to assuage his conscience before he left, began to make inquiries early the next morning. He asked the Inn's owner what he knew of the most recent occupants of Oakdale House, a couple by the name of Mr. and Mrs. Corner. He received the identical answer he would hear wherever he went that day. In the village of Usk, in the hotel, in nearly every shop, he was told the same story, given the same information. A young Englishwoman lived there, entirely alone, except for a second woman who, it was rumoured, was mad. The first woman had recently given birth, and the child's father was unknown. She was a widow, that was what she had told Gwyn Jones, who sometimes worked for her. Her husband, she said, had been drowned at sea.

All this time, Selene had been alone. She had borne his child—their child!—alone. She had not written him, never once asked for his help. He could discover in himself only one explanation for her silence and it shamed him. She did not believe he cared. Their quarrel in Paris, unresolved. His stiffness at Sydenham, where nothing truthful had been said. His notes to her here, so coldly formal. He had meant to protect himself, not hurt her. But because he had not risked himself, had not told her he loved her, she had not come to him for help. The enormity of their misunderstanding, its unjust consequence to her, the weight of his own cruelty, though unintended and a result of his fear, stunned him.

By late that afternoon, he had packed his things, paid his portion of the bill and hastily scrawled a note for his companions, asking them to continue on their excursion without him—that he would, for an indeterminate time, be delayed.

It was late afternoon. The baby was asleep upstairs, and I had been practising on the piano and attempting to sing—I've been told my voice fairly wounds any ear but my own—still, alone, I do love to sing. Then, responding to some small noise behind me, I turned. There he stood, wearing his same hat and same coat, exactly as I had bid him good-bye the night before. His cheeks were ruddy, deeply flushed, and he stood before me, a silent, enigmatic figure of either doom or deliverance. His was the image I had seen all morning, but had not dared believe.

"Selene."

Odd, one's mind, how frantically it darts about while the heart flies swift and straight for joy. My mind prattled on ...mortified...your singing, he heard you...at last, Selene Cook, you occupy a moment such as Mrs. Alexander or even Miss Broughton describe in one of their popular novels...

Yet that same moment achieved a sober integrity such novels do not convey. When two people yield their very souls to one another, that exchange is less passionate than it is noble, sanctifying the very place in which it occurs, changing that place forever, in this instance the drawing room at Oakdale House at the close of an afternoon beside a piano whose keys no longer bore the weight of my fingers which had risen up from their rote music to be grasped by the warm hands of the man who now stood beside me.

Such passion (and not as Miss Broughton and Mrs. Alexander have so partially described it) followed quickly enough on nobility's heels...for soon after William's fevered declarations (oh, his face— unforgettably tender, his eyes wildly lit, and for the first time in months I did gaze boldly upon his lips and was again weakened by their beauty) I looked upon him with fresh courage, memorizing distinct and miraculous features, features perhaps not uncommon, scarcely remarkable on anyone else, but still I found them, as I had always, beyond reproach.

It was then I began to realize how reserved William had turned, not in speech (wonderfully infected by love's eloquence), but his body seemed paralyzed, incapable of matching utterance to act. A suggestion sprang to my mind, which, by the force of its very mischief, persuaded me. I told William I must run quickly upstairs and check on the baby (whom I already knew to be fast asleep). I allowed myself a long look into his eyes, and this too, gave me strength.

"*Yes, of course, Selene,*" *though he looked puzzled, for I had cut off, in mid-sentence, an increasingly tedious account of how he had just learned the truth of my situation. I interrupted and with a light backward glance, went upstairs, then called down from the landing. "Come up," I said. "William, you must come up." Going into my room, in a few minutes more, I called again to him.*

At last, I heard his footstep on the stair, then his voice outside my door, "Selene, what is it?" There he found me waiting, undressed upon my bed, my heart beating like mad.

—

I say it. I am the most loved woman in all Wales, in all England, in all the world.

—

How is it we have become this single, rapturous creature, breathing together, thinking together, our thoughts rushing over each other's, we scarcely know who has said what, as if the same voice speaks, as if we occupy one mind, as if our very blood mixes in the same chambered heart. In sleep we turn together, and if we have moved apart, one of us wakens as if in some quiet distress and pulls the other close again. And when I gaze at my reflection in the looking glass and see my youth returned to me and my innocence through love, restored, I am reminded of that bright, singular joy surrounding Jules Bois, except that our happiness, William's and mine, seems the more precious for having been long denied and never before so completely expressed.

—

This morning I woke alone and could not at first find William. Finally, I discovered him at the far edge of the garden, holding a wheelbarrow heaped high with pale straw and helping Gwyn, whom I could just see, setting down clumps of straw over the plants to keep the cold off them. Feeling my gaze, William turned then and waved. I waved back, shouted good morning, then watched as a great rose-coloured banner (visible only to me) flung itself, flashing, graced, between our two hearts.

—

Today William and I took our daughter to be baptized in a chapel in Cardiff. I have named her Gwyneth, after the man who saved both our lives. We stayed the night in a hotel there, and as we stood together at the window, gazing down at the dozens of coal barges grimly lining the harbour, I thought how somewhere out upon that grey, depthless ocean was Elgeron Corner. I had told William about the exact nature of that marriage. It meant nothing, he said. It never existed. It was empty, as meaningless as his own.

—

How is it my life has become paradise? To whom do I give thanks? There are no words. Words can only fleetingly tag the heart's bliss. The world is fresh born and I, gravely schooled in solitude, I, who had been taken by a sharp thread of loneliness through the soul's labyrinth and had resigned myself from all human company, find I walk with Gwyneth and William in a daily heaven of accord and harmony. And on those nights when I am made one flesh with him, with my beloved, I am delivered into an exaltation of the soul.

—

Gwyneth's eye is not right. A whitish cast glazes its surface and she cannot seem to see past it. When we pass an object in front of both her eyes, the left does not follow, it stares straight ahead. And she has been unwell with a cough and fever. I try, too, not to become overly anxious about our diminishing funds. William's supply of money (from his wife, for his photography excursion) is nearly used up, and we now await my monthly cheque from Charles Blackburn. William talks of returning to his wife in London, of hoping (a mad hope, he admits) she might somehow understand and grant him a fair divorce.

With this hope in mind, William left us. He returned after only five days, delighted to find Gwyneth improved, but his own news, I fear, was very bad. Mrs. Herapath, whom I once counted as a friend, or at least a kindly acquaintance, has given him little choice. She says she cannot forgive his loving me, that I am a low fortunehunter and a *conniving cheat. She eventually had him turned out of his own house, refusing further conversation with him. He managed, however, to take away from his laboratory three trunkloads of books and scientific journals, all of which he studies night and day, losing himself in them. He sits up late most nights now, reading by candlelight while Gwyneth and I sleep beside him. He is wonderfully educated, able to read in French, in Latin, in German. He is still kind, very loving to us, yet I feel these books are more and more a precious comfort to him while I have become, along with our daughter, an unpleasant reminder of all we need, of all we do not have, of responsibilities he hasn't the faintest notion how to fulfill. I tried once to tell him I need nothing to be truly happy, but he became angry as if I had directly reproached instead of tried to reassure him. Now I say little and for the first time, though I have faith the love between our two <u>souls</u> is as strong as ever, that it is <u>eternal</u>, I no longer believe that love is unbreakable, for the world drives its rift deeper, makes demands. Life itself begins to separate us.*

*

William Herapath had never before considered knowledge to be cruel, but the additional strain the horses were under, hauling his several trunks of books back to Oakdale, suggested the possibility. He had not heeded his wife's first demand, that he break off his shameful liaison with a "low class fortune hunter ...the schoolgirl medium, no less," Maude had taunted him. All the power in her demand was most cunningly tied up with her wealth and his reliance upon it. He begged for compromise. "Let me return to her," he had bargained, "for a few months, say six, then I give you my word I will return exactly, as you wish. Should I stay with her, you may divorce me on grounds of adultery, leave me destitute, I don't care." He pleaded frantically while playing out in his mind quixotic, ephemeral schemes in which he could somehow retain Maude's financial security and still be near Selene. Though of late, he admitted to himself, an insidious part of his own nature had begun to criticize Selene's complacent acceptance of her situation. Her simplicity, which had initially fascinated him, had begun to irritate him. Her freeness of spirit, her lack of desire for physical comforts, once so intoxicating, now seemed faintly distasteful...unseemly...bespeaking an absence of good breeding, as Maude had pointed out, as well as a disregard for the refinements of education. Their values, he realized, did not match. Still they had a child together (this he had neglected to mention to Maude, half intending to, then retreating and saying nothing when he saw she was near acquiescing to his plea—he did not want to lose his advantage by delivering more shocking news). Perhaps he could persuade Maude to give him a monthly stipend for his research and from that, send a bit of money to Selene and the child, one day bringing them all legitimately and solvently together. Oh, it was absurd. An absolute quagmire.

His head ached fiercely what with the jolting of the rough country road, the cold winter sun and the insolubility of his dilemma. He could not know then that love's resolve would weaken, that he would choose to return to the house on Mornington Road, to his laboratory and his work, that he would attempt several honorably phrased letters to Selene, then leave them half-finished and unmailed, that he would excuse his cowardice, justify his silence, remind himself he had significant contributions to make in science, and that in Wales he could contribute nothing. That he would convince himself of this, but think guiltily of Gwyneth, of Selene, intending always to travel back to Oakdale, or bring them somehow to him. But the twin tyrannies of economy and science would blunt his conscience, muffle the protestations of his heart.

"Write to the poor creature if you like," Maude had initially said. "Tell her you'll be back within the year. But imagine," she had added in a light tone meant to reveal its poisonous intent. "Imagine introducing that young woman into your circle of distinguished acquaintances as anything but an experiment." Yet in the end, Maude relented. Six months she allowed him, with no money from her. Let him see what life without funds or society was like. She was confident he would be back, if not for her, then for the pragmatic support she was able to lend his dreams.

So was it knowledge that proved cruel or love? Were these, at least in his life, so incompatible? He adored Selene. He knew that just by seeing her again, as she ran to meet his coach. He knew with all the conviction of his own nature that he loved her. It was life together he could no longer predict, or worse, even imagine. Still. He had six months with her. He had until June.

7 Arundel Gardens
Ladbrooke Estates
London

My own dearest SPIRIT,

You have written faithfully to me over the years, and I want, in my prostration, a few more lines of comfort from you, written with the enclosed lead pencil, on the back of this letter—and replace it where you take this from—viz my bedroom drawer.

From your side, you can see if the doctors are working correctly for my restoration, and if you don't know, can't you get Pierpont or the other doctors to assist you in writing to me the best remedy—as I don't want to quit yet!

Of course, we have had no seances of late as my condition has not been suitable for months. Still, we know and feel you about us and hope you will reply as usual and put it in a small envelope which I enclose with pencil.

With Love and Kisses, which I have so often received from you,

Charles Blackburn

*

In her bedroom, at her writing desk, Octavia turned the letter over to reread her hastily penciled reply.

My Dearest FRIEND,

Your letter gave me both pleasure and pain, pleasure in thinking writing me still interests you, pain to think I cannot give you comfort by telling you you will recover. All is being done for you that is possible both on your side and mine. Many are waiting to welcome you Home, and know I shall be with you always.

You must believe you have had a long and useful life and have been just to all those connected with you. Look forward to us meeting, not as we have done, but in a perfect new unity and friendship.

I must not close without thanking you for all your great kindness to Octavia and those belonging to her.

Will you destroy this? I have been long in answering, for so many influences are at work in your room, it is not want of desire to write.

Believe me that always I am with you, your faithful, loving SPIRIT.

This is not good-bye.

L. Gordon

*

Five weeks after her husband's death, Octavia Blackburn was near the end of overseeing the packing and moving of her things and her mother's to their new home in Kensington Park Gardens. She had no wish to stay on in the Arundel house where Charles had died. The decision to sell this house where they had all lived together and move to a more luxurious residence in Kensington had been an easy one. After all, she had a surfeit of money from the terms of her husband's will, terms she had further influenced in her favour in the days before his death. The harder decision, the one she hadn't come to yet, was what to do about Oakdale. Selene's fate now lay entirely within her hands. Some kinder part argued for clemency, remembering their childhood, those occasions when they had, as sisters, been close. And it would be convenient to keep Selene in Wales, distant, requiring only a small monthly income. Part of her, the kinder part, as well as the practical, argued for this. But then Octavia remembered certain humiliations and personal defeats. She remembered taking care of her father, then Charles, having to manage both deaths. The joyless task she'd been given of caring for ailing, old people. Selene had missed all that, hadn't she? Most particularly Octavia remembered—and with fresh bitterness each time—the way Selene had called her a thief, accused her of stealing Charles Blackburn's fortune, had bluntly called her a common thief. Whatever had Selene done but the same, receiving the man's money in exchange for trumped-up assurances of an afterlife? Both of them had capitalized upon the lonely widower's grief, it was just that Octavia had proved the cleverer, had surpassed her sister by marrying him. Still, this old insult of Selene's had not ceased to sting and was, in the end, the compelling factor which drove Octavia to seek out her husband's solicitor and demand that he write a certain letter, dictated by her, to be sent to her sister in Wales.

*

It was mid-afternoon. Selene had just bathed Gwyneth in the clear river, while William lay on his back beneath a tree, sleeping, yet another book open on his chest as if replacing his heart. Books. Selene thought how she, too, had once read them, memorized their poetry, yet it seemed to her that books could be used for good or for ill, to widen or to narrow one's gaze upon the world. She sat in the sunshine with Gwyneth standing in her lap, naked and tugging at her damp hair, marking her cheeks with sweet little kisses. In the midst of Gwyneth's devotion, or perhaps because of it, Selene finally found strength to withdraw the letter from her pocket. She had carried this envelope about with her for two days. It contained, she already knew, a certain hard piece of news.

17 May 1875

Mrs. Corner,

Be advised that Oakdale House, following the death of Mr. Charles Blackburn earlier this month, no longer belongs to his wife and the sole inheritor of his estate, Octavia Blackburn. It has been purchased by a family in Kent who indicate a wish to take up permanent residency in one year's time, by May of 1876. I have informed Mr. Deeds, the new owner, of your situation. He has indicated his willingness to let you stay on until you shall have made your decision as to future plans.

As to yourself, enclosed please find a cheque from Mrs. Blackburn to cover all upcoming expenses until your departure from Oakdale House as well as an additional sum to assist you thereafter. I trust you will find your sister's decision agreeable and her monetary gift proof of her perennially generous nature.

Sincerely,

Malcolm E. Clarkson
Clarkson & Bates, Solicitors

Gwynnie dearest, no. Here, give that to me, let go. Gently Selene pried from her daughter's curious fingers the single thing that holds whatever is left of their security, the cheque from Octavia.

Several agonizing weeks of discussion have passed. It is now early June and William has fixed on a plan to return to London. He insists he will not send for us until he has found a decent place to live. I have made him take half the money Octavia sent me (for her, a surprisingly large sum). I tell myself it is a good plan because it is what William insists on.

I said good-bye to him while holding Gwyneth, who is fussy from still another slight fever and cough. The first day or two after he left us (and taking his books with him) I almost hoped he would turn back, come home and we would manage to find a small place here in Usk to live simply. But four, then five days passed, two weeks, and I knew he had carried out his plan. I waited for news, for a letter. None came, though I pestered Gwyn every time I saw him. Then, some weeks after William had left for London, I was distracted from that anxiety by a much more urgent concern—Gwyneth's worsening illness.

——

Before this day, I might have guessed that a child stillborn was the worst tragedy that could ever befall a woman. It is not. The death of a child you have grown to love better than you love the world is worst. It is not to be endured. I cut a lock of her beautiful hair and keep it beside me when I lie down (I do not sleep), as well as her dress, still spotted with mud (we had been caught out in the rain), the last she wore.

And no word, none, from William.

——

Nothing stops me from breaking this net of skin tinged with fear, nothing dissuades me from entering that sweet fruit of perception, what those who cannot see or do not choose to understand, call mad. My voices have returned, yet I find they speak not to harm but to instruct. And when they go quiet, I drop away from cruel time, that uncharitable road of hours I had been trained to move by and to obey. All proportion, all constraints of space leave and release me. In my sleep—I begin to sleep for days on end and a year is much like a day—existence becomes as a lengthless and luminous plain of rest. In dream I visit golden domed cities of light, am taken through libraries of glass whose spacious corridors hold books scripted in brilliant embellishments, in crystalline hieroglyphics. I am carried by tall beings, neither male nor female, their features lost to radiance. These speak without speaking. Whole chapters of their one mind flood into mine, absorbed, translated into ethereal tone. Gladly I forget my name, neglect food, sleep where I lay down. God does not abandon me, rather I am held in the mothercore of God, then the rhythmic core itself. This first spring, this first summer and season upon season thereafter, I wake nights to roam a green and spawning countryside, I walk until the sun breaks from its eternal hill of ash. And when the moon is fully white, when pale, corded clouds enflame the heavens, I run barelegged through meadows crisscrossed with glittering streams and shallow riffles of water, the energy of earth surging up through my naked feet, shooting sap up my two legs and my spirit is cleanly drawn like a fiery silver thread out of my chest near the region where it is said the heart dwells but never rests. Then I fly, skimming, soaring over a leafy counterpane of trees, I hover above stone-fenced fields where sheep stand close together, their great brown eyes dewy with starlight. I pierce their bodies, wing through the silken rivers and salt nettings of their blood, float above a marsh where mallards drift on the water's murky skin, then I am the teeming water itself, lapping beneath their downy bellies, supple around their webbed, limp feet, cooling the silver-fingered lengths of fish. I descend into ethereal-eyed leaves of trees, flow down through dream-veined branches, stoical trunks, trickling into the million starred roots. I kneel inside stones and accept their memories. I hear the one dream of a thousand birds, stand within the vast dimensions of their intelligence, I am encircled by a net of jewels, a shimmering web linked at origin and source by a thing I can only name, though the word itself fails, as love. Around all the earth fields unfold, pulsations and tides, a rising and falling, dissolving, creating. I do not know how many nights my soul, that eternal gossamer filament is drawn out from me... it might be one time or thousands. I am carried to the faerie world, its lucent terrain as real as any rough-trod human landscape I have suffered.

Days when I diminish back inside my flesh, it, my body, seems to me constricted, ill-fitting. My eyes see nothing. My senses bury me. My blood purls its dark sanguine path, I hear my heart's stubborn,

*inky roar. I stare at my feet, do not know them and think to laugh.
When I speak, sounds entangle and break, clotting the air, so I turn
away from the inchoate, sickish deception of speech. I keep to
myself, solitary in all I do. While he is here, the gardener keeps
kindly distant, working his row upon row of vegetables, his scarlet
cap moving like fruit among the slow leaves. On hands and knees he
traverses the ground. I hear him—he knows I grieve my child. Out
of a good heart, he does not approach and though it is difficult to
judge these things, I suppose I am glad.*

—

*Late September. A windy green afternoon axed open with light.
Gwyn leaves a letter for me, a stern whiteness on the table in the
kitchen. Inside, I find Octavia's money, the portion I had given to
William, returned unspent. Then a brief message. He is deeply sorry.
He cannot return. Within the fortnight he will write a full
explanation.*

*Holding the letter (strange I did not dream, or know, or see in
some vision this...), my recent dwelling in otherworlds lifts like a
mist, this way of living or not-living ends. It comes clear to me, too
clear, that I am to return for a few years more to this poorly sighted,
deeply glorious world.*

—

*Strange. How long have I lived in this house? How many hours
passed? How much slept, how much kept awake? How much eaten,
walked, observed, loved, suffered?*

—

Two trunks stood in the middle of the floor. The cherrywood
armoire empty as was the dresser, its top still slightly bowed and
warped. (One of Mrs. Deed's servants, in moving the armoire,
would discover a pair of manacles, a tiny key.) Though she stood
at its center, the room echoed as if she were already vanished. The
window was open wide, and Selene stood before it, leaning out a
little into the sharp, chill breeze and gazing at the river.

—

Houses. They are pure beings of emotion and thought and memory, possessed of skin, eyes, language, hearing. This house breathes as surely as I breathe within its walls. It has an intelligence, a spirit. Another family will take possession of it, come inside it, impress themselves upon its rooms, upon the very air that circulates through its corridors. And what of Eliza? Jules? William? Gwyneth? Myself?—transparent images, ghosts in the body of this house, sometimes felt or glimpsed, our scent caught in passing.

—

In October, 1875, having lived less than two years of her life at Oakdale House, Selene Cook made her way back to London, a small woman wearing a drab, brown and tan plaid dress. The coachman who came for her was a stranger. Without interest or conversation, he transported her, silently, down the wide straight road which dipped here and there only slightly as it took its course alongside the quiet-flowing Usk. Gazing out the coach window for as long as she could still see the little churchyard where her daughter lay buried, she finally turned forward only to observe a diminutive figure hovering on the edge of the wooded road. As the coach passed slowly by, she and this figure, of indeterminate age, but thin and finely boned, gazed as in a moving dream upon one another. Beneath the woman's eyes were grey crescents of exhaustion. A wide embroidery of scarlet honeysuckle stood out around the neck of her white nightgown. Her feet were bare and clean and shone like pearls. The woman lifted her hand slightly, a smile of weary recognition upon her lips, her whole face washed over with a pale tint of hyacinth.

THE CRYSTAL PALACE

The Herapath Residence
Mornington Road
London
April, 1886

Young Jenny Dobbs, quite enjoying her adventure, sat down to wait on the front steps, admiring the window box with its brilliant profusion of yellow primrose. The Herapath's housekeeper, a Mrs. Bixley, had informed her that Sir Herapath and his wife, entertaining guests for luncheon, were not to be disturbed. Then she would wait, Jenny Dobbs had replied. After more than an hour of checking out the window, Mrs. Bixley, in a fit of exasperation, feeling it was highly improper, it wouldn't do at all for this young woman, whoever she was, to be found by Mr. Herapath's company sitting like a great toad on the front steps, opened the door and fairly hissed at the girl to wait in the laboratory to the left of the foyer while she fetched her employer. Mrs. Bixley also said she hoped the girl understood the impudence of her act.

Having never been in a laboratory of science, Jenny Dobbs looked curiously about and concluded it wasn't all that different from her husband's grocery. Things lined up, catalogued, labeled. Except for those, she noted with a shudder, the stuffed, horrid-looking fox on the desk and directly behind it, on a counter-top, two lifeless blackbirds perched on sticks beneath belljars, nothing like the lovely goldfinch Miss Cook had bequeathed her.

"Yes? What can I do for you?"

At the sound of his voice, she turned and why, she reasoned with herself later that evening, should she have been shocked to see such an old man fairly glaring at her? She had known he was older than Miss Cook, that years had passed since the events Selene related had occurred. Still.

"Yes?" He repeated, clearly irritated.

She was sorry to disturb him. But she was here on behalf of Miss Cook. Miss Selene Cook.

William Herapath visibly paled and as if to conceal his reaction, moved quickly to his desk. Keeping his back to her, he began idly picking up pieces of paper and looking at them.

"Yes," he said in a much softer tone. "What is it?"

Briefly she told him of Selene's death, of her last request to deliver the letter she had written. With the mention of a letter, he turned and saw it in her hand, watched her set it down on a corner of his desk. There was a warm, jovial burst of laughter from another part of the house, the sound of the pianoforte picking out a tune of some sort.

"I won't disturb you any longer, Sir Herapath. I merely meant to keep my promise to deliver the letter personally. Miss Cook was a lovely person, she truly was. I am recently married, and she and I were becoming friends before she fell ill. We used to talk a great deal. I admired her."

He seemed almost to have forgotten anyone was there. He was holding the letter, turning it over and over. Then he looked at her, and for an instant, Jenny Dobbs saw what Selene Cook might once have seen in him, the compelling eyes, the dark, arrogant glance.

"I'm sorry. I didn't quite get your name, was it Jenny? Yes, well, Jenny, I thank you for taking the trouble to come all this way from where did you say, Battersea? You came by what means?"

"Omnibus, sir."

He was reaching impatiently, as if he wished her gone, into his pocket.

"Well, here you are, take this. I insist you take this for a cab ride back to your home. Your fulfilling your friend's request has meant a great deal to me, and so I wish you safely home."

"Thank you, sir."

Jenny took the omnibus back to Battersea, saving the money Sir Herapath had given her until she found a set of handpainted haircombs at a milliner's shop near her husband's that she especially liked.

That night, she lay beside her sleeping husband and thought of old Sir Herapath, remembering how his hands had trembled, holding the letter. She imagined him opening and reading it, wondered what pain or pleasure its contents brought him. She had said nothing to her husband about any of this. Meanwhile, he had mentioned over dinner having already found a new tenant for the flat Miss Cook had previously occupied, a young law student named Hampton. Jenny hoped it was the same young man she had seen her husband speaking to on the street the day before. He had been tall and very nice looking. Selene had once seen into Jenny's future and foretold a second marriage to a man her own age who would make her wildly, truly happy.

*

William Herapath returned to the dining room, apologizing for his brief absence. The letter was in his pocket; he planned to read it when everyone had left and his wife was resting, as she did now most afternoons. Battersea. How long had she been living there? He had thought she was in Europe, Belgium or Czechoslovakia, the two places Thomas Boynton had mentioned last time he had spoken of her. But that was so long ago. If he had had any idea how close she was... the very idea unnerved him. He patted the letter, reassuring himself of its presence, not allowing himself, not yet, to let the full news of her death affect him.

April, 1886

Beloved,

When I arrived in London (this in October of 1875), I did not yet believe your message, the one you sent me at Oakdale. I was determined to challenge you, to hear from your own lips, uncoerced, the terrible sentence you had so blithely pronounced on paper. I even had some fixed notion Maude had forced you to write those loveless sentences. But when I reached your home on Mornington Road (and what a flood of memories met me there!), my nerve failed me and for the following reason. As I stood down the street a bit, gathering courage to proceed, I saw several figures coming down your front steps. They turned in my direction and from an unobtrusive position, I watched them pass by. I recognized Looie, your governess, two of your older children and a baby being wheeled in a pram—no doubt the child Maude had been carrying while I lived in your home. Their little group appeared so happy, so merry, that my resolve to confront you that day, to expose our relationship to full light, seemed a terrible intrusion. It seemed wrong.

I walked until I caught a cab to Kensington Park Gardens where I had thought to visit my mother—as for Octavia, well, I frankly hoped she would not be at home. But as the driver helped me to search out the address, as we stopped before Octavia's newest residence since Charles Blackburn had died, its opulence made me too anxious (and angry), and I told the driver, who was by now quite frustrated with me, to move on.

Having reneged on two of my plans, I now instructed the driver, more confidently this time, to take me to Navarino Road, to The Dalston Association, to Mr. Boynton's familiar address. Thomas begged me to sit down in his study and tell him, as he said, everything. An impossible task, still, I told him all I felt I safely could. We spoke of Charles Blackburn, and when I gingerly inquired about you, he became agitated, saying that since your return from Wales in June you had adamantly refused any discourse of a spiritual nature, that all your experiments and articles were now confined within strict scientific perimeters. He was most sympathetic, however, to my plight and on the spot wrote letters of recommendation for me to take to friends abroad. Establish your reputation outside England, he advised, and then return—as other mediums had successfully done. He insisted I take the money he and his wife offered me. I left England for what would turn out to be some years. Of that time in my life, there is little I wish to tell. I traveled, gave seances set up for me in different parts of Europe. It was an adventurous time for me, but eventually I managed to return to London and settle here in Battersea, where I now reside, poor in health, indeed, very near this life's end.

I did attempt, one last time, only a month ago in March, to see you. Again I stood near your home, across the street this time, waiting until I saw you emerge. You were dressed very finely, William, and as I watched you climb into a waiting carriage, as I heard you laughing most heartily with its occupants, I saw, clearly saw, how content you had become—how satisfied. I understood you had chosen not to return to me, that you did not believe in any possibility for our happiness, that your passion for science, your fear of hardship, perhaps even your conscience, had turned you from me. These won over the heart in you, William.

I have lived quietly these past years. As I did in Wales, and now for my own pleasure, I float through realms other than this one. I do not particularly care where I stop and where other beings, those spirits I sense everywhere around me, begin. Again, as in Wales, loneliness alternates with aloneness, the first made bearable by the other's quality of joy.

I write this letter, William, partly to ask one thing of you. A favor. There is a journal left behind at Oakdale. It is hid in the outside wall beside the kitchen door. There is a loose, discoloured brick, larger than the rest, and if you remove it, you will find the hollow place where I hid my journal. Written down in it are messages I was given by those voices and spirits who told me they were angelic beings. I put down these messages in a code I was told to use—the letters backwards, the fourth and second letter of every word reversed. While I lived alone at Oakdale, these beings appeared to me, giving, as I said, a great many messages. Please, William, take this journal to the Society for Psychical Research. Tell them it is Selene Cook's journal, kept during her stay in Wales. I feel it may be of some use. Now that I am so near death, I wish most urgently that these messages be given out to the world, through the Society. What you may choose to tell them about us, if anything, is up to you.

I have sad news too. Gwyneth, our daughter, died of scarlet fever on September 28, 1875. She was buried in the small churchyard, the one I took you to visit when you first arrived at Llanbadoch. You may wish to visit her grave. It is beneath a larch tree.

My life has been rich in ways human society can neither count nor measure nor reward. I have been taught (and how I resisted the lesson!) that love is an invisible energy which cannot die. It changes form, appears to vanish, then reappears. You remember we once spoke of feeling as though we were one fiery light, one soul? It is true. There is no thing such as time, and this life is a shadow dream at best, pale glimpse of a glory no one of us can imagine. I have little fear of death. It is a passageway, and no one is ever left there alone or for long.

I love you, William, and wait until you and I, being brought face to face in yet another lifetime, will seem, instantly, as friends, to recognize one another.

Ever yours,
S.

Llanbadoch
Usk, South Wales
October, 1886

As she did each summer, Maude Herapath had removed Looie and the children to her parents' estate in Nottingham to escape London's stifling heat. William had agreed, as he did each summer, to join them in one month's time.

Now, though, he had just emerged from the small, crowded cemetery where, almost at once, he had spotted the larch tree and nearby, her gravestone.

GWYNETH
CHILD BELOVED
December 1874
September 1875

Earlier that morning, inquiring in the village of Usk, he had learned that Gwyn Jones and his wife had also both died, though he hadn't the heart to search for their graves in either this churchyard or the one he remembered as being further on toward Newport. He had stood before his own child's grave a long while before returning to the coach that waited outside the ironwork fence, before instructing the driver where he wished to be taken next.

It had been years since he had last seen Oakdale House, though since her letter had been delivered to him, William Herapath often imagined himself there because when he did, he always found her waiting. As he caught sight of the house from the road, as the mingled smells of the river and the trees and the land grew intoxicatingly familiar, he saw that what he had been told at the Inn of Three Salmons, where he had spent the previous night, restless and waking every few hours, was sadly true. Most of Oakdale had been destroyed by lightning. Before that, the house stood vacant for years. Its last occupants, a family by the name of Deeds, had left, claiming they saw figures on the staircase, heard a woman's voice in the hallway, that Oakdale House was haunted. He was told they had tried to sell it, reducing its price several times. No one came to see it. No one even inquired.

In the graveled driveway, he stepped down from the coach, telling the driver to lead the horses down to the river for water, that he wouldn't be long. With his heart beating absurdly fast, William Herapath walked in the direction where he remembered the kitchen to have been. Most of the wall still stood, though the wood door had burnt, the plaster had blackened, and a wild rose vine with a wealth of fragrant, white blossoms, seemed to spill over the damaged wall. Cautiously, he searched until he found the place she had described, found it and wondered why, in all the months he had lived here, he had never noticed that single larger brick, jutting out and lighter in colour than the rest. Taking out his pocket knife to peg off a portion of the vine, he tugged the brick back and forth, drew it out, set it on the ground and peered in. Blackness. He reached his hand into that surprisingly cold space and felt almost immediately the small leather journal. He drew it out and went around to the back of the house, which was mainly fallen in, its timbers badly charred. Settling his back against a low stone wall in the warm afternoon sunlight, he studied the small book of black morocco leather, not much larger than his hand.

Its cover was stiff, cracking slightly as he opened it. On the first page he found her name, Selene Rose Cook, the date, January 1873, then beneath, her address in Hackney. The sight of her handwriting caused a soft, anguished cry to break from him, and without thinking he lifted the book and brought her name to his lips.

it grows worse.
instructions. mischief. powers.
a trembling throughout.

He turned more pages, these not in any code, apparently written when she was a girl in Hackney. Here were entries about voices, fear of madness, seances, about lessons from a Mr. Herne and a Mr. Risdale. Then abruptly, following a page describing her intent to live for some weeks at William Herapath's home on Mornington Road (his name, he noted, twice underlined), the entries ceased. There followed a number of blank pages, then the code she had spoken of began. The handwriting itself was erratic, the backwards words taking on diverse styles as though written by someone with her eyes closed, climbing steeply over the page, then dropping off altogether. He began leafing quickly through the rest, a part of his mind considering this a possibly useful project, decoding her messages before the journal was given to the Society as she had asked—he was quite taken with this idea when he came upon a terrible, ruinous thing. After the first several pages in code, the rest became indecipherable, the ink washed away. Dampness, rainwater, had seeped onto all the pages, utterly destroying them. Whatever messages from the spirit world Selene had heard and faithfully copied down were reduced to inky smears, with here and there a word or letter faintly legible but, by itself, signifying nothing. He sat awhile, then got up and walked to the front of the house and stood in the driveway, its graveled curves choked thick with weeds. As he prepared himself, reluctantly, to leave this place he had so loved, it was then he thought he glimpsed her, just for an instant and then the picture, or vision—whatever it was—faded. He distinctly saw her standing naked in the river, gleaming with water, her back to him. She was singing, and just as he remembered, her voice was sweet and slightly off-key.

Chiding himself for being an old, weak-hearted fool, William Herapath turned and climbed stiffly up into the coach. It would be a long ride to Newport where he planned to stay the night at a comfortable inn recommended by a friend. Still, part of him longed to turn and see her there in the river. No. He withdrew from his pocket the little journal. He would not give it to the Society. Why should he? It was ruined. Unreadable. No one would know what it meant. Besides, he had so little left of her. Unable to stop himself, he turned and as he had known, saw nothing but the grey, flat, west-flowing river. *A dream, a shadow, a glimpse.* A day, she had said, when they would come face to face and know one another again. He pressed the book in his hands, swearing an oath that he would not, when they met again, confuse erudition with truth. That his courage would not fail him. That he would find a way to marry knowledge to love.

He thought of his wife, of Maude, of her humility in taking back a husband who did not love her. Perhaps he should, for the remainder of his life, devote himself to her. If it would not be love, then it would be love's reflection he could live by. He considered those libraries where he had spent hours, days, no, years of his life, the hundreds of books and articles he had read, the few he had managed to write and been chiefly disappointed by how far short they fell of his intentions, his dreams for them. He considered the years of research in his laboratory, the dozens of expensive instruments he had used to calibrate and to weigh, labouring to break down and to catalogue the world's immense mystery. As he held Selene's ruined journal in his hands, its pages overwritten with decay, his imagination was briefly lit by a vision of radiant, golden-domed cities of light, of libraries fashioned all of crystal, of books glittering, infinite row upon infinite row, like purest diamonds. The distance between his crude laboratory, his dull books and this brilliant vision overwhelming him as he held her small journal and wept, was a mystery he could not hope, without her love and her wisdom, to decipher or to bridge.

Crystal Palace
Sydenham, South London
December 1898

"Exceedingly grave occasion, eh?" Sir Rudyard Volkman spewed crumbs, his mouth functioning quite like his character, Sir Herapath dryly noted, in a kind of untrustworthy swivel. Herapath sawed away at his slice of goose, his silence compelling Volkman, across the green-ivied table, to replay his feeble wit. "Covey of relics crammed down the maw of Old Iguanodon, wouldn't you say?"

Herapath chewed. His dinner was dead cold and half cooked, defeated by the problematic business of serving several dozen Royal Fellows inside the reconstructed skeleton of a dinosaur. He loathed being there, suddenly detesting the self-congratulatory atmosphere of this insular group of scientists to which he belonged. The notion that he attended such functions chiefly to eavesdrop upon his own obituary had begun to plague him, though he was easily, along with Volkman, among the youngest of the scientific company present, all black-frocked as priests and scarcely separable from the phalanx of butlers hovering behind them. He was among a privileged rank of deteriorating specimens seated within an ivoried cage, an immense skeleton which filled the entire north wing of the Crystal Palace. Gathered thus under the sternum of a female Iguanodon from the Jurassic age, Sir William Herapath and his chosen company poked away at their Christmas dinners.

"Why so seedy, Herapath?" Volkman now sprayed insult along with morts of his orange-sauced goose. "No doubt old Trowbridge will be singing your praises any time now." Volkman was referring to the current President of the Royal Society of Fellows, who now stood on a dais in the neck region of the Iguanodon, intoning the lifelong achievements of each of his guests. Damned obituaries. Each met with a smattering of applause, further muffled by the Iguanodon's poor acoustics. Though the setting was apt, Herapath mused—all of them fossils, these various inventors of the hydraulic crane, the compound steam engine, the steam turbine engine, ductile steel, synthetic fiber, the siphon recorder, the underwater torpedo, the kaleidoscope, discoverers of amyl, thallium, cathode rays, electrical precipitation and argon, achievements seized upon and utilized for the industrial glory and profit of England. Herapath regarded the Christmas centerpiece before him, the dark green ivy and pyramids of oranges and pears, the gilded varieties of nuts, the candelabra blazing richly. If he could make his way to a gentlemen's room (he had a need painful and urgent now, to relieve himself), he might cheer up.

Not dignifying Volkman with any response, after all, hadn't the man kept up a vicious nipping at his heels for years now, Sir Herapath leaned back to ask directions of the butler stationed behind him.

Afterward, he did feel better, so much so he considered eschewing his social obligation altogether. The Crystal Palace was a vast edifice housing exhibits of all the world's industry with a natural bias toward the superiority of things English. Herapath found himself near the entrance to the famous Winter Garden with its broad avenue of gleaming marble statuary, triple-tiered fountains plashing rhythmically and row upon row of potted ornamental palms. He could hear faint traces of the Hallelujah Chorus being sung by the choir of six hundred. He entertained the heretical possibility of absenting himself from the banquet, wandering instead through a glassy labyrinth of ethereal voices and brilliant geometries of winter light, jeweled prisms of light breaking through thousands upon thousands of glass panes fitted into iron transepts and naves, as six hundred voices soared heavenward in this crystal cathedral dedicated to all the recordable achievements and observable glories of man, the Englishman in particular. But no, his devoted butler had got him by the elbow, and was now steering him back to his assigned spot.

"If you'll forgive me, Sir, the others are awaiting your return."

"Sir William Herapath, born June 17, 1825, former editor of *The Liverpool Photographic Journal, The Journal of the London Photographic Society, Chemical News,* and *The Quarterly Journal of Science* ...discoverer of thallium, the cathode ray, inventor of the radiometer and the spinthariscope...author of books on aniline colours and beetroot sugar, former President of the Royal Society, the British Association for the Advancement of Science, the Chemical Society, the Institution of Electrical Engineers and the Society for Psychical Research..." he heard it, the whole impressive chronicle of himself. As the accolades progressed, the list of his honorary degrees and professional accomplishments, discoveries and inventions (the failures all deleted—yet it was chiefly these, his failures—which had taught him most), he heard his obituary, if that's what it was, and allowed it to warm him like a tonic. He was rather fond of this lopsided portrait of himself—eminent, distinguished, brilliant. As the applause gained in vigour, as he rose from his chair and bowed (beckoning to his now familiar butler for a third dish of plum pudding), Sir Herapath, newly affable, nodded to each of the gentlemen around him, colleagues, peers, the hot infusion of praise enlivening his senses. Then Volkman, wormy pest who would not be stifled, no matter how many obscuring arrangements of ivy, no matter how many pyramids of citrus were heaped between them, spoke.

"Pity Trowbridge omitted the most famous business."

"What's that?"

"Come, come, judging by the present company, we've each got a leg in the grave. That scandal with the little medium. Rumour has it that young girl played quite the parlour trick on you. What was she like in the spirit cabinet, behind the psychic veil as it were, Herapath? Gratify the curiosity of an old colleague. Oh, damned inconvenient. Trowbridge is starting up with me now. Far shorter list than yours, old man. I'd better cock an ear before he's done."

*

Later that night, as his wife of some forty-seven years slept, William Herapath went quietly downstairs to his laboratory, lit the coal fire and began searching out those things he had too weakly, too sentimentally, too long held onto. The packet of letters, the still shining lock of her dark brown hair, a length of diaphanous cloth, the photograph of himself standing protectively beside her small, shrouded figure. And her journal of worn morocco leather kept hidden among his possessions for years; he was loath to admit it, but since the Royal Society's banquet, since Volkman's ugly questions and insinuations, he had begun to experience an anxious regard for his own future eminence. It seemed clear that these few tokens, these remembrances of her, should be destroyed. Nothing should compromise his place in history. So for the first of what would be countless similar occasions before his death in twelve more years, William Herapath stood before the fire, his hands filled with the damning evidence of their love. Calling on a lifetime's discipline, he ordered himself to pitch the letters, the journal, all of it, into the flames.

Instead, he sat down, slipped the topmost letter from the ribboned bundle and unfolded its neat pages to the closing passage—

My life has been rich in ways human society can neither count nor measure nor reward. I have been taught (and how I resisted the lesson!) that love is an invisible energy which cannot die. It changes form, appears to vanish, then reappears. You remember we once spoke of feeling as though we were one fiery light, one soul? It is true. There is no thing such as time, and this life is a shadow dream at best, pale glimpse of a glory no one of us can imagine. I have little fear of death. It is a passageway, and no one is ever left there alone or for long.

I love you, William, and wait until you and I, being brought face to face in yet another lifetime, will seem, instantly, as friends, to recognize one another.

Ever yours,

S.

AFTERWORD

Selene of the Spirits was initially inspired by what few facts still surround the lives of Florence Cook, a young Victorian woman who enjoyed a brief popularity in London's spiritualist circles, and Sir William Crookes, a chemist, amateur photographer and psychical investigator who attempted within the controlled environment of his home laboratory, to calibrate, to weigh and to confine to measurement Miss Cook's soul.

These minor figures of British social history caught my attention by seeming accident. I had been returning a biography of Madame Blavatsky to my local library (Madame Blavatsky being one of the more charismatic figures in the nineteenth century's spiritualist movement), when a much smaller book, drab looking, published over thirty years ago, its jacket a dusty plum color, seized my attention. Without quite knowing why, I took this book home and read of the documented professional relationship between Miss Florence Cook and Sir William Crookes, along with the author's more personal and passionate contention that these two had had a clandestine and ultimately tragic love affair.

This strange little book, complete with photographs, held my imagination. I began, over the next year, to research the subterranean, bizarre, sometimes comical, occasionally erotic world of Victorian spiritualist circles. I was particularly intrigued by current feminist speculations on the unique avenues spiritualism afforded Victorian women for self-expression, for freedom of movement, for the enjoyment of liberties otherwise condemned, including dressing as men, cursing, and sometimes marrying well above their social class. I was also interested in the methods by which spirit mediums, who typically afforded grieving persons some small and hopeful access to the world of the dead, were examined by scientists, self-appointed investigators who attempted by various unusual means to prove the authenticity of spirit voices and apparitions. While these aspects of my research proved fascinating, I returned again and again to the attraction between seventeen-year-old Florence Cook who seemed to possess some authentic psychical powers (albeit augmented by certain "parlour tricks" she had been taught by Mr. Herne and Mr. Risdale) and

William Crookes, scientist and married father of nine children, who invited her into his home so that he might study and photograph her in the privacy of his laboratory. On one level, these two minor figures in British history became vehicles through which I could note existing sociological tensions between spiritualist circles and the square boxes of cameras, the rigid, often linear categories of experiment. On another level, the love story unfolding in this environment fascinated me still more.

I completed the novel's first draft in six weeks' time. Often, as I wrote, I could scarcely move the pen fast enough across the page, fast enough to catch the words of a voice I distinctly heard. During those six weeks, I secluded myself, kept visible company with no one. While working on a second draft of the novel, I received a completely unexpected invitation to visit Florence, Italy. Around that same time, an old friend by the name of Florence resurfaced in my life, and when I went to visit a local psychic for the first time, she immediately said a woman by the name of Florence was in my spirit field, influencing and protecting me, did I know who that might be? As for Sir William Crookes, rechristened William Herapath in the novel, he seemed to insist on a larger part in the story than I had initially allotted him. In several small, uncanny ways, he made his discontent known. While attending a conference on the uses of narrative in teaching science, I was seated beside a well-known physicist from Maryland who within minutes of our meeting, made a knowledgeable reference to Sir William Crookes, the British chemist. After I indicated my own interest, he disclosed detailed information about a man I had thus far managed to find only the driest and briefest of references to. And after her visit to the St. Francis de Assisi church in Taos, New Mexico (the same church I was once married in), my friend and research assistant, Allyson Stack, brought me a pamphlet distributed by the church, outlining the history of the famous "Mystery Painting," on permanent display in their rectory. The pamphlet referred to a Sir William Crookes who, for a short time, had been in possession of the painting in London where he had investigated its inexplicable luminosity. Finally, I consulted with a close friend and psychic, Mary Osmond, who, in a phone conversation lasting several hours, related many colorful and specific details about the life of Florence Cook which I had not come across in my more conventional methods of research. In part because of this information, I began to alter the story, even releasing one character from the book entirely, and giving William Crookes the role he seemed not only to deserve, but to insist upon.

As the writing and rewriting of this novel began to take on a sheen of otherworldliness, I became increasingly aware of the presence of these two people. I began to feel I was writing not only a love story but a ghost story as well, with the principal ghosts hovering nearby, trying in subtle, persistent ways, to influence and perhaps correct me.

From working so long on *Selene of the Spirits*, I have come to believe these two, Florence Cook and Sir William Crookes, did have a passionate, if clandestine and ultimately tragic, love affair. Furthermore, I have come to hope they will "be brought face to face in yet another lifetime" and seem "instantly, as friends, to recognize one another," and that this time, on this occasion, William will choose the path of the heart and arrive at the place where she stands, in wisdom and in love, waiting.

Melissa Pritchard
May, 1998

ABOUT THE AUTHOR

MELISSA PRITCHARD is the author of two collections of short stories, *Spirit Seizures* and *The Instinct for Bliss*, as well as a previous novel, *Phoenix. Spirit Seizures* was the recipient of a number of prizes, most notably the Flannery O'Connor Award. *The Instinct for Bliss* received the 1996 Janet Heidinger Kafka Prize for fiction by an American woman. Pritchard's stories have appeared in numerous journals, including *The Paris Review, Story, The Southern Review*, and *Ontario Review*, and have been selected for many anthologies, among them *The O. Henry Awards, The Pushcart Prize*, and *Best of the West*. She was recently awarded a Howard Foundation Fellowship from Brown University to complete her fifth book of fiction, a collection of stories tentatively titled *Her Last Man*. She lives in Tempe, Arizona, where she is an assistant professor of English and Women's Studies at Arizona State University.

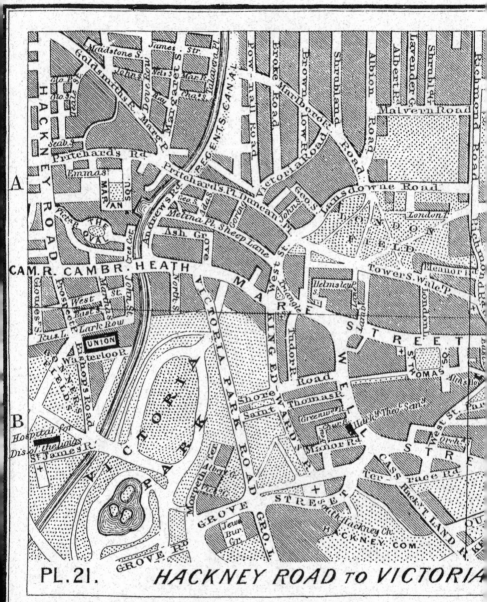

PL. 21.   *HACKNEY ROAD to VICTORIA*

PUB. BY H. C. COLLINS, PATERNOSTER ROW, LONDON.